Beth Carpenter is thankful for good books, a good dog, a good man and a dream job creating happily-ever-afters. She and her husband now split their time between Alaska and Arizona, where she occasionally encounters a moose in the yard or a scorpion in the basement. She prefers the moose.

Books by Beth Carpenter

Harlequin Heartwarming

The Alaskan Catch
A Gift for Santa
Alaskan Hideaway

Visit the Author Profile page
at Harlequin.com for more titles.

To Drew and Kelsey, with love.

"While you're here, in Alaska, you can count on me as a friend."

"A friend?"

"Yeah, a friend, Sabrina. You know. People you like, who you enjoy spending time with. Who will pick you up when you have to leave your car at the shop or take care of your dog while you're out of town or tell you when you're about to marry the wrong person." Leith probably shouldn't have said that last part, but Sabrina just smiled.

"And you want to be my friend."

"Yes, I do."

"All right, then. Friends it is." She smiled up at him, her dark eyes shining, and he was suddenly overcome with a more than friend-like urge. He touched her face, stroking his finger over the wondrously smooth skin of her cheek. Her eyes grew wider.

He bent to kiss her, stopping just an inch away. Suddenly, he wondered if maybe he'd assumed too much. But then she reached up to slide her arms around his neck and pulled him closer.

Dear Reader,

How far would you go to feel secure? When Sabrina was a girl, her father's business failed. Rather than stay to deal with it, he left Sabrina and her mother to start a new life with another woman. Overnight Sabrina lost her father, her home and her way of life, and her mother was in no shape to help her adapt. Sabrina learned that the only person she could trust to take care of her was herself. For Sabrina, everything was different.

It's never easy to start over. I've always been an avid reader, but it wasn't until much later in my life that I started writing. I had much to learn and it took time and effort, but eventually I was published. This is my fourth book for Harlequin, but I still feel a little giddy when I tell someone I'm an author.

So if you're ever frustrated because it seems like you're starting from scratch, remember that's how dreams come true.

I hope you'll stop by to say hello at bethcarpenterbooks.blogspot.com, where you can find my links to Facebook, Twitter and email. While you're there, you can subscribe to the newsletter to keep up with all the book news, plus recipes and fun giveaways.

May your fondest dreams come true.

Beth Carpenter

HEARTWARMING

An Alaskan Proposal

—

Beth Carpenter

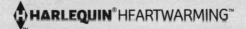

Recycling programs
for this product may
not exist in your area.

ISBN-13: 978-1-335-51052-5

An Alaskan Proposal

HARLEQUIN®
www.Harlequin.com

Printed in U.S.A.

CHAPTER ONE

HARD TO BELIEVE people did this for fun. Sabrina climbed over a sodden log and hurried around a boulder to catch up with the rest of the group. A sudden gust whipped the hood of her borrowed plastic poncho across her face, momentarily blinding her. In that instant, she stepped on a wet root and slipped, falling to her knee. A flash of pain shot up her leg.

"Are you okay?" Clara, Sabrina's temporary supervisor, offered a hand up.

"I'm fine." Sabrina managed to puff the words out between gasps for air. She accepted Clara's hand and got to her feet. "Thanks." She rubbed her knee. There would be a bruise tomorrow, but it wasn't bad.

"It's not far now," Clara said. "And I think we're winning."

"Great." Sabrina forced a smile, but she needn't have bothered. Clara had already turned and hurried up the trail, which left Sabrina to bring up the rear.

What was she doing here, climbing a moun-

tain, in Alaska, in the rain? Sabrina didn't
hike. She didn't wear ugly boots and plastic ponchos. At least the old Sabrina didn't.
The new Sabrina—the one she'd pretty much
created out of thin air—loved spending time
outdoors. At least that was the story she'd
sold Orson Outfitters' management during
her job interview, and that was the story she
intended to live up to. Today's team-builder
outing was her first test.

You'd think all those hours at the gym
would have prepared her for this, but it turned
out running on a treadmill and hiking rough
trails weren't quite the same. Her muscles
complained, forcefully. Still, she couldn't
quit, or everyone would know she was an
impostor. Somehow, Sabrina continued to
put one brand-new hiking boot in front of
the other. Twenty minutes later, they were
still trudging uphill, the rain was still coming down and everyone around her was still
acting happy about it. What was with these
people? Every place she'd ever worked had a
resident whiner—someone who made a fed-
eral case out of running out of staples or complained about the quality of the coffee—but
she hadn't heard a peep of dissension from
this crowd.

Then Clara, who was at least fifteen years

older and probably thirty pounds heavier than Sabrina, broke out into a song, but she still didn't slow down. Several others joined in. How did they have enough breath for singing and climbing? Maybe all of Sabrina's new co-workers were animatronic robots. That would explain a lot.

Just about the time her legs were seriously considering a mutiny, they crested the top of a rise and saw the company van and another truck parked beside a canopy emblazoned with the Orson Outfitters name. "We're first!" Clara called out. Everyone cheered. Sabrina cheered along with them, just happy she didn't have to climb anymore.

The van's driver was relaxing in a folding chair beneath the canopy. Sabrina would have tried to snag that job, but the woman who'd volunteered to drive all the supplies to the rendezvous point looked to be about eleven months pregnant.

Two guys dressed in matching navy rain jackets were unloading something from the back of a pickup with a Learn & Live logo on the door. What were they doing here? Maybe they were part of the special surprise Walter had promised the group.

Sabrina collapsed onto a big rock and swallowed the last of the water from her bottle.

Clara plopped down beside her. Sabrina was lucky to be training under Clara in her first assignment. Clara was one of those people who always assumed the best about everyone, which meant she tended to attribute Sabrina's lapses to rookie jitters rather than ignorance. "Great climb, huh?"

Sabrina nodded. "Challenging."

"Oh, yeah. We were determined to get here first this year. Walter's group usually beats us up. Oh, look. Here they come." Clara bounced up and hurried over to the other trail to deliver some good-natured razzing.

Sabrina watched from where she was. A brief expression of disappointment crossed Walter's face when he saw their group had already arrived, but he grinned when Clara teased him. Their store manager was quite a character, about five-four with a walrus mustache and an oversize personality.

He'd insisted that Sabrina call him Walter when they met on her first day and pumped her hand with such enthusiasm he'd all but sprained her elbow. "Great to have you here, Sabrina. I have high hopes for this new management-trainee program. We've been telling Corporate for years the managers need to understand how the stores work before they can make good decisions at the corporate level, and they finally listened."

"Thank you, sir. I'm glad to be here."

"Trust me, you drew the best assignment." He straightened the chunk of turquoise that secured a bolo tie around the collar of his plaid shirt. "I know you're on probation and that only the top half of the trainees will move on to the next level of management, but you don't need to worry. You'll learn everything you need to know from this crew. Anchorage has been number one in sales for the past three years running, and we're not planning to surrender that title anytime soon. The secret to our success is passion. The people who work here love the outdoors, and they enjoy sharing that enthusiasm with our customers. That's my main criteria when I choose employees."

Sabrina could certainly see Walter's passion for his job. She just hoped she could convince him she shared his excitement. "I can't wait to get started."

"Good. I think first, we'll put you on the register with Clara, so you can get an overview of the store before we move you to one of the departments. How does that sound?"

"Great idea." Sabrina had worked retail all through high school and college, so running a cash register would be a piece of cake, and would give her time to study up on the rest of the store.

"Welcome aboard."

It turned out she'd arrived just in time for the big annual team-builder. Today only involved half the store employees. The other half, who were working at the store today, would be doing their team-builder tomorrow. Sabrina would lay odds that tomorrow Walter's group would be the first to the top of the hill. He clearly didn't like to lose.

Walter and some of the others were shedding their raincoats. The rain seemed to have stopped. Good—Sabrina could get out of this plastic wrap. Everyone else seemed to have jackets made from the latest high-tech waterproof fabric. She'd sold a couple of them in the store this week. Sabrina didn't even own rainwear. Well, technically there was that vintage Laura Wilkes umbrella she'd gotten at an estate sale, but Sabrina considered that more art than protection. Dealing with rain hadn't been a big part of her life as a fashion buyer in Scottsdale. But that was then.

Now Sabrina was doing the nature thing in Alaska, and she wasn't equipped for it. Fortunately, Clara, being the experienced mom she was, carried extra folding ponchos in her glove compartment and had loaned Sabrina one at the beginning of the hike. It had done the job, but Sabrina was glad the rain had finally stopped and she could peel it off.

She stretched, and then turned to see one of the guys from Learn & Live looking toward her. Even from this distance she could see the intense blue of his eyes, and those eyes were sweeping over her from head to toe. He frowned. Sabrina did a casual scan to see if she'd spilled something on her clothes, but her leggings seemed fine. So did the French blue pima cotton cardigan, her favorite sweater. It could have been a little thicker, though, she realized as a sudden breeze cut through the knit. She rubbed her hands up and down her arms to warm them. When she looked up again, the guy had turned away and was talking with Walter.

Now that everyone was removing their raincoats, Sabrina realized most of them had on gray or blue cargo pants and some sort of fleece vest in a primary color. Nobody else wore anything close to leggings. Oops. Sabrina prided herself on always dressing appropriately, and it seemed the appropriate things to wear on company hikes were clothes from the company store. It looked like boxy vests and ugly pants were in her future.

Walter called for everyone's attention, congratulating Sabrina's group for being first up the mountain. Judging from the applause and cheering, it was a big deal. He called them all forward and hung medals around their necks. When it was Sabrina's turn, he patted her shoulder. "Nice job for someone who's only been here four days. Congratulations, Sabrina."

"Thanks." All she'd done was follow the rest of her team along the trail, but it was still nice to be recognized. And it was nice that he remembered her name. It had taken her old boss three weeks to quit calling her Semolina, and she was never quite sure if it was deliberate. The medals were just novelty items—a plastic disk painted gold with the word *winner* stamped on it—but it was all good fun.

Once Walter had given out the medals, he gestured to the two men from the Learn & Live truck to come over. They'd both removed their raincoats and were wearing long-sleeved zip-necks under fleece vests, with the same logo as the truck embroidered on the chest. The first guy towered a foot over Walter. With his wavy blond hair and relaxed grin, he looked like he'd just put away his surfboard. The other guy, the one who'd been frowning at Sabrina before, seemed more serious. He was a couple of inches shorter than his coworker, which would put him around six feet, with brown hair and those incredible blue eyes. Walter's cheeks plumped over his mustache. "Everyone, I want you to meet Leith Jordan and Erik Peterman, from Learn & Live. They're going to be giving us a demonstration on survival skills."

Survival skills? Wasn't that like making huts from tree branches and eating bugs? No, thanks. Surfer-dude Erik talked for a few minutes about a course they'd set up a little farther along the trail, where they were going to be giving the lessons in orienteering. Sabrina didn't know what that was and wasn't sure she wanted to find out. When Walter asked for volunteers to stay behind and cook lunch, Sabrina's hand was the first one up.

"Great. Thanks, Sabrina, Will and Amy. The rest of you follow Erik and Leith."

Will was one of the few people in the store whose name Sabrina remembered, other than Clara. He looked like a high-school student, but when he'd sold Sabrina the hiking boots yesterday, he seemed to know all about them. He'd steered her toward this slightly more expensive pair. It pained her to drain her anemic checking account for ugly footwear, but she had to admit, the boots he'd recommended kept her feet dry and comfortable despite the rain and rough trail.

Will introduced Sabrina to Amy, the pregnant lady, who seemed to be his supervisor. "You're the management trainee, right?" Amy asked.

"That's right."

"So, you'll be working in Seattle once you finish up here?"

"Yes, assuming I make the cut. They only plan to move the top half of trainees to the next level, based on evaluation scores."

"Walter will take care of you," Will said.

"He's right," Amy said. "I've been with the store for seven years. Once you're part of his team, Walter treats you like family. Although, I don't know why you'd want to live in Seattle. I was there last year, and I couldn't believe the traffic. There are some nice hikes in the area, though."

"That's what I've heard." The other management trainees wouldn't shut up about the trails during breaks in the orientation meetings. Sabrina had just smiled and nodded. "I hope I get the chance to try them out."

Amy gestured toward the van. "We'd better get started if we're going to have everything ready by the time they get back. Will, can you get the cooking crate out, please?"

Will carried a yellow-and-black plastic case from the back of the van. He opened it to reveal various pieces of equipment that looked as though they might belong in a science lab. Huh. Maybe Sabrina should have gone to the survival demo after all.

Amy pulled out a rolled bundle and, through some feat of origami, turned it into a table. "I'll cut up the veggies and make the dip. Can you two build the fire, heat the beans and handle the grill?"

"Sure," Will volunteered before Sabrina could say anything. "Where do you want the table?"

Sabrina had to admit, Will was a nice kid— he moved Amy's table and equipment under the canopy and arranged everything for her so she could sit while she worked on the vegetables. Meanwhile, at Amy's suggestion, Sabrina unloaded a bunch of logs from the van and stacked them near a circle of stones in a clear area not too far away. A few minutes later, Will returned, shaking his head. "I wish she'd have that baby. I keep thinking one of these days it's going to pop out in the middle of the shoe department."

"When is she due?" Sabrina asked.

"Yesterday. Walter told her she didn't need to do the team-builder this year, but she didn't want to miss it. You want to build the fire, while I get the rest of the wood?"

"Why don't you build the fire, and I'll haul the firewood? You shouldn't be stuck with all the heavy lifting."

Will gave her an odd look, but he didn't argue. Of course, as a management trainee, she technically outranked him. Probably.

She tried to watch how he built the fire, but since she had to make a couple of trips for firewood, she missed a few steps. She was pulling the last of the wood from the van when her finger got pinched between two logs. "Ouch." She shook her hand. *"Cielos!"*

"What's wrong? You break a nail?"

Sabrina spun around to find the survivor guy with the blue eyes pulling something from the back of his truck. Leith Jordan, according to Walter. She looked down at her hand, where a big scratch ran across her polish and the ragged edge of a fingernail hung by a thread. She grimaced. That was going to take some time to repair tonight. "As a matter of fact, I did. Don't you have anything better to do than sneak up behind people?"

"Sorry." He looked more amused than apologetic. "You're new with Orson, aren't you?"

"Yes. Why? Do you know all the people from the store?"

"No, but I'm in there a lot and I haven't seen you before." He looked down at her boots and shook his head. "I'd remember you."

What did that mean? There was nothing wrong with her boots. They were exactly like the ones Clara was wearing. Besides, he wasn't with Orson, so his opinion didn't matter.

"I'd better get these logs to the fire." Sabrina gathered up the wood she'd dropped and returned to the fire ring without looking back.

Whatever Will had done in her absence must have worked, because flames were licking at the wood. He stepped back. "I'll light the grill and handle all the meat and veggie burgers and stuff. Okay?"

"Sure. What should I do?"

"Uh, well, I guess you just need to watch the fire and heat up the beans."

"Sounds good." Surely she could manage that. "Thanks, Will."

He set up the grill close enough that he could talk with Amy while he cooked. Bushes and boulders partially blocked the view between Sabrina and the other two. That worked out well for her, because it allowed her to paw through the chest Will had brought and try to figure out what everything was without him watching.

The fire seemed to be burning nicely, so she threw a couple more logs on. The flames died down. Oops. Using a stick, Sabrina raked one of the logs toward her and the fire jumped up between the two logs. Okay, that looked good. Digging through the crate, she found a metal box labeled *camp stove*. Better and better. But when she opened the box, the contents held no resemblance to any stove she'd ever seen. She put it aside for the moment.

The crate held a dozen big cans of baked beans. Probably half of them were for the group tomorrow. Sabrina dug a little more and found some sort of metal circles surrounded by rings of silicone—trivets maybe—and something that looked like a manual can opener, except it didn't have any handles. How was she supposed to heat beans without a pan? Eventually, she found some tongs but still no cooking containers.

She peeked around the rock. Will was whistling as he unpacked a bunch of stuff from an ice chest. She could ask him how the stove worked, but then he'd know she was a fraud. And if one person in the store knew, soon the whole store would, including Walter.

She picked up one of the cans. It was a metal cylinder, right? Just like a small pan. Why not just put the cans into the fire and let them heat?

Once they were hot, she could take them out of the fire with the tongs. Yeah, that would work. And she wouldn't have to deal with the camp stove. Problem solved.

She added more wood to the fire, careful to leave spaces between the logs for the flames. Then she set the cans of beans onto the coals near the heart of the flames. The labels caught and burned away, but the cans seemed stable. Now all she had to do was wait.

It wasn't long before the main group returned, laughing and joking. Clara trotted over to Sabrina. "Sorry you missed out on the fun. Those Learn & Live guys are great. I'll tend the fire and you can go do the equipment try-outs."

"The what?"

"You know, where we try out all that shiny new equipment we're going to be selling this season. Walter said to send you over. You'll be working in one of the departments, so you need hands-on experience more than I do."

"Oh. Okay. Well, the beans—"

"Sabrina," Walter called, waving his arms. "Over here."

"Don't keep the boss waiting," Clara said. "I'll take care of the beans. Go."

Sabrina went. Her coworkers crowded around the van, where Walter was handing out packages to everyone. The breeze kicked up again, and without the fire to warm her, Sabrina felt goose bumps rising along her arms while she waited her turn. Walter passed an orange backpack to a guy with a gray ponytail and picked up a long, thin nylon sack that appeared to contain something heavy. "Sabrina. This one's for you." She stepped closer and Walter leaned in so only she could hear. "Thanks for volunteering to help with the food. That shows leadership. But now it's your turn for some fun. Here, this new tent design is supposed to make for a faster, more intuitive setup without compromising structural integrity. Give it a try and let me know what you think."

"All right." Sabrina accepted the nylon bundle and looked around. Where did this testing take place?

"There's a flat spot over there," Walter suggested, waving his hand toward a spot a little past the fire.

"Perfect. Thanks." Sabrina smiled at him and carried the tent over. She waved at Clara as she walked by. Okay. A tent. Let's see what she had to work with. Sabrina opened the drawstring at the top of the bag and dumped everything out. Hmm. A bunch of nylon, two short bundles of colored sticks, small metal sticks with hooks on the ends and…oh, instructions.

Good. She grabbed the paper and looked at the picture. Step one: spread tent on the ground.

Clear enough. She unrolled the nylon and spread it in a neat rectangle. Presumably the heavier side was the bottom, and the net side went up. So far, so good.

Step two: assemble shock-corded tent poles. Was that stick in the picture the big one or one of the little ones? Another gust sent a shiver up her arms. She stamped her feet. It was hard to concentrate when she was so cold.

"Problems?"

Sabrina jumped and turned. Those blue eyes, watching her again. This was starting to get weird. "No, I'm just reading the instructions."

He looked over the pieces she'd set on the ground. "Looks like it sets up just like the old design except they color-coded the poles, shortened the sleeves and used minicarabiners to make setup faster."

Minicarabiners. Uh-huh. "Yeah, well, I'm approaching it like a customer who hasn't ever set up one of these tents," Sabrina said. "I want to make sure the instructions are clear, even to a novice."

"I see." His lips twitched into a small smile. Sabrina couldn't be sure whether it was a friendly smile or if he was laughing at her, but she suspected the latter. She made a point of turning her back to him while she read, shivering as she did. Maybe he would go away. "Shock cord? What the heck is a shock cord?" she muttered to herself. "*Cielos*, these pictures are confusing."

"What did you say?" He was still there. "*Cielos?* What does that mean?"

"Nothing." Just something her grandmother used to say when she got flustered. Heavens. But he didn't need Sabrina's life story.

"Where's your jacket?"

She gave up and turned to look at him. "I'm wearing it."

"That's all you brought?" He shook his head. "Where are you from, anyway?"

"Arizona. And I'm fine."

"Scottsdale?"

"As a matter of fact, I used to work in Scottsdale."

"I figured." He unzipped his fleece vest and removed it. "Here, wear this."

"What? No. I'm okay."

"I don't think you are. Shivering, mumbling, confusion. All symptoms of hypothermia."

I'm not mumbling because I'm hypothermic. I'm mumbling because I'm annoyed. She thought the words but managed not to say them. Instead she repeated, "I'm okay."

"Are you wet?"

"No. I was wearing a rain poncho."

"Then you're probably not hypothermic, but you're obviously cold. Take the vest."

It was tempting, but she hated to be in anyone's debt. Especially someone who seemed to disapprove of her. "Then *you'll* be cold."

"I have a fleece jacket in the truck."

Of course he did. The survival expert would always be prepared. Another cold gust convinced her. "Fine." She pulled the vest over her sweater and zipped it closed. Still warm from his body heat, it covered her from her shoulders to her thighs. "Thank you."

"You're welcome." He continued to stand there. She pretended to be studying the instructions, hoping he'd walk away, but he remained where he was. "I'm Leith Jordan."

"Sabrina Bell."

He nodded. "So, Sabrina. Why are you here?"

"For the team-builder, obviously."

"No, I mean why are you in Alaska? Why didn't you stay in Arizona?"

"I came for the job."

He raised an eyebrow. "You came all the

way to Alaska to work at the Orson Outfitters store?"

"Not that it's any of your business, but I'm
training. Headquarters hired me as a management trainee, and the first part of that is
to work in different positions in one of the
local stores."

"Oh, so Alaska is just a temporary stop
for you."

"Yes."

"That makes more sense. Why are you pretending you know anything about camping?"

She looked around sharply to see if any
of the other employees were within earshot,
but it was just the two of them. She picked
up one of the metal sticks and examined it as
though she intended to do something with it.
"I told you. We're supposed to be testing the
products, and part of that testing is to see if
the instructions are clear."

"If you say so."

"I do." She rattled the paper and tried to concentrate on the instructions. She felt warmer
already. Now, if she could just figure out step
two.

He handed her the blue bundle of sticks.
"The shock cord is the bungee cord running
through the tent poles. It holds the short poles
in line while you fit them together to create

a long pole, which fits through the sleeve at the crown of the tent."

"Well, yeah. That's what the instructions should have said. I'm going to have to let them know these wouldn't be clear to a beginner." Sabrina studied the sticks, and sure enough, they were all threaded onto a stretchy rope. As she unfolded them, they snapped together. Ingenious. Now, if she could just get rid of Mr. Know-It-All, she might have a shot at figuring out this tent. But he showed no signs of leaving.

Without another word, he lifted the top of the tent and held a blue fabric sleeve that matched the pole so that all she had to do was slip the pole through the sleeve. Okay, that made sense. Once it was in place, Leith arched his end of the pole and secured it through a grommet at the base. Sabrina followed suit with her end of the pole. Suddenly, the tent was standing. She assembled the red sticks and threaded the pole through the red sleeve, again with Leith's assistance. He began securing the hooks on one side of the tent to the poles. She did the same on her side.

Leith unrolled the final piece of nylon. She took two corners and helped him center it over the poles. Leith handed her the thin metal pieces. "Now you just need to stake out the corners."

"Right. Let me just see if the instructions say that."

Leith grinned. "For testing purposes." Now she was sure he was making fun of her, but she didn't care.

"Exactly." She picked up the instructions and turned the page. "Stake corners." She pointed at the diagram. "Right here." She set down the paper and pushed one of the stakes through a grommet into the soft ground, anchoring the corner. Leith did one of the other corners. He wasn't so bad after all.

Bang! Sabrina whirled toward the sound of an explosion. Something came whizzing out of the fire and flew several feet before crashing into a rock. Something about the size of a can.

"Oh, *cielos*! The beans." Sabrina rushed toward the fire.

"I don't know what happened." Clara stared wide-eyed at the fire. A silicone-sided pan of beans simmered nearby on the camp stove Sabrina hadn't been able to figure out.

"It's my fault." Sabrina looked around for the tongs. Before she could grab them, another can exploded and sailed off to the right, knocking over the stove and spilling the beans onto the ground.

"Get back." Leith pulled Clara away from the fire. "Sabrina, you, too."

"I just have to get the rest out before they go off." Sabrina grabbed the tongs and reached into the fire, extracting a blackened can.

"What is it?"

"A can of beans." She dropped the can in the dirt and tried to locate the next one.

Leith grabbed a shovel and pushed the logs apart. "How many are in here?"

"Six." She spotted another can and pulled it out. "Two more."

Leith pushed in his shovel, scooped out another can and dropped it on the ground, away from the fire. Sabrina spotted the last one, but before she could get to it, it went off, zooming out of the fire like a missile and spraying a trail of beans all over the tent she had just erected before it landed in a bush. Sticky sauce dripped down the sides of the tent.

"You're sure that's all?" Leith asked.

"That's it." Sabrina turned to see Clara and all the other employees gathered behind her staring at the tent and at her. Super. Walter pushed through the crowd.

"What happened here?"

Sabrina swallowed. "It was my fault. I thought it would save some mess and equipment if I heated the beans in the fire."

Walter narrowed his eyes. "You put the cans in the fire without opening them?"

Sabrina nodded.

"Any casualties?"

"Only the tent."

Walter marched over to the tent. He examined the beans oozing down the fabric, then unzipped the tent and crawled inside. A moment later, he popped out, smiling. "Not a drop inside, and the rain fly wasn't even completely staked. I think we have a winning design here. Sabrina, please clean that tent before you return it to the store. Everyone else, looks like we'll have to do without beans today, but Will says the burgers are ready. Let's eat."

With a few headshakes and some laughter, the rest of the employees drifted away. Sabrina picked up a spatula and went to scrape baked beans off the fabric.

Only Leith followed her. "You have to be careful. When the contents of a can are overheated and the steam can't escape, pressure can build up past the tolerance of the can."

"Thanks, Admiral Hindsight." She "accidentally" flicked the spatula so that beans flew in his direction, but she missed. "Any other words of wisdom?"

He flashed a snarky grin. "Well, I could tell

you the best way to wash a tent, but I'm sure an experienced camper such as yourself already has a preferred method." And with that helpful comment, he turned and went to join the others crowding around the grill, leaving her to clean up her mess.

CHAPTER TWO

LEITH PULLED THE truck into its assigned parking spot near the back door at Learn & Live. Erik jumped out and opened the tailgate.

Leith grabbed the checklist and followed. "Do we need more maps for tomorrow's demo?" he asked, his pen hovering over the clipboard.

Erik pawed through the supplies in the crate. "No, looks like we have plenty."

Leith checked off the item and locked the truck. They headed inside the office. As soon as they stepped into the lobby, a black-and-tan dog dashed out of Carson's office. Leith knelt to give her an ear rub. "Hey, Tal. There's my girl."

Their boss, Carson, followed her out. "Good. You're back. Did the Orson Outfitters demo go okay? Anything you need to change before doing it again tomorrow?"

"No problems." Leith stood but continued to stroke Tal's head. "I think they all got something out of it."

Erik laughed. "Except for Explosion Girl."

"Explosion?" Carson narrowed his eyes. "You were teaching orienteering. How can that explode? Was anyone hurt?"

"No," Leith assured him. "It wasn't at our demo. For some reason, this management trainee Orson Outfitters hired decided she should put cans of beans directly into the fire."

"Oh, yeah?" Carson grinned. "I thought that was an urban myth. Did they really explode?"

"Launched a couple of cans like rockets. One of them splattered a tent that was a good twenty feet away. We managed to get the rest out of the fire before they turned into grenades." Leith shook his head. "She was clueless. Brand-new hiking boots, no jacket. She'd obviously never been camping a day in her life."

"She was cute, though," Erik pointed out.

"The cute ones are the most dangerous." And Leith should know. His ex-wife used her looks like a precision tool. "They're so used to everyone falling over backward to make them happy, they don't realize nature can kill you no matter how pretty you are."

"Uh-huh." Erik nudged Carson. "That must be why our white knight over here gave her his vest."

"Nuts. I forgot to get it back from her." Now Leith was going to have to decide whether chasing her down or paying for a new company vest was the lesser of two evils. That was what he got for being a nice guy. He probably should have stayed far away from Sabrina, but it was painful to witness her struggle to set up a simple tent. Then when he'd noticed she was shivering, he couldn't just stand there and watch.

When Carson raised his eyebrows, Leith shrugged. "It would look bad for the company if someone went hypothermic on our watch."

Carson snorted. "I'm happy to hear the company's reputation is so important to you."

The break-room door opened and Zack walked out, his phone to his ear. "It's too bad you couldn't get the ones you wanted, but I think daisies sound fine. No, really, they'll look great. Okay, babe, I've got to get back to work. Love you, too. Bye."

Zack pocketed his phone and rolled his eyes. "If any of you guys decide to get married, my advice is run off to Vegas. Weddings are killers."

"No worries here," Leith said. He'd been through a wedding and a marriage, and after that experience he planned to stay as far away from both as humanly possible. If he could get away with it, he'd skip Zack's wedding, but he was one of the groomsmen.

"So, who's the plus-one you're bringing?" Zack asked Leith.

"Plus-one? What are you talking about?"

"The wedding. Caitlyn says you RSVPed that you're bringing a guest. Who is she?"

Oh, great. Leith's sister had volunteered to send in his RSVP card when she did her own. He should have guessed Volta was up to something. She probably had someone all picked out she was planning to fix him up with. "That was a mistake. You can tell Caitlyn I'm not bringing anyone."

"No way, dude. If you said plus-one, you're bringing someone to fill that chair. I don't care if it's your grandma. Caitlyn has been going nuts trying to figure out how to arrange the tables. She has all these relatives who she can't put too close together or she says there will be blood. She's finally managed to find the perfect seating plan. If one little thing changes, it'll mess it all up. I'm not going to be the one to make her head explode."

"Speaking of explosions," Erik said with a sly smile. "You ought to ask Explosion Girl. She's probably great at weddings."

"Who's Explosion Girl?" Zack asked.

Leith just shook his head, so Erik explained

about the beans. Zack laughed. "Sure, bring her. She should liven things up."

"I'll take it under advisement." Leith stepped away to drop the keys to the company truck into a drawer. "Who are you bringing?" he asked Erik.

"I invited this woman I met from the parks department. She's just here for a month, on some government project. No strings. The most important quality in a relationship."

"That's what I used to think, until I met Caitlyn," Zack said. "Someday you're going to want some strings."

"No way. Leith will back me up, right?"

"I'm not getting in the middle of this." After his own marital disaster, Leith was inclined to agree with Erik, but he didn't want to upset Zack. He had to admit, Zack had been a lot happier since Caitlyn had come into his life, even if she was a little obsessive about the wedding plans. He just hoped their marriage was more successful than his had been. Not a high bar.

Carson cleared his throat. "Well, if we're about done with advice for the lovelorn, maybe we can get a little work done around here?"

They all scattered. Leith went to his desk to fill out his time sheet and a summary of the day's events. While his computer booted up, he thought about his options.

Weddings made his skin itch, but since he'd been drafted as a groomsman, he couldn't miss this one. Now, thanks to Volta, he was going to have to find a date. And it better be soon, before his sister coerced him into taking out whatever new friend she had in mind for him. The last woman she'd set him up with, six months ago, had been a walking disaster. That two-hour date had to have consumed at least ten years of his life. No, if he had to have a date, he was choosing her himself. Volta didn't get a vote.

That decided, he opened a spreadsheet and went to work. Work, he understood. He could worry about this other stuff later.

SABRINA RANG UP a sleeping bag the color of a roadwork sign and a snap-together salt-and-pepper shaker for a woman with a long braid hanging down her back. The customer checked the tag. "This says it's comfortable down to forty-five degrees. Do you think that's accurate?"

Sabrina had spent most of her off time during the last two days since the great bean incident reading product descriptions on the company's website, but that didn't help with questions like this. "Honestly, I haven't tried out this particular sleeping bag, so I'm not sure." Sabrina called to Clara, "Do you think this bag would keep you warm at forty-five?"

"Sure, if you're wearing sweats or thermals to sleep in. It's a great bag."

"Oh, good. Thanks." The customer waved at Clara and left the store. Clara finished ringing up her customer and handed him the sack of merchandise. For once, no one was waiting in line to check out.

Clara wandered over to Sabrina's register. "That's our most popular summer bag. You're probably used to a lighter one where you come from, huh?"

"Mmm. Does it come in any colors besides orange?" Sabrina had found the best way to deflect Clara was to ask a question. Clara loved to talk, and Sabrina had already picked up a few nuggets of wisdom she could pass on to customers and sound as if she might know what she was talking about. Besides, she was curious. Surely not everyone wanted a sleeping bag in a color that could be seen from space.

But before Clara could answer, Walter hustled over to the registers. Today his bolo tie slide was a silver horseshoe. He hadn't said anything since the team-builder, but Sabrina kept expecting him to call her in and expose her as the fraud she was. Her stomach tightened in anticipation, but he just smiled. "Say, Clara, do you mind if we borrow Sabrina for a little while? Tim needs some help with a display in camping."

"That's fine. Randy will be back from lunch in fifteen minutes. If I get backed up in the meantime, I'll call for help."

"Great." Walter motioned for Sabrina to walk with him. "I saw on your résumé that you've worked in fashion, so I thought you might have some experience with display."

"Yes, I have." Sabrina used to enjoy creating displays when she was working retail in high school and college. Even after she'd gotten the buyer job, she'd often sent out tips and ideas to the local stores. But she wasn't sure her flair for fashion accessories was going to be a big help with a camping display. Still, the basics of form and balance she'd learned in her design classes should apply across the board.

Walter introduced her to Tim, a tall, skinny guy with thick glasses. Tim looked more like a chemistry professor than a camping enthusiast, but he was setting up the tent Sabrina had almost destroyed in less time than it had taken her to shake it out of the bag. Fortunately, she'd found tent-washing tips on the internet and managed to get the bean stain off the rain fly, no thanks to survival expert Leith Jordan.

Now, that guy made her nervous. Everyone at the store seemed to take her at face value, but Leith wasn't buying her act. His disdain for her inexperience had been pretty clear at the team-builder. In fact, she'd just about reached the conclusion he was going to expose her to all her coworkers, when he'd suddenly started being nice and loaned her his vest. Which she'd washed and now had to figure out how to return without asking anyone in the store where to find him. She didn't want to call attention to the fact that she'd been unprepared for the weather. Among other things.

"Hi, Sabrina," Tim said. "Would you mind grabbing me a couple of 'biners? I want to hang this canoe from the ceiling."

Beaners? She wondered if this was some sort of joke aimed at her, but he didn't look as though he was joking. "Sure." Beaners. Whatever those were. Sabrina scanned the area for anything that looked likely.

"Aisle ten," Walter prompted, before walking away.

"Thanks." Sabrina hurried over to the aisle.

It seemed to contain miscellaneous camping gadgets. She found cooking utensils, lanterns, some sort of special toilet paper and a bunch of C-shaped hooks with levered latches.

Will, the guy who'd built the fire at the team-builder, walked past, presumably on his way to the shoe department. "Hi, Sabrina. What are you looking for?"

"Beaners."

He gave her a puzzled frown and gestured at the hooks. "Right there."

"Oh, duh." Sabrina gave a little laugh. "Right in front of me. Good thing it wasn't a snake." *Quick, change the subject.* "So, has Amy had her baby yet?"

"Soon. She called in while her husband drove her to the hospital this morning. Asked me to finish the inventory without her." He grinned. "She says she's going to name the baby after me. Course, her husband, Bill, is really named William, too."

"That's convenient. Well, I'd better get these to Tim. See you later, Will." Sabrina grabbed a few medium-sized hooks, which she now realized were labeled as carabiners. Ah, like the clips on the tent. *Carabiners equals 'biners.* As if she didn't have enough trouble with camping terms, they were using nicknames for tools.

Hopefully, Will would just assume she was blind, rather than ignorant.

She brought the carabiners to where Tim was now on a ladder, threading ropes over beams. "There you are. I thought you'd deserted me."

"Sorry. I ran into Will and he said Amy is having her baby."

"I heard. Maybe she'll take some time off now. She was over there stocking shoes last week even though she could hardly bend over. Did Will say she's doing okay?"

"I don't think he had any updates yet."

"I'm sure we'll hear something soon. Can you give me one of those?"

Sabrina handed him the carabiner. The employees here all talked to and about each other like they were all part of one big family. At least that was how Sabrina assumed families functioned. She really didn't have a lot of experience. It had been just her and her mom since she was twelve, when her dad left.

That was when Sabrina discovered security was an illusion. That counting on someone else for love and support was a gamble. Sabrina didn't believe in gambling. The only person she could absolutely depend on was herself. And that was why she had to keep this job.

She thought she'd done all the right things.

In college, she'd been tempted to go into fashion design, but chose the safe route of fashion merchandising. Only it turned out not to be so safe. The department store where she'd been working as a buyer went bankrupt. With her experience and references, Sabrina had assumed she'd be able to find a similar position, but in-store sales were down all over, and everyone was cutting back.

There was a rumor circulating that one of the senior buyers at McCormick and Sons was about to retire. McCormick's had always been Sabrina's dream job. A family-owned chain of upscale department stores based in Scottsdale, they had the reputation of hiring the best and keeping them forever. Once you were a part of McCormick's, you were set.

Sabrina had tried to wait it out, but the buyer stubbornly refused to retire. Time went by and Sabrina's carefully accrued savings dwindled. A friend of her mother's mentioned this management trainee program with Orson Outfitters in Seattle. Sabrina applied there along with several dozen other places, but Orson's was the only company that showed interest.

At the time she applied, she'd assumed they were a casual clothing company. It wasn't until they'd contacted her requesting an interview that she'd researched the company and discovered they made and distributed outdoor equipment, with clothing making up only a small portion of their product line. But after five months of unemployment, and her cash reserve almost gone, Sabrina was determined she was going to get the job with Orson Outfitters, even if it meant she had to fudge a little about her outdoor experience.

"Sabrina? Another one?"

"Oh, sorry." She handed Tim the second carabiner.

"Attention, everyone." Walter's voice came over the speaker. "We have a new member of the Orson family. It's a boy, nine pounds, eleven ounces."

Everyone cheered. Tim grinned. "Wow. Almost ten pounds. And my wife thought an eight-pounder was big. We'll have to go by and see Amy and the baby after work." He tied the ends of the ropes into loops and passed them to Sabrina. "Can you use a couple more carabiners to clip these onto the gunwales of the canoe, so we can hoist it up?"

Okay, Sabrina didn't know what a gunwale was, but the only reasonable place she could fasten a carabiner onto a canoe had to be the posts across the top. She clipped the ropes to the canoe, front and back. "How's that?"

"Good. Pull on those lines to raise it?"

She tugged on the lines, lifting the canoe off the ground, while Tim guided it into place from the ladder. Once they had it in position, he tied it off. "Great. I just need to set out a chair in front of the tent, and I'll be all done."

She thought about offering to create the display. She had an idea about arranging two chairs in front of the tent with a few stones suggesting a fire ring, like the one at the team-builder. She could set a bird-watching book and some binoculars on one of the chairs, and hang one of those cute lanterns she'd spotted in aisle ten somewhere. Maybe lean a paddle in place to draw the eye toward the canoe. But the more she was around other employees, the more likely it was that her secret would come out. She'd better not risk it. "I should get back on the register."

"Okay. Thanks for your help, Sabrina."

"No problem. See you later." Sabrina returned to her post next to Clara. This was ridiculous. She was supposed to be gaining practical experience as a preliminary to moving into management, but instead she spent most of her energy avoiding any conversation that would expose her ignorance.

Only the top half of the candidates working in the stores would be chosen to move to the next round of the training program. If Walter didn't give her a high rating in a little over three months, she would once again be searching for a job. And so far, the only impressive thing she'd managed to accomplish was to blow up a few cans of beans.

If she was going to keep this job, she needed a crash course. And obviously she couldn't get it from any of her coworkers. There was only one person in Anchorage she could think of who might be able to help her without giving away the whole thing. After all, he was already suspicious, and training people to survive outdoors was what he did for a living. So be it. She'd contact him. Because, obnoxious though he might be, Leith Jordan was her best bet if she wanted to keep her job.

TIRED AND A little damp, Leith rolled into the office after a long day of watercraft survival training in the swimming pool at one of the local high schools. He unloaded the kayaks and headed to his desk to fill out his reports. Everyone else had gone home for the day. Before he could even sit down, his phone rang. Volta.

"Hi, sis."

"Hi. Want to come for dinner? I made a big pot of spaghetti and meatballs."

Leith's stomach growled at the mention of food. He loved Volta's spaghetti. She usually only made it when she was having a bunch of people... Wait. "Who else is coming?"

"Just some people from work. You know most of them."

Nicely evasive. But he knew her. "And who don't I know?"

"Oh, well, there's a new nurse. She just came from the military. She has some great stories. So funny. You'll like her."

"Uh-huh." As good as a homemade spaghetti dinner sounded, he was too tired to fend off his sister when she was in matchmaker mode. "Yeah, well, I'm pretty wiped out. I think I'll just head on home."

"Oh, but you have to come. I already told—" She stopped talking.

"You already told who what?"

"I, uh, already told Emma you were coming. She'd be so disappointed if her uncle Leith didn't show up."

They both knew it wasn't Emma she'd been about to mention, but he let that pass. He did want to see Emma. He'd helped her put together something for show-and-tell last week, and he wanted to see how it went. "Okay, I'll be there, but I do not want a setup. Are we clear?"

"Who said anything about a setup?"

"I did. I mean it, Volta. I'm not going out with your friend. Remember Mina?"

"That was a fluke. How was I supposed to know she had a dog phobia?"

"What about what's-her-name with the purple hair?"

"Jaci was sweet."

"Jaci wanted to plan our wedding before we'd even ordered appetizers."

"She was joking."

"I don't think so."

"Okay, whatever. Just come for dinner in an hour."

"All right. You want me to bring anything?"

"A better attitude. See you then." She ended the call.

Leith set his phone on the desk and started on the report. If he could finish in the next fifteen minutes, he'd have time to swing by his house for a quick shower and to collect the dog before heading to Volta's. But he was only halfway through when he heard the chime signaling the front door opening. "Hello? Anyone here?"

Nuts, he'd forgotten to lock the door behind him. "We're closed. Sorry." He strode into the reception area. Explosion Girl herself was standing there, a striped tote bag tightly gripped in hands tipped with shiny pink nails. What was Sabrina doing here?

She looked a little different than she had on the mountain. Her dark hair was down, waving across her shoulders. She wore a multi-colored scarf, which looked like a watercolor painting, draped around her neck over a bluish dress that stopped just above her knees. *Cute* was an understatement. His eyes followed the curve of her calf down to highly impractical pink shoes, before his gaze quickly returned to her face. Big eyes the color of milk chocolate stared back at him, as though she was as surprised to see him as he was to see her. But she was the one who'd come to him.

"Can I help you?"

"Oh, uh, I hope so." She reached into her bag. "I wanted to return your vest. Thanks for loaning it to me last week."

"You're welcome." Good—now he didn't have to chase it down. He took the vest, but she wasn't making any move to go. Now what? "Was there something else?"

"Yes. It's just, um, you teach classes, right? On outdoorsy stuff?"

He chuckled. "That's not exactly the term we use, but yes, we do."

"So, if I were to want to learn about camping and whatever, you know, just the basics, do you have classes on that?"

"Actually, most of our classes are a little more advanced than that. We teach survival techniques, first aid, river rescue, that sort of thing."

"Oh."

"Besides—" he couldn't help a little teasing "—you implied that you already have camping skills."

"But not necessarily Alaska camping skills. I'd like to learn... Oh, what the heck—I've never been camping in my life, and if my manager finds out, I'll probably lose my job." Her lip trembled, and her eyes opened wide. He got the uncomfortable feeling she wasn't that far from tears. He hated tears.

"Okay, so let me get this straight. You told Walter you were an experienced camper when he hired you?"

"You're on a first-name basis with my boss?" she squeaked. He wouldn't have thought it possible, but her eyes opened even wider.

"Everyone is on a first-name basis with Walter. Orson Outfitters sponsors practically all the outdoor events in the state, and Walter's always out there greeting people. Why did you lie to him?"

"I didn't lie to Walter. My camping skills just never came up. Headquarters hired me as part of their management training program. The first part of the program assigns all the trainees to different stores so we can understand the business at the retail level. In the interview, they asked if I enjoyed the outdoors." She raised her chin. "I do. I like sunshine and flowers and...all that stuff. If they chose to interpret that to mean I like to camp..." She shrugged.

"I don't get it. Why would you want to work for a company in a business you don't even like?"

"I might like it once I learn about it. You never know. But whether I do or not, I need this job. I was a buyer for Cutterbee's department store, but they went bankrupt, and nobody's hiring right now. I'm a hard worker. Whether you help me or not, I intend to give this job my all. I just need a little help getting up to speed."

He remembered hearing about Cutterbee's going under. He'd never understood why anyone would shop at overpriced department stores full of impractical items, but he could see that clothes with fancy labels would be right up Sabrina's alley.

Why should he help her? Whether it was

a direct lie or only implied, she got the job with Orson Outfitters under false pretenses, and Leith had more reason than most to despise liars. On the other hand, when the cans exploded at the team-builder, Sabrina didn't try to deflect the blame or make excuses. He respected that. Besides, he could see the desperation in her eyes. For some reason, the thought of losing her job terrified her.

"Look, like I said, we don't really teach basic woodcraft. Maybe you could register for a course from the University of Alaska, Anchorage, this fall."

"Fall is too late. My assignment here ends September first, when the store managers send in their evaluations. Only the top half move on to the next level of training. Besides..." She paused, taking a sudden interest in the worn vinyl floor.

"Besides, what?"

She took a breath and looked up. "After putting down deposits on my apartment and utilities, I'm a little short on cash right now. I thought maybe we could work out some sort of barter arrangement?"

This should be good. What possible skills could she have that he would find useful? It wasn't as though he needed his hair braided. "What did you have in mind?"

"I don't know. What do you need done? I'm pretty good at interior house painting."

His kitchen could use a coat of paint, but that would mean having her in his house and that sounded like a bad idea. Besides, considering her perfectly groomed appearance, he had trouble picturing her doing manual labor. He suspected her biggest talent was looking good. Which, now that he thought about it, might just solve his problem.

"Suppose I offered to spend a day teaching you to be 'outdoorsy.' Would you be willing to accompany me to a wedding Saturday after next?"

She took a half step backward, like she was afraid she might be walking into a trap. "You're asking me on a date?"

"Nope. Strictly a business arrangement. For all appearances, we would be on a date, but actually I just need a plus-one for the wedding to keep my sister off my back. One and done."

"Why would your sister care whether you had a date for a wedding?"

"It's a long, boring story. The point is, I need a fake date. Are you game?"

She tilted her head to one side and pressed her lips together while she considered. Pink lips to match her fingernails and shoes, of course. "That doesn't seem fair. A couple of hours at a wedding versus a whole day of instruction. Is there something horrible about this wedding I should know about?"

"Horrible?" He laughed. "No, it should be very nice. Dinner and dancing afterward. It's outdoors, so bring a jacket. But I'll tell you what—if you want to trade hours one for one, I'm teaching a class on Wednesday afternoon, and I could use an assistant. Are you free?"

She checked her phone. "I work Wednesday morning and then I'm off until Friday, when we're starting the big Memorial Day weekend sale. But I don't see how I could be of much assistance since I don't know anything yet."

"You'll see. Here, give me your phone number and I'll text you the address for the class Wednesday. On Thursday, we'll do a day's instruction in woodcraft, and a week from Saturday is the wedding. After that we're square. Agreed?"

"Um, yes. Agreed." She offered her hand, and he noticed that her fingernails were not only pink, but each one also had a paler pink flower painted on it. She wasn't going to fare well away from running water and electricity.

But that was her problem. He took her soft hand in his and shook it. This should be entertaining, if nothing else.

CHAPTER THREE

SABRINA FOLLOWED THE directions to the address Leith had given her, which appeared to be a middle school. As she turned in, a line of yellow buses pulled out. She found an empty parking spot and got out of her car, wondering how she was going to find Leith somewhere in the building.

She still wasn't sure why he seemed to think she would be any help as an assistant, unless he just intended for her to fill water glasses and erase whiteboards. Maybe he'd come up with this assignment as a boondoggle, to make her feel she was earning her lessons tomorrow. She hoped not. There were few things Sabrina hated more than feeling useless.

She started toward the main entrance, but as she reached the edge of the parking lot, she heard someone call her name. "Sabrina. Over here." Leith waved from beside a pockmarked white Land Cruiser two rows over. He walked over to join her, carrying a large duffel. His eyes skimmed over her and he pulled his eyebrows together. "I should have told you to wear pants, but we'll manage. Ready for the class?"

"Um, sure." She walked with him, trying to match his long strides. She'd chosen this outfit deliberately: an A-line navy skirt, a silk T-shirt in a subtle tone-on-tone paisley, and an Anne Li raspberry blazer she'd scored after a trunk show. She'd had to alter it, of course, since she wasn't as tall as the model, but sometimes being a size four paid off. Sabrina had given many a presentation in this outfit, and it always made her feel competent and in charge. "Why should I have worn pants?"

"You may need to get down on the floor, but as I said, we'll manage."

The floor? "What is this class?"

"Babysitting."

"What?" She hurried to catch up, wishing she hadn't worn heels. "Why are you teaching babysitting?" She'd thought Learn & Live was about outdoor survival stuff.

"I'm not teaching the whole course. I'm just today's guest instructor." They had reached the main office. Leith signed them in and led her down the hall to a classroom. Inside, a dozen or so young teenagers, mostly girls but a couple of boys, sat in chairs at the front of the room and chatted with a happy-faced woman with brown curls. When Leith walked into the room, the teacher jumped up and beamed at him.

"Welcome back. Students, this is Leith Jordan. Oh, and you brought someone this time."

"Yes. Hi, everybody." Leith waved. "As Mrs. Livingstone said, I'm Leith and this is Sabrina."

"Hi, Leith. Hi, Sabrina," the kids chanted, more or less in unison.

"Let's jump right in. Does everyone have their dummies?" Leith asked as he unzipped the duffel bag. He pulled out a first-aid kit and a life-size baby doll.

All the kids reached under their chairs and pulled out dolls. Leith handed his to Sabrina. She took it, and after a quick glance at the kids, she cradled the doll in her arms like most of them were. Sabrina had never spent much time around babies.

Leith had her sit in a chair. "Okay. Now suppose Sabrina here is taking care of this baby. Maybe she's been feeding him, or the baby has been crawling around on the floor. All of a sudden, she notices the baby is distressed but can't seem to make much noise. His skin looks a little blue. Who knows what's wrong with the baby?"

Sabrina hoped she wasn't supposed to come up with an answer because she had no idea. The kids whispered among themselves. After a minute, one of the girls raised her hand. "It's having a heart attack?"

"Probably not, but good guess. Think about it. What would make your skin turn blue?"

"He can't breathe," someone said.

"Exactly. And what is the most common reason someone suddenly can't breathe?"

There was a moment's silence. "Choking!" another of the girls blurted out.

"Yes!" Leith flashed the girl a smile, and Sabrina almost dropped the doll. Wow. When he smiled a genuine smile, not just the snarky smirks he'd thrown at her before, everything changed. His rugged face grew animated and the cobalt blue eyes, framed by thick dark lashes, seemed to be creating a magnetic force field. Sabrina wasn't the only one who felt it, either, judging by the way all the girls suddenly leaned forward.

"So what do you do when someone's choking?" Leith asked.

"The Heimlich," the first girl said.

"Right. Have any of you seen the posters in the cafeteria about how to administer the Heimlich maneuver?" Several hands rose. "Good. We'll practice that in a few minutes but right now we have a baby choking. Babies are fragile. We can't give them the same treatment we'd give an adult or teenager. Here's how to treat a choking baby."

Leith took the doll from her and demonstrated how to position the baby, supporting it with one hand while slapping it on the back five times with the heel of his other hand. "Not too hard. We don't want to break any ribs, but hard enough to dislodge whatever is blocking the airway." He had all the students practice, going from one to the other to check their positioning and technique. Then he explained the next step to take if that didn't work and had them practice that. Sabrina was impressed. He really seemed to know his stuff, and he had the kids' full attention. By the time they'd finished the lesson, she felt like even she would be able to treat a choking baby.

When Leith was satisfied everyone had it down, he moved on. "Now, what if you're not babysitting a baby. What if it's an older child? Sabrina, can you stand up, please?" She did, and he moved beside her. "Okay, so little Sabrina is agitated. She isn't saying anything. Maybe she's bringing her hands to her throat." Now Sabrina understood what Leith meant by being his assistant. Her job wasn't to help him teach; it was to play the victim.

That, she could do. Sabrina wrapped her fingers around her neck and pretended to gasp as if there was something stuck in her throat.

"Hands on the neck are a classic sign, but even if a person isn't doing that, suspect choking if someone who was eating suddenly seems panicky. But unlike the baby, Sabrina can talk. Let's ask her. Sabrina, are you choking?"

"Yes," Sabrina answered in a stage whisper, tilting to one side and giving a couple of fake coughs. "Please save me."

Leith grinned. "Remember, if she can answer you, her airway isn't completely blocked. Let her try to cough it up herself. But if she can't, that's when the Heimlich comes in. Let's try it again. Sabrina, are you choking?"

Still holding her hands on her neck, Sabrina nodded. Leith moved behind her and put his arms around her, explaining to the class how he was positioning his hands just below her ribs. "And then I'd push in hard to drive the air from her lungs and dislodge whatever is blocking her airway. We won't do that today, because I could injure her that way. A cracked rib is a small price to pay for saving a life, but let's not risk it today."

"Excellent decision," Sabrina croaked. The kids laughed.

"However, I do have a training vest in my

bag. First, I want you to pair up and see where to position your hands, and then we'll get out the vest and practice."

The kids broke into twos and practiced. Once he was satisfied everyone had the basic idea, Leith had Sabrina wear the vest. "See, this foam plug is the food that's obstructing the airway." He stepped behind her and positioned his hands over the air bladder in the vest. "Now let's see if I can do it properly." He tightened his arms around her and gave a hard thrust to the vest. The foam plug popped out. The kids cheered.

All the kids in the class took turns using the Heimlich maneuver on Sabrina. It took some of them several tries, but Leith coached them patiently until they had all succeeded. Sabrina was glad when they moved on to the next lesson, until she discovered it involved head wounds.

"You have lots of blood circulation in your head, and so heads tend to bleed heavily. Suppose Sabrina fell against a piece of furniture and cut her head right here." He pulled a red sticker from a sheet and stuck it to her forehead. "Who can tell me how to stop the bleeding?"

"Put a tourniquet around her neck?" one of the boys suggested, grinning.

"That would do the trick, all right, but it would also stop the blood from getting to Sabrina's brain, and remember, you're getting paid to keep Sabrina's brain safe. Let's try direct pressure instead." He pulled up a chair. "Sabrina, can you sit down, please?" Leith took a gauze pad from his kit and pressed it to her forehead. "Here, push here."

Leith turned toward the kids. "Position. Examine. Elevate. Pressure." He ticked off the words on his fingers. "If you're a chicken about blood, remember to PEEP."

Sabrina groaned. "That pun is more painful than my head wound." Everyone laughed, including Leith.

Before the day was done, Sabrina had been bandaged and splinted, and had her arm put into a sling. Also, while Leith was busy with some of the kids practicing CPR on a dummy, she'd explained to three girls who asked how she'd created the ombré effect on her fingernails and told them where to find an instructional video on the internet.

At the end of class, Leith held up some papers. "Great job, everybody. For me to certify you in first aid, you'll need to pass this test. So, before we start, let's review. What's the first thing to do if you think an older child is choking? Kara?"

"Ask them."

"Good." Leith moved on through all the lessons. Between Leith's goofy memory aids and the practice sessions, these kids had it down. Leith really was a good teacher. Sabrina only hoped she would be able to learn as much about the outdoors tomorrow as he'd taught these kids today. Because if she could, it was just possible that this unusual plan of hers might work.

LEITH SWALLOWED THE last of the coffee in his travel mug while he waited for the light to turn green. He'd been a little surprised to find that Sabrina was living in this part of town. Not that there was anything wrong with this particular neighborhood, but most of the houses here were old and small. Based on the way she dressed and the amount of money she must spend on manicures, he would have thought she'd have chosen a shiny new apartment in a trendy part of town.

She'd surprised him yesterday, too, when she'd accepted her role as training dummy with good grace. In fact, the melodramatic way she'd acted out the injuries really helped keep the kids focused. The other day at the office, when she'd declared herself a hard worker, he'd had doubts. In his experience, hard workers didn't talk about it; they just did it. But he was starting to think she might be the exception to that rule. He hoped so, anyway, because if he was going to get through all the lessons he had planned for today, she was going to have to put in some effort.

It still bothered him that she was hiding her lack of experience from her employer. He'd been lied to and taken advantage of, and it stank. But she was trying to acquire the skills she'd claimed to have. And was her deception any worse than what he was doing, having Sabrina pretend to be his date to the wedding?

Dinner at his sister's had gone just about the way he'd expected. Volta, with all the subtlety of a locomotive, had seated him next to the new nurse at the table and kept throwing out random pieces of information designed to force them to bond. "Leith, Marley's blood type is B negative, just like yours and mine. That's only two percent of the population. Interesting coincidence, huh?"

What did you say to something like that? Marley had seemed like a perfectly nice person, but after going through a divorce three years ago, Leith had decided the safest route was to avoid getting involved with women, period. So, when Volta made a point of asking him if he had a date for the wedding in front of Marley so that he'd almost be forced to invite her, it had given him great satisfaction to assure her that, yes, he did have a date. He'd almost laughed out loud at the expression on his sister's face when her plot failed. Fortunately, Marley didn't look all that brokenhearted. She was probably glad to have gotten out of Volta's trap unscathed as well.

Leith couldn't understand why his sister was so fired up to find him a girlfriend. As far as he knew, Volta had been on less than a dozen dates since her daughter, Emma, had been born seven years ago, seven months after Volta's husband had died in an avalanche. Leith worried about his sister sometimes, but he didn't push her. So why did she feel entitled to push him?

Anyway, this nondate with Sabrina would take care of that problem for the time being, and all he had to do was teach her a few basic camping skills. How hard could that be?

He found her apartment building, a weathered fourplex split-level. Her door was down a half flight of steps. He knocked. A minute later, she opened the door a few inches, pulling a restraining chain tight. "Oh, hi. You didn't have to come get me. I thought you'd just call my cell."

"No, I…" He'd been lectured by his mother that a gentleman always walked a lady to and from her doorway. Of course, she'd meant on a date, and this wasn't a date. "Never mind. Are you ready to go?"

"I think so. Let me grab some yogurt for lunch."

"No need. I brought food to cook. That's part of the lesson."

"Oh, thank you. In that case, I'm ready." She closed the door to unhook the chain and slipped out before he could see into her apartment. Today Sabrina wore tight jeans, a long-sleeved shirt and an Orson-brand fleece vest. She carried a small leather backpack that was obviously more for looks than practicality, since it wouldn't last a day in the rain. At least she was wearing enough layers this time, and the sky was clear today. The jeans weren't the most practical, although he had to admit, they fit her well. She carefully locked the door and turned to him with a smile. "I appreciate you doing this for me."

It was a disarming smile, but three years ago, he'd developed immunity. "No problem, as long as you keep up your end of the bargain. Remember, you still have to do that wedding next week."

"Yeah, but weddings are fun."

"Maybe from your perspective. From mine, camping is fun. Weddings are a pain. But one of my best friends is getting married, so I got stuck as a groomsman. I even have to wear a suit."

Sabrina laughed. "You're a true friend to sacrifice so much. Where are we going?"

"I thought we might head over to Ekulna Lake, do a little hiking and set up a mock camp. Sound okay?"

"You're in charge."

Sabrina approached his ancient Land Cruiser without the usual comments about what a dinosaur it was. One point in her favor. Whatever she drove probably required premium fuel.

As they approached, Tal jumped up from her spot on the back seat and stuck her nose out the window he'd left open a few inches, madly wagging her tail.

"Oh, you've got a dog! Hi, sweetie," Sabrina crooned. "What's your name?"

"Talkeetna." Leith reached past Sabrina to wrench open the stubborn passenger-side door. "Tal for short."

"Hello, Tal." Sabrina climbed into the seat and twisted around to reach for the dog. "Oh, my goodness, your ears are so soft. You're just a big love bug, aren't you?" All the while, she was rubbing Tal's head, and Tal was eating it up, thumping her tail against the seat back. A long thread of drool dangled from her lip, but if Sabrina saw it, it didn't faze her. "Is Tal a boy or a girl?"

"Girl." Leith slammed Sabrina's door closed and went around to the driver's seat. "Better buckle up."

Sabrina fastened her seat belt. "She's so soft and fluffy. How long have you had her?"

"Almost six years. I got her as a puppy." Not long before Nicole decided she needed a graduate degree from an out-of-state college and moved in with a guy in Seattle who she'd insisted was only a roommate. Leith couldn't believe he'd fallen for that story. He patted Tal's head. Happily, this female in his life had remained loyal.

"I love dogs, but I've never had one," Sabrina said.

"You didn't have a dog when you were a kid?"

"No." Sabrina's effervescence lost some bubbles. "We couldn't af— Have pets."

Her mother probably didn't want dog hair on her nice furniture. Everything about Sabrina— the trendy clothes, shiny hair and flashy fingernails, which, he noticed, were pale green today to match her shirt—shouted upscale. Any outdoor activities she'd experienced growing up probably took place at the country club. Some people would envy her. He wasn't one of them. His brief experience in high school with country-club life only made him more appreciative of what Alaska had to offer.

Leith drove out of the neighborhood and merged onto the Glenn Highway. He glanced toward Sabrina. Should he mention her clothes? He was supposed to be training her in woodcraft. "I see you're wearing a fleece vest today."

"Yes. I bought it yesterday."

"Good. The vest will be useful, but jeans may not be the best hiking pants, especially up here."

She tilted her head at him. "You mean because cotton is hydrophilic?"

Huh. She must have been reading the company catalogs. "Yes. If they get wet, jeans take forever to dry. But also because they're tight on your thighs, and when you're lifting your feet to climb uphill, that extra effort tends to tire you out."

"Okay, but these jeans have Lycra, so they stretch." She paused. "What did people wear outdoors before synthetic fabrics? Wool?"

"Mostly."

"I know wool is warm when wet, which is one reason they use it for tweed hunting jackets in Britain."

Leith didn't know anything about British hunting jackets, but it made sense. "It's not supposed to rain today, so your jeans should be fine. And I just have a short hike planned."

"I looked at some nylon hiking pants at the store, but they're going to have to wait until the next payday."

He glanced at her before returning his eyes to the road. "I guess they don't pay trainees a lot, huh?"

She shrugged. "They pay reasonably well. But, you know—student loans, moving expenses, security deposits. And I need to replenish my emergency fund."

"Emergency fund?" He grinned. "What? For fashion emergencies, like shoe sales?"

She didn't look amused. "Emergency fund so I can pay the rent if I don't make the cut in September and I'm unemployed again."

This didn't quite jibe with the lifestyle he'd imagined, but it was hard to feel too sorry for her. Even he could tell those jeans she was wearing didn't come from a discount store, and her manicure probably cost as much as the hiking pants. But there was no use getting into an argument about how she spent her money "I hope you'll learn enough today that you will make the cut to management."

"Here's hoping."

Sabrina was quiet during most of the drive to the lake. Leith got the uncomfortable feeling she was annoyed at him. She stared out the window at the birch trees, with their yellow buds just starting to turn to green. In the distance, snow still covered the top half of the Chugach Mountains. He tried to think of something to say to improve her mood, but nothing came to mind.

Finally, just before they reached the exit, Sabrina spoke. "It is beautiful. I was starting to wonder what all the fuss about Alaska was about, but now that the sun has come out and I can see the mountains, I'm starting to understand."

"It's been a wet spring, and breakup is never the prettiest season," Leith acknowledged, relieved that she seemed to have forgotten his stupid joke. "Give it another two weeks, and you'll be amazed at how green everything is."

They reached the trailhead parking lot. Sabrina pulled on the handle, but the door jammed. Before Leith could get around to help her, she slammed her shoulder into the door and knocked it open. Without comment, she slid out. "What a pretty lake. I love that color. Somewhere between azure and lapis."

"Looks blue to me." Leith opened the tailgate to grab Tal's leash and went around to let her out.

Sabrina turned, and her eyes widened as she looked at something over Leith's shoulder. "Oh, a dog." She trotted past him.

Leith looked up. *Oh, nuts.* "Sabrina, wait." He pushed Tal back into the car before she could see what was going on and escalate the problem.

"I'm just going to check out that dog," she called back to him. "There's nobody else here. It must be a stray."

"Don't go any closer." Leith slammed the door and hurried around the car after her. The dark gray animal at the edge of the woods startled and ran for a few steps before pausing to look toward Sabrina.

Sabrina slowed to a walk, creeping forward while gently crooning. "Here, pup. You're a big guy. Are you lost? I think you're wearing a collar. Do you have a microchip? I'll bet your family is missing you."

"Stop!" Leith finally yelled loud enough to get through to her. She turned. The creature at the corner of the parking lot looked toward him as well.

Sabrina scowled at him. "What? I just want to help that dog. He seems shy. I wonder if someone abandoned him."

"The reason he's shy around people is because he's not a dog." Leith grabbed her elbow and dragged her back toward the safety of the Land Cruiser. "He's a wolf."

CHAPTER FOUR

"NO WAY." SABRINA looked up at Leith's face, expecting to find that he was teasing her, but he wasn't smiling.

"I'm serious. We need to stay back." He nudged her closer to the car.

Sabrina squinted at the animal, who was now hovering at the very edge of the woods, holding his head low as though ready to run. "Are you sure? I think he's wearing a collar."

"He is," Leith agreed. "A radio collar." He opened the car door and reached under the seat, pulling out a pair of binoculars. After focusing, he handed them to Sabrina. "Take a look."

She put the binoculars to her eyes, and the animal jumped into focus. A black collar with a boxlike attachment under his chin almost disappeared in the dark gray fur. Now that she could see him more clearly, he looked a little rangier than most dogs. He lifted his head to stare straight at her with amber eyes, and then he was gone.

"A real wolf." Sabrina returned the binoculars to Leith. "That's incredible."

"Yeah. You don't see wolves often, especially this time of day. They're generally too skittish."

"Were we actually in danger?"

"Probably not. They had a little trouble with a pack north of Anchorage several years ago following people and attacking their dogs, but I haven't heard much about them lately."

"Do wolves ever attack people?"

"Almost never. Every case I've heard of is a lone runner attacked by a pack, and in the middle of winter when food is scarce. This wolf seemed to be alone. I suspect he got separated from his pack and that's why he's wandering around this morning, trying to find them."

She nodded. "Does this mean we can't stay here?"

"I'd suggest we give him a fifteen-minute head start while we make as much noise as possible unloading the equipment, and then carry on with our plans. We'll keep Tal on a leash today, just in case."

"Good." Sabrina walked to the back of the Land Cruiser. "Because this lake is lovely."

Leith eyed her, his eyebrows raised.

"What?"

"Honestly, I thought you'd be scared."

"Why should I be? From what you said, a wolf fifty yards away is not much of a threat. Now, scorpions in your bed. That's scary."

"You found scorpions in your bed?"

"Once. I didn't sleep much that night." Scorpions weren't the only scary things around the apartment building they'd moved to after Sabrina's dad declared bankruptcy and disappeared from their lives. She'd seen a cockroach in the hallway that looked like it could take on a Chihuahua in a fair fight. And some of the people living in the building were even scarier than the roaches. But she didn't like to think about those days. She smiled at Leith. "So, what's my first lesson today?"

"Eager to get started?"

"Got to get that management position."

"Right. Well, I figure since your goal is to impress with your product knowledge, we should experience as many different activities as possible today. I thought we'd start with how to load a backpack and take a short hike first. Then we can set up in one of the campground spots."

"Sounds good."

He pulled out a red backpack. Sabrina wasn't surprised to see the Orson Outfitters logo on the flap. "First, I'll show you how to adjust the straps so that the pack fits you. Then we'll load it up."

Once he had all the buckles and belts adjusted, the pack felt quite comfortable on her back. At least when it was empty. He had her take it off and load it up with a tent, a sleeping bag and other equipment, then put it back on. It didn't feel too bad. "How much does this thing weigh?"

"About twenty-five pounds. Rule of thumb is not to carry more than twenty-five percent of your body weight."

"I think sometimes my purse weighs this much." Sabrina buckled the waist strap and followed Leith and Tal along the flat trail that circled the lake. Maybe the climb during the team-builder had toughened her up, because she wasn't having any trouble keeping up with them.

They reached a Y in the path. Leith looked back at her. "Doing okay with that pack?"

"I'm fine."

"Good. Then we'll go a little farther." He took the path off to the right.

Sabrina followed. The pack grew heavier, but he'd said it was a short hike, so she didn't want to wimp out. This path seemed harder than before. Eventually she realized they were climbing steadily uphill. Leith glanced back a few times, but he never slowed down. Sabrina was sucking wind when he finally stopped.

She stopped, too, resting her hands on her knees and drawing in vast lungfuls of air. Tal came to stand in front of her, staring. The dog had probably never seen a human panting so hard. After a few minutes, Sabrina had recovered enough to speak. "Sorry. I can't climb any farther without a rest."

"That's okay." Leith handed her a bottle of water. "We're here."

She gratefully accepted the water and gulped down half the bottle. "Where's here?"

He offered his hand. "Come see."

She took his hand and he led her a few steps out of the forest, toward the edge of a bluff overlooking the lake. She dug in her heels several feet from the edge. "This is close enough."

"What's wrong?" He studied her face. "Oh. Not a fan of heights?"

"No." She hated this. It was embarrassing to be the one who couldn't do something simple, like cross a bridge. The one whose fear inconvenienced everyone in the group. She knew the danger was in her head, but her pounding heart never listened. She tried to shrug it off "Not from ledges."

He nodded. "No problem. Here. If we stand

on this rock away from the edge, you can still see."

He climbed onto a boulder and Tal scrambled up beside him. Leith reached down for her. The boulder was at least ten feet back from the edge. Sabrina took his hand and climbed onto the rock. He was right. It did give a magnificent view without that sense that the earth was falling away. And he'd done it without making her feel small.

Sabrina shaded her eyes with her hand and looked outward. The lake stretched out below them, a few puffy white clouds reflected on the deep blue surface. Furry dark spruce lined one edge of the lake. On the other side, cerise buds scattered like confetti across the branches of white-barked trees. "It's gorgeous here."

"I thought you'd like it."

She looked up at him and that amazing smile was back. The blue eyes were watching her again, but now they seemed friendly. It was obvious that Leith was in his element. Sabrina realized she was still holding his hand, and she wasn't sure she wanted to let go. After a pause, Tal pushed between them and the spell was broken. Sabrina dropped his hand, rubbing along Tal's head to cover her sudden awkwardness.

"It's almost worth the climb."

Leith raised an eyebrow. "Almost?"

Sabrina sucked in another deep breath. "Totally worth the climb. Just maybe not while carrying another fourth of a person."

He laughed. "You did well." He jumped down from the rock and she followed. "It will be easier going downhill. We'd better get started if we're going to cook in camp today. By the way, I brought supplies to make chili. Is that okay with you? I should have asked if you eat meat."

"I love chili."

"With kidney beans?"

She grinned. "You trust me with a can of beans?"

"Absolutely. I figure that lesson is one you'll never forget."

"You're right about that. I just wish it hadn't been such a public lesson. I'm afraid Walter and the others will never forget it, either."

"Don't worry about it. Someday, it will be one of those funny stories they tell each other about how they knew you before you were a big shot."

"You really think so?"

"Why not? You say you're willing to do the work. You've lined me up to teach you the skills you need, which shows excellent judgment. How can you lose?"

"Too bad Walter can never know about my excellent choice of instructors."

"You can impress him in other ways. Maybe volunteer to staff the Orson Outfitters' sponsor table at one of the events this summer."

"Great idea. Thanks for the suggestion."

"No extra charge. Let's go." He set a brisk pace on the return trip, but as he'd said, it was easier going downhill.

Once they reached the parking lot, they dumped their backpacks into his car and Leith drove to the campground. "Since we're not staying overnight, I could take us to a picnic area for the practice camp, but I want to show you how to build a fire, and they're only allowed in designated campsites."

Only four of the campsites were occupied, three with giant RVs parked and one with a tent. Leith drove away from the others and stopped at an isolated spot near the lake. He got out of the car, so Sabrina followed him. His gaze swept the campsite and then he turned toward her. "What do you think of this spot?"

Sabrina looked around. A metal picnic table was chained to concrete sunk into the ground. Beside a gurgling creek was a flat place under some trees where she assumed the tent would go. A round metal firepit sat in the clearing, with an unobstructed view of the lake. "It's beautiful. But I can tell by that little crinkle in the corner of your eye there's something I'm supposed to notice."

He laughed. "You're good."

"Not good enough to figure out the problem with this campsite."

He nodded toward the creek. "Today, there's no problem. But if this warm weather keeps up, the water coming off the glacier will cause the creek to rise, and you might wake up in the middle of the night with the creek running through your tent. In a public campground like this, the host will probably put up a sign not to camp here, but it's something to keep in mind for wilderness camping."

"Wilderness camping? Is that out in the open without designated campsites?"

"Exactly. But today, this will work just fine. I'll go back to the gate to check us in, and we can get started."

Sabrina insisted on paying the ten-dollar camping fee. Leith protested, but they were using Leith's gas and Leith's food even though this was all for her benefit. She filled out an envelope, enclosed two fives and dropped it in a slot in a post beside the campground sign. A handwritten note on the bulletin board warned that someone had spotted a wolf in the area and to keep your dogs and children close, so the wolf must have tracked through the campground after leaving the parking lot.

She returned to the campsite, where Leith had stacked an armload of wood beside the fire ring. Tal wagged her tail and whined at Sabrina, clearly upset to be tied to a tree. Sabrina hurried over to stroke her head. "Does she have to be tied up?"

"I'm afraid so." Leith gave the dog a pat. "She's pretty good about staying close, but in case she spots a squirrel or something, I don't want her wandering off with that wolf around. Come on. Our first lesson is fire building." He handed her a bucket. "Go fill this with water from the creek."

Was he kidding? "Water. To make a fire."

"Never start a fire unless you have the equipment ready to put it out. Safety first."

"Oh, I get it." She filled the bucket and wrestled it back to camp, while he watched. He could have helped. On the other hand, she was supposed to be learning to camp independently, and lifting buckets of water was probably good arm-toning.

When she got to the edge of the fire ring, he did take it from her and set it against a log. "Ready to learn how to build a fire?"

"One second." Sabrina closed her eyes and took in an exaggerated breath. "I'm unleashing my inner pyromaniac." She opened her eyes. "I'm ready."

Leith didn't laugh but his mouth twitched. "Good thing I brought a fire extinguisher and first-aid supplies." He nodded toward a large canvas case with a red cross on the front.

"I'll try to keep it under control. Okay, how does this work?"

Leith took a knife from his pocket and showed her how to create kindling from a branch. She was surprised to discover that fires were literally built; she'd always assumed it was a figure of speech. But Leith showed her how to create an intricate arrangement of tinder, kindling, twigs, sticks and then logs with spaces in between for air circulation. "Now you just need to strike a match."

"Where do you keep the matches?"

"You didn't bring matches?" Leith raised his eyebrows as though it was a serious question, but the laughter in his eyes gave him away.

"I guess I missed it on the invisible supply list you gave me. Do you have any matches, survival guy?"

"Why, as a matter of fact, I do." Leith reached into his pocket. "In fact, I have two matchboxes, so one must be yours." He handed her an orange plastic cylinder. "Don't go into the wilderness without it."

The Learn & Live logo stamped on the side of the box identified it as a promotional goodie. Sabrina clutched it to her heart. "Thank you. I'll treasure it always." She unscrewed the top and removed a match.

"Striker's on the bottom."

"I suspected as much. I once lit a candle, all by myself."

"Impressive." He smirked.

Sabrina tossed a twig at him before she knelt in front of the fire. "So, just hold the match to the dry grass, right?" At his nod, she struck a match. A slight breeze she hadn't noticed before blew it out. She sneaked a look at Leith, but he didn't seem to be laughing at her. Yet. She struck another match, this time cupping her hand around it until she could touch the flame to the tinder.

The flame caught for a second, and then sputtered out. Sabrina blew out a breath of frustration. She moved so that the wind was at her back and struck a third match. This time, the grass caught fire and burned, lapping at the kindling she'd shaved from a branch. As she watched, the kindling started burning and began to ignite the twigs.

"It's going!" She turned to Leith, grinning.

"I mean, I realize it took me three matches, but I lit a fire!"

"Three matches isn't bad. You get a gold star for fire building. Now, while we let the logs burn to coals for cooking, I'll unload the food, and you can pitch the tent. This is last year's version of the one you, uh—"

"Almost destroyed?"

"You said it, not me." He handed her the tent bag, which she dumped out.

"It's green." She rolled her eyes. "What a surprise."

"What have you got against green? It matches your vest."

"I know. And it matches the camp chairs in the store, and the midweight sleeping bags, and most of the rain jackets. It's like whoever designs the products for Orson only has eight crayons to choose from. I can't figure it out. I've been looking online at our competition. There are beautiful designs in outdoor gear. Why do ours have to be so...plain?"

"Did you see the prices on those brands? Orson Outfitters is known for producing high quality at reasonable prices. That's why people like it. They don't spend a lot on stuff that doesn't matter."

"It is good quality." Sabrina unzipped her vest to show him the lining. "The workmanship on this vest is excellent. The seams are straight and well finished, they used a heavy-duty zipper, and the stitching on the wind-proof lining is perfect. But it's boxy. It's like they just made a smaller version of a man's vest without changing the shape."

"They probably did."

"It shouldn't cost any more to curve the seams and use more interesting colors."

"I don't see what's wrong with green."

"Nothing. I love green. But why couldn't it be forest green, or sage green, or emerald? Or they could use the nap of the fleece to create some textural interest." He was looking at her as though she was speaking a foreign language. She laughed. "Sorry. Back to the tent. I can handle this. Now that I know what a shock cord is."

This tent was just like the other one except that the fabric and the poles were solid green. She followed the same steps and threaded the first pole through the sleeve, as she had on the other tent, but when she was finished, it was too long to fit into the grommets.

Sabrina let out a groan of frustration. "Why doesn't it work?"

Leith set down a Dutch oven and came to see. "Oh, I should have mentioned. The poles aren't the same length. That's why they color-coded them on the new design. I've made the same mistake before. I should mark those poles somehow."

"I'll do it." Sabrina set down the poles and trotted to the car for her leather backpack. She burrowed around inside until she located a bottle of nail polish. "Ta-da. I'll mark them for you. *L* for *long* and *S* for *short*?"

Leith was shaking his head. "You bring nail supplies on a camping trip?"

"Hey, you brought that enormous first-aid kit." She pulled out the brush and painted an *L* on the end of the longer pole. "I'm a whole lot more likely to break a nail than a bone."

"Maybe so, but if you do break a bone, you'll be glad to have the first-aid supplies to splint it."

"Good point." She carefully painted an *S* on the other pole. "But you must admit, the nail polish came in handy."

"I admit nothing." He looked over her shoulder. "Be sure to mark the other ends of the poles, too."

Sabrina snorted and looked up to see him grinning at her. "I'll do that. With my useless nail polish. To make setting up your tent easier next time."

Once the polish dried, she successfully set up the tent. Leith showed her how to make chili over the fire in a cast-iron Dutch oven, but while that was cooking he had her practice lighting a camp stove and boiling water. It turned out that those metal trivets with silicone rings she'd seen at the team-builder expanded to turn into pans.

He demonstrated inflatable sleeping pads and folding cots, mentioned the importance of using biodegradable products when camping and debated the pros and cons of mummy-style sleeping bags versus conventional bags. She'd never remember all of it, but at least some of those terms she'd read on the company website were starting to make sense.

"Chili should be ready. Are you hungry?"

"Starving," Sabrina admitted.

"These are the latest silicone camping bowls from Orson." Leith handed her an orange disk. "They're heat-resistant and foldable, just like the pans."

Sabrina pushed on the center and it popped open into a bowl. "Cool."

"And they're not green."

"You're right. Orange is a favorite, too, I've noticed. For some reason our summer bag is only in orange."

"I know. I have three." Leith used a thick mitt to grab the Dutch oven by the bale and lift it off the fire. When he opened the lid, the aroma of cumin and chilis filled the air. Tal whimpered.

Sabrina almost whimpered as well. "That smells so good."

Leith tossed Tal a dog biscuit and handed Sabrina a big spoon. "Help yourself."

She ladled the rich red chili into her bowl and carried it over to one of the folding chairs. Leith settled into the other chair. He scooped up a spoonful and held it up like a toast. "To outdoor adventures."

"Outdoor adventures. And successful careers." Sabrina blew on her spoon and then took her first bite. It was as good as it smelled. "Yum. I'm a good campfire cook. Who knew?"

"Not bad," Leith agreed. "A little heavier on the jalapeños than usual."

"Oh? Can't take the heat?"

"Oh, I can take it," he said, taking another spoonful of chili. A minute later, Sabrina noticed he took a big gulp from his water bottle, and she smiled to herself. Next time she'd dial down the jalapeños a little. And then she remembered that, unless they served chili at the wedding, there wouldn't be a next time. This was a business arrangement, not a friendship. Too bad because she'd enjoyed her time today with Leith more than she ever expected to.

It was just as well. She needed to spend the

next three months learning everything she could learn about Orson Outfitters and impressing Walter and her coworkers with her potential. Then, if all went well, she'd start her management career in Seattle and she could finally settle in. Make some friends. Maybe even get a dog once her job was secure.

Of course, she'd thought her job had been secure at Cutterbee's. She'd been getting regular salary bumps and good reviews. Over the last two years, Sabrina had seen some disappointing sales reports, but she hadn't realized the chain was in trouble until the day they declared bankruptcy. She wouldn't make that mistake again. Before she'd interviewed with Orson Outfitters, she'd read several stock-analyst reports, and they all gushed over the healthy balance sheet and growth potential.

"Eat up." Leith's voice broke her out of her reverie. "We've got lots to cover this afternoon. Camp dishwashing to start."

Sabrina scooped another spoonful of chili. "Can't wait."

BY THE END of the day, Leith noticed Sabrina's eyes glazing over while he was trying to explain how to correct for magnetic inclination when using a compass, a classic sign of information overload. He decided to forgo the lesson on reading topo maps. Besides, he needed to head home. His niece was staying with him tonight. He pocketed the compass. "Time to break camp."

Sabrina smirked at him. "What are we breaking it with?"

He chuckled. "Those same two hands you've been using all day long." He unzipped the tent and started stuffing one of the sleeping bags into a sack. "You've done well."

She grabbed the other bag and followed suit. "You don't have to sound so surprised."

"I am surprised. I figured you'd get tired or bored about an hour in and demand to go home."

"Nice to know you had such faith in me. I hope I didn't upset your alternate plans." Her voice dripped with sarcasm.

Leith grinned at her. "Nope."

"Well, I guess since you fulfilled your promise for a whole day of training, you'll still want me to attend that wedding."

"Yep. And you don't have to wear fleece. Or green, unless you want to."

"Good to know."

Together, they disassembled and packed away the rest of the camping equipment. Leith showed her how to make sure the fire was out. While he arranged everything into the back of the Land Cruiser, Sabrina volunteered to take Tal for a quick walk before they left for Anchorage.

"Why don't you take her along that trail beside the lake? I'll be done here in just a minute."

They weren't back by the time he'd finished packing everything, so he shut the tailgate and went looking for them. A distant splash drew his attention. A moose swam across a little bay on the far side of the lake. Sabrina stood a little farther up ahead, her hand on Tal's head. She stared across the water, so absorbed that she jumped when Leith rested a hand on her shoulder.

She glanced back at him and then returned her gaze to the moose. He whispered, "I wondered what was keeping you."

"What is that?"

"A moose. A young bull."

They watched until it reached shore and scrambled out on unreasonably long legs. The moose looked in their direction and flicked his ears before turning to plod away. Only after he'd disappeared into the forest did Sabrina turn to Leith, her eyes sparkling. "That was amazing, to see him swim like that."

"It was." He'd seen, maybe, hundreds of moose in his years in Alaska, but for him, it was always a treat. He would never have thought Sabrina would feel that way, though. He would have expected her to be excited, maybe to try to snap a picture to post online, but not to be affected as deeply as she obviously was.

"I can hardly believe I didn't imagine it. First a wolf, and now a moose. In one day."

"That's hardly typical," Leith told her. "You're lucky."

"I am." She smiled at him. "Thanks for bringing me out here."

"You're welcome. Shall we go?"

"Unless you have some other supercool animal ready to run by me, I guess I'm ready."

"No, I think that was probably the grand finale." He reached to take Tal's leash and accidentally brushed his fingers against her hand. Her skin was soft and smooth, as though she'd never done any work. She'd worked hard today, though.

They climbed into the car and started home. As he drove, Sabrina asked a few questions. "In the store, they have this fire-starter-in-a-tube stuff. It didn't seem that hard to start a fire today. Is it just a gimmick?"

"Today was warm and dry, and more importantly, the wood was dry. If you'd been trying to start wet kindling, that paste could come in quite handy."

"Good, because yesterday a customer asked me if he needed some and, based on the description in the catalog, I said it couldn't hurt. I'll feel a little more comfortable with questions now that I've experienced using the products."

"One day of camping hardly makes you an expert. You haven't even spent a night outdoors."

"But it's a giant step in the right direction."

They were past Eagle River and almost to the outer edge of Anchorage when he remembered he hadn't mentioned Emma. "My niece is staying with me tonight, and I need to pick her up. You don't mind if I swing by for her before I drop you off, do you? It would save me a trip back across town."

"Of course I don't mind." Sabrina tilted her head. "Do you spend a lot of time with your niece?"

"When I can. Her mom works as a flight EMT, and she's on call tomorrow. Emma usually stays with my mom and dad, but they're on vacation right now, so Emma's staying over with me."

He waited for the inevitable question about

Emma's father, but it didn't come. Instead Sabrina asked, "How old is she?"

"Emma? She's seven." He exited the highway and started toward Volta's house. "One thing, though. You know how I mentioned I need a date to the wedding to get my sister off my back?"

"Yes."

"Well, since you'll be meeting her..."

"Oh, you need me to pretend we were on a date, rather than a lesson."

"Exactly."

"I can do that, although I still don't understand why. But then, I don't have any siblings, so maybe there's a family dynamic I'm not grasping."

"Yeah, it's weird. Ever since my divorce three years ago, Volta has been trying to fix me up, and she had this new coworker all picked out to go with me to the wedding. That's why I told her I already have a date."

"Fix-ups are the worst."

"Tell me about it."

"This woman I used to work with had a son my age, and she was determined we were destined for each other. Eventually I went out with him, just to get her off my back. I've never had such an awkward evening in my life. The guy was some kind of computer guru, which is fine except he spent the entire evening lecturing me about the pros and cons of Linux. In a monotone. I'd try desperately to change the subject, and he'd just keep on talking. The worst part was going into work the next day, with his mother all starry-eyed over this great romance she thought she'd arranged. How do you tell a person she's raised the most boring man on the face of the earth?"

Leith laughed. "What did you say?"

"I think I said something about him overwhelming me with his genius. Fortunately, he was no more enthralled with me than I was with him. I guess I wasn't an appreciative enough audience."

"You got off easy. I spent one evening with a fix-up my sister arranged. One dinner, a little awkward conversation and I took her home. And yet she called me every day for a month. I think she only stopped because she moved to Pennsylvania. I still get emails from her with cute kitten photos once in a while."

"Are you a fan of cute kittens?"

"Not anymore."

"Was she a good listener? Maybe we should put her in touch with the computer guy."

"Let's not." He pulled into Volta's driveway. The front door flew open and Emma ran outside. "Uncle Leith!"

He got out of the car and caught Emma as she threw herself at him and wrapped her arms around his neck. "Hey, shortcake."

Emma gave him a big hug and then scrambled down to press her hands against the car window. "Hi, Tal."

The big dog ran a slobbery tongue over the inside of the glass. Sabrina climbed out on the other side of the car. Emma ran around to greet her. "Hello."

"Hi. I'm Sabrina." Sabrina offered her hand.

Instead of shaking it, Emma took her hand and studied her fingernails. "Pretty." She looked up at Sabrina. "Are you Uncle Leith's new girlfriend?"

Sabrina looked at him helplessly. Leith jumped in. "Sabrina and I have only been out once. That doesn't make her my girlfriend."

"Oh." Emma took Sabrina's hand and led her toward the front door. "How many dates make you a girlfriend?"

"That's a good question." Sabrina looked back at Leith, smirking. "Leith, how many?"

"Well, I'm not sure." How did he get into this discussion? "I guess it depends."

Emma stopped and looked at him, hands on her hips. "On what?"

"On different things. What kind of dates,

how people feel about each other, stuff like that. Are you all packed to come to my house? I'm taking you to that birthday party tomorrow, right? Did you already buy a gift, or do we need to go shopping later?"

"We got one, and Mommy already wrapped it. What kind of date did you go on?" She saw right through his lame attempt at distraction. Emma could be a lot like her mother when she had a subject she liked.

"We went hiking," Sabrina offered. "And we made chili over the campfire."

"Did you kiss?"

"Emma." Volta had stepped outside and was trying hard not to bust a gut. "Remember when we talked about how some things are private, and you don't ask people about them?"

"I thought that was not asking people how much they weigh."

"Yes, and questions about kissing fit into that category as well. Go get your backpack so you can go with Uncle Leith." Once Emma had run inside and was out of earshot, Volta grinned at Leith. "I admit, I'm a little curious myself, but I won't ask. Come on in." They stepped inside her living room and she turned her attention to Sabrina. "Hi, I'm Volta."

"Sabrina."

Better make this good. Leith reached for

Sabrina's hand and held it in his. "Sabrina is going with me to the wedding next week."

"That's great. It'll be a chance for Emma and me to get to know you better."

"I'll look forward to that." Sabrina lifted Leith's hand and gave it a visible squeeze before stepping closer to a wall filled with pictures. In the center of a big frame, Volta had arranged photos of Emma inside the letters of her name. "This is so cute. I love that name—Emma."

"Me, too. Mostly because it's a nice, easy-to-spell name." Volta pointed out a newborn picture in the *E*. "Right after she was born, my mom said I should name her Eileithyia, after the Greek goddess of childbirth. I think she was kidding, but I'm not entirely sure."

"Wow. That would be a challenge to spell."

"Mom loves weird names. She wanted to name Leith 'River.' River Jordan, get it? Dad vetoed, so she found a name that meant 'river.' Then when I was born, it was Dad's turn and he's an electrician, so he named me Volta. Can you believe anyone would do that to an innocent baby?"

"I like it. It's like a superhero name. My mom named me after a movie title she saw on the TV schedule in the hospital. She'd never even seen the movie. The title character could have been a serial killer, for all she knew."

Volta shook her head. "Parents. Gotta love 'em."

Emma ran back into the room, dragging a purple duffel bag almost as big as her. "I'm ready."

"Did you bring everything you own?" Leith grabbed the bag and slung it over his shoulder.

"I've got my clothes, and the present for Jamie's birthday party tomorrow, and my sleeping bag, and Rufus."

"Of course—Rufus." Emma couldn't sleep without the almost-life-size stuffed basset hound Leith had made the mistake of giving her for Christmas a couple of years ago. Why couldn't he have chosen a teddy bear instead? "Tal will enjoy the company."

"Me and Rufus and Tal can have a sleepover in my room."

"Hugs." Volta gave Emma a squeeze and a kiss before sending her on her way. "It was nice meeting you, Sabrina. I'll look forward to talking with you at the wedding."

From the glint in Volta's eye, she was already planning the next wedding—between him and Sabrina. Like that would ever happen. Even if Leith did want a girlfriend, a high-maintenance city girl like Sabrina was the last person he would get involved with, but Volta didn't need to know that. And he'd be the last person to crush his sister's dreams.

CHAPTER FIVE

AFTER MAKING SURE Emma was buckled in the back seat beside Tal, Leith climbed in behind the wheel and backed out of the driveway. Emma waved goodbye to her mother, but almost the second they were out of sight of the house, the questions started. "Uncle Leith, have you ever been to a wedding before?"

"Yes, I've been to weddings."

"Are they fun?"

"Um…" Leith exchanged glances with Sabrina, who was pressing her lips together to keep from laughing. "For some people, I guess."

"I got a new dress. It has flowers on it."

"Hmm." Leith was never sure what he was supposed to say when Emma started talking about things like clothes. He was good at taking her fishing, or playing tag, or helping with homework, but clothes were a mystery.

"I can't wait to see you in your new dress," Sabrina said.

"I got shoes, too."

"What color?"

"White. And they have little flowers on the top."

"To go with the flowers on your dress. That will look great."

"Do you have flowers on your dress?"

"Maybe. I haven't decided which dress I'm going to wear yet. One of them has flowers."

"Wear that one," Emma declared. "We can be twins."

"All right, then. I will." They pulled into the parking lot of Sabrina's apartment building. Leith pulled her leather backpack from the back of the car. She took it from him. "Thanks for today. I learned a lot."

"You're welcome. I'll see you for the wedding, then?"

"I'll be ready. Bye, Emma. See you there."

"Bye-bye." Emma waved until Sabrina disappeared inside the building. "She's nice."

"Yeah." Leith couldn't argue with that. He pulled out from the parking lot.

"And she's pretty."

"Uh-huh."

"Why didn't you kiss her goodbye?"

"Emma…"

"You said you were on a date. At the end of a date, you're supposed to kiss."

"Where did you hear that?"

"I saw it on TV."

"Well, first of all, just because you saw something on TV, that doesn't make it true. Not every date ends with a kiss, especially not first dates."

That stopped Emma for about two seconds. "The wedding will be your second date. Will you kiss her then?"

"Emma, remember what your mom said?" He glanced into the rearview mirror at her. "Some things are private."

Emma grinned. "You are gonna kiss her."

He wasn't, because it wasn't a date, but if he said so Emma would surely tell her mother, and Volta would start up with the matchmaking again. "That's between me and Sabrina."

Emma started singing to herself. *"K-i-s-s-i-n-g..."*

Where did she get this obsession with kissing? He just hoped it was a passing fad, like last year when she'd decided to be a dog. She'd worn her hair in two ponytails and barked instead of talked for almost a week.

Emma held her hands above her head and spread her fingers. "Maybe for the wedding, Mommy will paint my fingernails a pretty color like Sabrina's. Do you think so?"

"I don't know, Emma." He hoped not. He liked Emma the way she was, not afraid of bugs or dirt or the occasional bruise or scrape. He didn't want her to think she needed to impress people with nail polish or fancy dresses. Maybe Sabrina wasn't the best role model. He decided to change the subject. "I think I'll grill tonight. You want me to make hot dogs or burgers?"

She thought for a moment. "Which one does Sabrina like best?"

"I don't know, Emma. It doesn't really matter, since Sabrina isn't here. What do *you* want?" His tone was sharper than he intended.

"Hot dogs, I guess," Emma mumbled, and he felt like a jerk for raising his voice.

"Sorry, Emma. I didn't mean to lose my cool there. Hot dogs it is." He pulled into his garage and opened the door to let Tal jump down. "Maybe you can take Tal into the yard and play fetch with her while I unload."

Emma brightened. "Okay. Come on, Tal." They ran into the house to grab a ball.

Leith smiled and stopped at the mailbox before grabbing Emma's duffel out of the car. A thick envelope on top had an Oregon return address. He dumped Emma's stuff into his guest room and returned to the kitchen to open the letter. Nicole's name jumped out at him.

He sank onto a kitchen chair and skimmed the cover letter, then read it again, slowly. An annulment. His ex-wife was getting married again, and she wanted their marriage annulled. Dismissed. Poof. As though it never happened.

As though they'd never agreed to love and honor one another. Never lived as husband and wife. As though all the time and effort he'd invested in trying to make her happy, not to mention his savings and a big chunk of his salary to pay her tuition and expenses while she went to graduate school out of state, didn't count. As though it was all a joke.

Maybe she had played a joke on him. It could be that, even though she was the one who'd pushed for marriage, she'd never really intended to spend her life with him. Perhaps she'd always planned to move on to some other place and some other guy once she got what she wanted. But he'd meant it when he said "I do." As far as Leith was concerned, their marriage had been real. And the fact that Nicole had now decided it was inconvenient to have been married before didn't erase what they had.

Forget it. He wasn't signing anything. They'd been married and divorced, and he was still living with the fallout from that. Nicole was just going to have to live with it, too.

Leith tossed the papers into a drawer and returned to the garage to unload the camping equipment. When he picked up the tent, a small bottle fell to the garage floor and rolled to the wall. He bent to retrieve it: the nail polish Sabrina had used to mark the tent poles.

Leith frowned. Nicole used to get weekly manicures. He always thought it was a waste of money, but she'd insisted it was important to look professional if she wanted to move up at the bank where she'd worked. Then she'd decided looking professional wasn't enough, that she needed an MBA to get to the next level. And while she'd earned that MBA, she'd decided that little bank in Alaska wasn't enough anymore, and neither was Leith.

He should have seen it coming. He should have realized before he married that they were too different to make a go of it. He tossed the bottle of polish back into the car to return to Sabrina. He certainly had no use for it.

ON MONDAY EVENING, Sabrina straightened the dollar bills so they all faced the same way, then counted them. Despite having made several cash drops throughout her shift, her cash drawer was packed full. It would take longer than usual to balance out tonight.

"Good work, everyone." Now that the doors were locked, Walter was walking through the store, congratulating all the employees on a job well done. Sabrina had been involved in some big sales, but she'd never seen anything like the response to the Memorial Day sale at Orson's. The giant tepees of popular products they'd set up on the sidewalks outside had been reduced to rubble. Every register had been open, and still the lines had snaked past the camping department and almost back to where the shoes and boots were. Walter had been circulating among the waiting customers, chatting and offering samples of protein bars and trail mix.

He drifted over to her register station. "How goes it, Sabrina?"

She raised a finger to ask him to wait while she finished counting. "One-seventy-five, one-seventy-six and one-seventy-seven." She made a note and turned to Walter. "Great. I'm amazed at the turnout this weekend. Is the Memorial Day sale always like this?"

"We usually get a good response, but this may turn out to be our best yet. It will probably be quiet for a day or two. I think you're about done here, don't you?"

"Done?" Oh, no. Was he letting her go?

"Time to move to another department. You've obviously mastered the register and had a chance to see what merchandise is selling. I was planning to put you in camping or fishing, one of the bigger departments, but Marianne has a family emergency and needs to spend a couple of months in Arkansas caring for her sister. I thought you could take over women's wear until she gets back, if that's okay with you. It's a working supervisor job, split between supervision and working the sales floor. I know you were probably expecting to work in one of the main departments, but it would really help us out."

"No, women's wear is fine. Great, in fact." Her day with Leith made her feel a lot more confident about camping, but she still couldn't identify half the products in the camping department. And she hadn't even delved into fishing. "When do I start?"

"You're off tomorrow, right? Come to my office on Wednesday, and I'll get you started." He wandered over to Clara's register and Sabrina could hear him praising her on the efficient way she'd managed the checkout line. Sabrina had worked under a lot of bosses, good and bad, and Walter was one of the best. He genuinely cared about his employees, and they were devoted to him. The more she got to know Walter, the worse she felt about her deception.

But if she worked hard enough, she could make it up to him. She'd learned so much from her day with Leith, and she'd been poring over camping websites and catalogs. Now Walter was trusting her with a department, and Sabrina was determined not to let him down.

The burst of excitement over the new assignment got her through the final half hour of her shift, but by the time Sabrina crossed the parking lot to her car, she was ready to drop from exhaustion. She wanted nothing more than to go home and put her feet up. But as she waited at a traffic light, she remembered she'd used the last of her coffee. She was tempted to delay shopping until tomorrow, but if she did, she'd hate herself in the morning.

She pulled into the parking lot of a grocery store a few blocks from her apartment. Ten minutes later, she returned to her car, carrying in her shopping bag a pouch of fresh coffee, half a dozen bagels and a tub of cream cheese for a celebratory breakfast tomorrow. On the way to her car, she passed an old truck parked beside a van. In between the two vehicles, a man suddenly yelled, "Stop that, you little—"

At the man's feet, a tiny dog looked up from a torn package and snarled. The man aimed a heavy boot at the dog's head, but the dog jumped aside. It growled at the man, who grabbed a tool from the back of his truck. "I'll teach you to snarl at me."

"Stop it," Sabrina shouted. "Don't hit that dog."

The man fixed his bleary gaze on her. "Who are you?"

"It doesn't matter who I am. Leave the dog alone."

"You can't tell me how to treat my dog." He took a step toward Sabrina, still carrying a tool like the one she recognized from the spare-tire kit in her trunk.

Sabrina swallowed and looked around the parking lot. A few people milled around the front of the store, but no one was near enough to see what was happening. Should she scream?

The man took another step closer, but she held her ground, even though her heart was pounding. Suddenly, he threw the tool in the back of the truck and jerked open the door. "You like that little mutt so much? Take him." He revved the engine and Sabrina barely had time to jump back as he shot out of the parking space. He roared off, not before giving her a rude hand gesture.

The dog gulped the last bite from what Sabrina could now see was a package of lunch meat. Clumps of hair and dirt made it impossible to see what color he was, but shiny black eyes surveyed her. Sabrina crouched and held out a hand. "Hi, there."

The dog watched her for a moment before returning to his conquest. He picked up the empty plastic pouch, gave it a good shake and tossed it in the air. Only then did he approach Sabrina. He sniffed her hand and quickly drew back. Sabrina stayed where she was. Once he'd determined she wasn't coming after him, he came closer and eventually allowed her to scratch him under his chin. After she'd petted him for a few minutes, she picked him up. He didn't resist. She ran her hand along his ribs and could count each one.

"Poor little guy. Had to steal your supper, did you?" She stroked the little dog's head, and his tail wagged. She carried him to her car, setting her groceries in the back seat and the dog in the front. "Wait right here, and I'll find you something better to munch on."

She hurried into the store, located a small bag of kibble and ran it quickly through the self-scan. When she returned to the car, the dog was on the back seat, tearing into her tub of cream cheese. Sabrina laughed. "Oh, well. You probably needed it more than I did. Come on. Let's go home."

The dog jumped onto the passenger seat and wagged his tail. Sabrina pulled out of the parking lot. "I can't keep you, you know. I'm only here for the summer, and I don't know for sure where I'll be after that. Besides, I signed on the lease that I don't have pets. If I were to keep you, I'd have to pay a security deposit and extra rent."

He watched her intently as though he understood exactly what she was saying. During the short drive home, he crept over the console into Sabrina's seat and laid his head in her lap. She reached down to run her hand over his head. "You're sweet. Don't worry—I won't just drop you off at the pound. I'll find a good place for you."

Her exhaustion forgotten, Sabrina carried her bag of groceries and the dog inside. He scrambled all over the apartment, sniffing every corner and wagging his tail as though he approved. Sabrina gathered up the can of paint and paintbrush she'd left out after putting a coat on the baseboards. When she opened the closet door, the dog ran inside, sniffed all around and then came out and looked at her as though assuring her it was safe for her to enter. She laughed and set the paint on the floor beside her sewing machine.

How did one go about finding a home for a dog? She should probably post a photo on the internet. But if she was going to put up a doggie dating profile, he needed to look his best. They'd start with a bath.

Sabrina filled the kitchen sink with warm water and got her shampoo out of the shower. She picked up the dog. He cuddled against her chest until she carried him over to the sink, when he began to struggle.

"It's okay," Sabrina crooned. "The water's warm. See?" She reached in and scooped up a little water in her hand, and then smoothed it over the dog's head. He struggled harder, his claws catching on her work polo.

"Okay. This isn't working." She set the dog on the floor. He pranced across the living room. Sabrina shook her head. "Don't get cocky, little dog. I'm changing clothes, and I'll be back for round two."

Her second attempt wasn't exactly a resounding success, either, but eventually she was able to get the dog in the water and soap him up. "See, it's not so bad. This is nice. People take bubble baths to relax." She reached for the sprayer to rinse him, but as soon as she removed one hand he squirted out from under the other one and leaped out of the sink. He landed on the kitchen floor, shook suds all over the cabinets and ran to the bedroom, where he burrowed into a basket of clean laundry.

When Sabrina ran in after him, he popped out of the laundry basket and wagged his tail as though they were playing a game. "You little stinker. Now I'm going to have to make another trip to the Laundromat."

She captured the dog and returned him to the sink, where she was finally able to rinse the soap out of his fur. She wrapped him in a thick towel and carried him to the chair in the living room, where she held him in her lap while carefully working the mats from his hair with a comb. This part, he didn't seem to mind. In fact, when she stopped combing for a moment, he nudged her hand to encourage her to continue.

The poor dog looked even skinnier with his fur all plastered to his body, but since he'd just finished a pack of lunch meat and half a tub of cream cheese, Sabrina figured she should wait to feed him dog food. After all, he only weighed about ten pounds, and he'd probably consumed at least half a pound of groceries.

He jumped from her lap and grabbed a pencil off the floor. It must have gotten knocked off the countertop during the bath. He carried the pencil to her, but when she reached for it, he turned his head away, teasing her. It took her three tries to grab the pencil. As soon as she did, the dog bounced across the room, ears up, looking at her expectantly. She threw the pencil. He chased it down and brought it back to her.

They played for several minutes before the dog stopped to roll on the carpet, grunting happily. His brown-and-black fur, freed from dirt and tangles, settled into silky tufts, forming shaggy brows above his bright eyes. If she hadn't witnessed the transformation, she wouldn't have believed this was the same dog as the one in the parking lot.

"You're so cute. I'll take your picture and post it, and I'm sure we'll find someone nice to adopt you." She pulled out her cell phone but stopped before snapping the photo. How would she know whether the people who answered the ads would take good care of him? The dog might end up in a home like the one he'd just come from. In fact, if she posted, the former owner might claim him, and might even accuse Sabrina of stealing the dog.

Maybe she should look into shelters. She

could research them first, make sure they were no-kill and took good care of the pets. The dog grabbed the pencil again and brought it to her for another round. Yeah, she should probably research shelters in Anchorage. Tomorrow. Because tonight, she was too busy playing with a dog.

BACK AT WORK two days later, Sabrina adjusted the collar of an orange T-shirt so that it showed half an inch above the yellow one she'd layered over it on the hanger. She wanted to feature warm colors, since women's apparel was tucked into the back of the store, far away from the sunshine coming through the front windows, and directly under a large air-conditioning vent.

Walter had introduced her to Marianne that morning. The older woman had thanked her repeatedly for taking charge of the department when she would be away. "This is the worst possible time to leave, but my sister has some complications with her second pregnancy and could use someone to take care of her and her little boy. He has special needs. She's a widow—long, sad story—but, anyway, she needs me." She checked her watch. "My plane leaves at three, and I still have a few things to pack. I should probably be going."

"Go ahead," Sabrina urged. "We'll be fine."

Marianne moved a stack of folded shorts on a table two inches to the right. "Okay, well, you've got the shift schedule. It's a good crew, hard workers, but they're all part-timers, so none of them could take over. I really appreciate you agreeing to fill in."

"It's my pleasure," Sabrina assured her, again. "Everything will be fine here. You've given me your phone number if I have questions. Go on. Take care of your sister."

Marianne finally left, but not before giving Sabrina a hug and passing a last lingering glance over the department. As soon as Sabrina was sure she wasn't going to come back to share one more detail, she started planning changes.

The department was clean and neat, almost too neat. The severe organization discouraged customers from browsing through the racks and upsetting the order. Each type of clothing hung on a rack of its own, sorted by size. There were no mannequins, no displays, just neatly stored clothing. Sabrina suspected Marianne would have been an outstanding personal organizer.

Sabrina started with creating a few end-of-rack displays. Over the layered T-shirts, she added a green fleece jacket, adjusting the zipper to half mast and tucking the cuff of one sleeve into a pocket to mimic movement. She stepped back to take in the total effect. Not bad, considering what she had to work with.

"What are you doing?" Autumn, the salesperson scheduled for the evening shift, had arrived, which meant Sabrina's shift was about over. Sabrina had seen Autumn around, but never met her before.

"Hi. I'm Sabrina. I'll be filling in for Marianne for a while."

"Marianne told me you'd be starting today." Autumn looked at the jacket doubtfully. "What's this?"

"I'm putting together some displays."

"Oh." Autumn bit the side of her cheek. "But the T-shirts go over there."

"Uh-huh." Sabrina couldn't quite see where she was going with this.

"Marianne is a stickler that everything needs to be on its proper rack, sorted by size, so customers can find what they're looking for."

"Well, that makes sense." Sabrina stepped forward to straighten the zipper pull. "But what if a customer comes back to look at the jackets, but when she sees the T-shirt with it she decides to buy both?"

"I guess we'd sell more." Autumn studied the ensemble Sabrina had created. "That looks good. I've never thought about layering two T-shirts."

"Thanks."

"Marianne says her sister's baby isn't due for, like, two months. I guess what she doesn't know won't hurt her, right?"

"Right. And if sales go up maybe we can convince her to loosen up a little."

"Yeah, maybe." Autumn grinned. "If you believe in miracles."

Sabrina laughed. "So tell me. If you're shopping for a T-shirt, what's the first thing you look for?"

"Color, I guess."

"Me, too. That's why I was thinking we might sort the T-shirts by color and then size. The color block makes a graphic statement and it's easier for customers to find their size in the color they want."

"Yeah, okay. I'll work on that during my shift."

"Great! I guess I'll see you tomorrow, then. Thanks, Autumn." Sabrina had enjoyed her half day in the department, but she wanted to hurry home to make sure the dog was okay. It was her first time leaving him alone for more than half an hour. According to their website, the shelter she'd researched wasn't open for drop-ins until tomorrow, so she'd have him for at least another night. She stopped to drop off her name tag and collect her purse from her locker. As she hurried to the front of the store, she passed the pet section and paused. She was going to need a collar and leash if she wanted to take the dog for a walk.

Surprisingly, the pet section was by far the most stylish part of the store. Collars came in leather or nylon, in all sorts of colors and prints. After a few minutes of deliberation, she chose a collar and leash with subtle variations of green and black in a curlicue pattern. A reflective thread wove through the design for increased visibility. There was even a coordinating microfiber dog scarf, although it was a better size for Leith's dog than the little dog she'd taken home. Too bad, because it wasn't expensive, and she really loved that print.

In fact… Sabrina picked up the scarf and returned to women's apparel, where Autumn was busy arranging the T-shirts. "Did you forget something?"

"I just wanted to check this color." Sabrina held the scarf against one of the green jackets. It blended perfectly.

"Is that one of the dog bandannas?"

"Yeah. Nice print, aren't they?"

Autumn laughed. "Yeah. Maybe we should sell them here."

Sabrina didn't laugh. "Maybe. See you tomorrow." She checked out using her employee discount and headed home. Taking advice from a dog-care website, she'd used a packing box to pen the dog in the kitchen while she was gone. She'd lined the floor with newspapers and provided a pillow, a bowl of water and a chew toy. Hopefully, he'd had a comfortable day alone.

When she inserted her key in the lock, an excited bark sounded. Sabrina hurried to shush him before the neighbors heard and reported her. She wasn't keeping the dog, but she didn't want to have to explain that to her landlord.

As soon as she stepped inside, a furry missile launched through the air and collided with her chest. She instinctively caught him. "Hey, what are you doing out here? You're supposed to be in the kitchen."

He wiggled higher in her arms to lick her chin. Sabrina laughed. "Stop that. It tickles. Yes, I'm glad to see you, too. Guess what? I got you a present. A new collar and leash. Just let me change, and we'll go out for a walk, okay?"

She set the dog on the floor. He dashed over to the kitchen and bounded effortlessly over the box to reach his bowl, where he noisily lapped up some water. So much for her careful preparations. A quick survey of the apartment showed an overturned wastebasket and a shredded tissue, but no lasting damage, fortunately. He hopped back over the box and ran to sit at her feet and stare at her as if to ask why she was wasting time.

It took a little longer than usual to change clothes, since the dog insisted on sniffing each article of clothing and her shoes before she could put them on, but a few minutes later, she was ready. She fastened the collar around his little throat and snapped on the leash. As soon as she straightened, he tugged her toward the door.

Sabrina laughed. "We'll go, but don't get used to this. If I get off work in time tomorrow, I need to take you to the shelter to find you a forever home. Understand?"

The dog tilted his head and stared at her for a moment, those bright eyes tugging at her heartstrings. Then he turned and scurried toward the door, tail wagging. His message was clear. He'd worry about tomorrow *tomorrow*. Today was for fun.

THE SUN WARMED Sabrina's shoulders as she jogged out of the woods. White daisies fluttered in the breeze across the open meadow between the trees and the street. The dog scurried along beside her, his short legs almost a blur when he ran. His tail never stopped wagging, which inspired her to make another lap around the park before heading home. The treadmill at the gym had never been this much fun. She was going to miss the little guy.

She paused to let him sniff an interesting rock. Some child had dropped a handful of daisies on the pathway. Sabrina picked them up and sniffed. No odor to speak of, but there was something so happy about a daisy. Once the dog had finished marking the rock, she started jogging again, this time toward home.

Inside her apartment, she unsnapped the leash and the dog ran to the kitchen for a drink. Sabrina pulled a jar from the kitchen cabinet and filled it with water for the daisies. Cute. The dog sniffed his bowl, so Sabrina poured in some kibble before she went to shower. She was reaching for the towel when she heard a soft scratching at the bathroom door. She opened it a crack and the dog ran in and sat on the rug, looking up at her.

She dried off and reached for her clothes. "Did you need something?"

The dog simply wagged his tail at her voice. Sabrina reached down to give him a pat, and his tail moved faster. He was a living Geiger counter, only he measured affection. The closer she got, the faster he wagged.

Once she was dressed, Sabrina returned to the kitchen and checked the refrigerator. Leftover arroz con pollo caught her eye. While it heated, she set the daisies in the center of the table and added a straw place mat and a cloth napkin. When her father left and they lost the house, her mom could barely drag herself out of bed sometimes. Meals were hit-and-miss. Eventually, Sabrina discovered that even if dinner was just spaghetti from a can, if she set a pretty table, it tasted better. And if she set the table for two, sometimes her mom would eat with her.

The dog sat quietly beside her chair as she dined, watching each morsel make the trip from her plate to her mouth. She smiled at him. "I'd share, but according to what I read, too many scraps aren't good for you." The dog tilted his head as though thinking that over. She laughed. "Maybe just a bite." She offered a few grains of rice, which he accepted daintily.

After dinner, she pulled out her fleece vest and the green dog scarf she'd brought home. She laid the vest on the counter and moved the scarf around to different areas until she had a plan. She dug out her sewing scissors and a ruler and went to work. She had cleared off the table and set up her sewing machine when her phone rang. She smiled.

"Hi, Mama. How was the cruise?"

"Wonderful. Amazing. We had so much fun. I wish you could have come."

Yeah, tag along on what was, for all intents, a honeymoon. Mama had married Mason a year ago, but this cruise was his first chance to get away from his job. Sabrina was sure he would have loved having his new stepdaughter there. "Maybe someday. How is Mason?"

"He's fine. Says he must have gained ten pounds from all the food on the cruise, but he didn't. All that walking was good for both of us. He's working late today, catching up on everything he missed while he was on vacation. Glad I don't have to worry about that anymore." Her mother laughed.

Sabrina didn't. Her mother's decision to stop working when she remarried worried Sabrina. She would have thought Mom would have learned something from all those years she struggled. Sure, Mason seemed to be a nice, dependable guy, but so had Sabrina's dad. They used to tell her their love story, like a fairy tale. How Mama had gone to work as a receptionist at Dad's business. He'd claimed he'd known from the first time he laid eyes on her that she was the woman he would marry.

And he had. Mama was only twenty when Sabrina was born and she quit working at Dad's business. Mama had relished her new role. They lived in a beautiful new house, in a beautiful new neighborhood. Mama used to throw beautiful dinner parties for their friends. She would spend days cooking and preparing the house. Sabrina used to help, folding napkins just so, sampling the fancy hors d'oeuvres. Sometimes, Sabrina would peek from her perch at the top of the stairs, watching all the ladies in their pretty dresses and sparkling jewelry, the men elegant in their suits.

And yet those friends had disappeared when the marriage fell apart, and their beautiful life was over. Sabrina remembered the night it happened. Hearing raised voices, she'd crept down the stairs and listened to her father break her mother's heart. The business had failed and the house had been mortgaged to the hilt, and he was planning to declare bankruptcy and start over somewhere else. With someone else—ironically, his former secretary.

That was when Sabrina and her mother had moved to that ratty apartment in a part of the city Sabrina had never seen before. Mama filled out some job applications, but two years as a receptionist and twelve as a stay-at-home mom didn't make for a stellar résumé. Not that she was trying very hard to find a job, or to do anything else. The shock of the husband she loved abandoning them had taken all the spirit out of her.

It fell to Sabrina to hold it together. She'd been the one to manage the tiny check her father sent every month, to set the rent aside in an envelope and shop for bargains in the little grocery store on the corner, next to the library.

That local library was Sabrina's saving grace. She spent hours there in the comforting company of books, escaping into other places, other lives. The librarian would talk with her, ask questions about her mom, generally make sure Sabrina was okay. It was a comment from the librarian about family that led Sabrina to ask her mother about her parents.

Over a dinner of peanut butter sandwiches, she'd asked, "Do I have a grandmother?"

"You do. My parents are your grandparents."

"Where do they live?"

"Here. In Phoenix."

She had family here? "Are they nice?"

Mama shrugged. "Nice enough, I suppose."

"Why haven't I met them?"

Mama had turned away and gazed out the window at the blank wall of the next unit instead of looking at her. "My parents, well, they opposed my marriage. They said I was too young, especially since he was ten years older than me. Your father took it personally. After we married, he didn't want me to have anything to do with them." She mumbled something that sounded like "burned bridges."

At that point, Sabrina didn't much care about her father's hurt feelings. Grandparents. Some of the kids at school talked a lot about their grandparents, how they would take them out for ice cream or buy them presents. It sounded like heaven to Sabrina. "Since Daddy's gone, can we talk to them now?"

"No. Not now." Mama stood up and opened the refrigerator. "You should eat more vegetables. Do you want a carrot?"

But Sabrina refused to be distracted. "Why not now?"

Mama sighed. "I have some pride left. I'm not crawling back to them for help. Maybe once I get on my feet, find a job and a better place to live. Then maybe I'll call them. But not now."

Sabrina couldn't get the idea of grandparents out of her mind. If Mama wouldn't call them until she got a job, Sabrina would make sure she did. On her next trip to the library, she'd checked out two books on job hunting and one on how to dress for business.

"Are these for your mom?" the librarian had asked.

"Yes. She's going to find a good job." Maybe if she said it enough, it would be true.

Mama glanced at the books, but she never got around to reading them. It didn't matter, though. Sabrina read them from cover to cover, learning all about applications and résumés and interviews. She read about how important it was to dress differently for different sorts of jobs, based on the impression you were trying to make. She found it fascinating.

When she'd returned the books to the library, the librarian asked her if her mom had found a job.

"Not yet," Sabrina had replied. "But she's working on it."

"I don't know what kind of job she's looking for, but a friend of mine mentioned her insurance agent is looking for a receptionist."

Receptionist. Mama had experience as a receptionist, and all the books said experience was important. This was meant to be. Sabrina was sure of it.

It took a little longer to convince her mother. Months of disappointment had left her wary, but finally she agreed to at least fill out an application. Sabrina helped her get ready, to fix her hair and put on some of those nice clothes she had in her closet. But something wasn't right. According to the book, a job applicant in fields like insurance, banking and accounting needed to appear solid and trustworthy. Mama looked like she was going to a fancy lunch out with friends. At Sabrina's suggestion, she'd removed most of the jewelry and brushed her curls into a smoother hairstyle. Sabrina added a scarf to cover the borderline too-low neckline of her blouse. And suddenly, Mama looked like someone you'd trust with your money and your secrets.

And it worked. She got the job. It didn't pay all that much, but added to child support, it was enough that they were able to move to a better apartment a few months later. Mama kept her promise to contact her parents. Grandy died the next year, but at least they reconciled.

After his death, Abuelita convinced Mama that they should move in with her. It was a modest house, nothing like the one they'd had before, but it was clean and tidy and in a good school district. And there was love. All the skills Mama didn't want to learn—knitting and embroidery and sewing—were fascinating to Sabrina. Abuelita had lovingly taught her how to combine fabrics, how to adjust patterns, how to hand-stitch an invisible hem. But six years later, Sabrina lost Abuelita, too. If only she could get back those first fourteen years she'd spent without a grandmother—something else her father had taken from her.

"Sabrina, are you still there?"

Sabrina jumped, causing the dog to leap to his feet. She smiled at him. "Sorry. Yes, I'm here. What did you say?"

"I asked how that team-builder you were telling me about went."

Right. The team-builder. The one with the exploding beans. Mama didn't need to know about that. "It was fine. It rained at first, but it cleared up. My team won a prize."

"That's great! I knew they'd love you!"

"I don't know about that."

"Of course they do. But I hate that you're all the way up there in Alaska. You know if you change your mind, you can always stay here while you look for something better."

"I'm not sure Mason would like that."

"Yes, he would. He adores you."

Sabrina doubted that. Mason was always

polite, but she suspected he just put up with her because of Mama. Or maybe she was projecting her feelings onto him. "I'm good here."

Mama paused. "I do need to tell you something. It's about your father." Mama's voice had become serious.

Strange, when she'd just been thinking of him. Mama seldom mentioned him anymore. "What about him?"

"He died."

"Oh." Her father was dead. How odd. Sabrina paused, waiting for some emotion to hit her, but it felt like her mother was passing on news of some stranger she didn't know. The father Sabrina remembered had disappeared long, long ago.

A few seconds passed before Mama spoke again. "Sabrina? Are you okay?"

"Yes, of course." Sabrina shook her head to clear it. "When did he die?"

"Last month, I gather."

"Thanks for letting me know." Sabrina didn't want to talk about her father. "Tell me more about your cruise."

Sabrina listened while her mother rhapsodized about tropical beaches, fine dining and their elegant cabin aboard the ship. It all sounded glamorous and glittery, just like the life she'd had when she was married to Sabrina's dad. Sabrina hoped history wouldn't repeat itself, and that this marriage would last. For Mama's sake.

CHAPTER SIX

LEITH ADJUSTED HIS rearview mirror and tried to straighten his tie, but it insisted on canting to one side like it was looking for an escape route. He knew the feeling. Giving up, he climbed out of his car and went down the stairwell to Sabrina's apartment. Somewhere in the building, a dog barked. After a few moments, Sabrina opened the door. "Hi."

Wow. She'd twisted her hair up on top of her head in the front, exposing sparkly earrings that dangled from her ears. The rest of her hair waved over her shoulders. Just as she'd promised Emma, Sabrina wore a dress with flowers on it. At least the bottom half had flowers. The lacy top of the dress was the color of alpenglow and hugged her slender waist, where the scallops of lace met the flowing skirt. "You look…" He almost said "beautiful," but that would send the wrong message. This wasn't a real date. "Nice."

"Thank you." She smiled. "You clean up pretty good yourself."

Leith felt like a paper doll, dressed in someone else's clothes, but that came with the territory. He looked down at Sabrina's peach-colored toenails peeping from silver shoes. "Thanks. Only thing is, those shoes you're wearing—"

"They're Bianchis. You don't like them?"

"They look good. I just don't think you'll want to wear them to this wedding."

"Why not?"

"Because it's at a reindeer farm, and the heels would stick in the ground."

"Reindeer farm?" She stared at him. "For real?"

"Yes. Sorry. I probably should have mentioned that."

"Yeah. That would have been helpful."

"I said it was outside."

"I thought you meant like on a paved terrace in a garden, not on a farm. What do you wear to a farm wedding? Do I need to change my dress?"

"No, you look great. Just your shoes."

She sighed and opened the door farther. "Come in while I change."

He stepped into the apartment and looked around. A round table covered with a colorful cloth sat in the center of a beige carpet. Beside it was a deep red wooden chair.

Two walls were painted a warm ivory. A wicker-framed mirror hung on one of them. The other two were dingy white, although one of them had lines of blue tape along the baseboard and ceiling. A wide swath of ivory paint ran along all the edges beside the tape. A couple of whiter patches revealed where someone had patched gouges or holes in the wall to prepare it for painting. Looked like the landlord had jumped the gun a little on renting out the apartment.

The room opened to the kitchen, where a large cardboard box was pushed against the ends of the cabinets, blocking the way. Sabrina stood on one foot and pulled her shoe off the other. A loud thump sounded and the box in the kitchen moved an inch.

"Hey. Stop that." Sabrina hopped toward the kitchen while pulling off her other shoe. Before she got there, the box moved again, and a little terrier shot out between the box and the cabinet.

It ran up to Leith and stopped, looking up at him, head tilted. A furry toy dangled from its mouth. Most dogs, especially terriers, would have been barking up a storm at a stranger in the house, but this one just studied him. "Hi, there." Leith squatted down and reached out a hand.

The dog sniffed his hand and started wagging its tail. Cute dog. It almost looked like one of Emma's toys. Just the sort of dog he would expect Sabrina to choose. Leith scratched under its chin and looked at her. "So, you got a dog after all."

"No, he's not mine." Sabrina came to run her hand over the dog's head. "Or rather, he came into my possession by accident, but I can't keep him. I'll be taking him to a shelter soon."

The toy in the dog's mouth looked brand-new, as did the collar he wore. He wagged his tail at Sabrina and dropped the toy into her hand. She threw it across the room for him to chase.

"What do you mean, he came into your possession by accident?" Leith accepted the toy from the dog and threw it again.

Sabrina explained about an argument in a parking lot. As he listened, Leith stopped playing with the dog and straightened to stare at her. "The man came at you with a tire iron? Good grief, Sabrina. What were you thinking?"

"I couldn't just let him hurt the dog."

"So you had to confront him yourself? You could have taken down his license number and called the police."

"Yeah, I'm sure they'd have dropped all their cases looking for stolen cars and drug dealers to chase down a guy who kicked a dog."

She was probably right, but still, how could she put herself at risk like that? "You could have been killed."

She shook her head. "I don't think so. He was staggering around like he'd been drinking. I doubt he could have caught me even if he'd tried."

"What? What if he did catch you?"

"There were other people in the parking lot who probably would have come if I screamed."

"You'd bet your life on *probably*?"

"It wasn't that big of a risk. Look at you. What if a bear decided to eat you when you were out in the woods? It's possible, right?"

"Sure, it's possible, but unlikely."

"Just like this. It's over now, and the dog is safe. Wait here a minute while I find some better shoes." She turned and flounced through a door to another room, the little dog at her heels.

Leith took a long breath and willed his heart rate to slow. He wasn't sure why Sabrina's story upset him so much. As she said, it was over. It wasn't as though he'd never been in dangerous situations, but he didn't dwell on them afterward, except to learn lessons. Maybe that was why. He got the idea that, in the same circumstances, Sabrina would do it all again. And all for a dog she didn't intend to keep. Allegedly.

He wandered over to look into the kitchen, behind the packing box. A pillow topped with a soft fleece blanket sat in one corner. A no-tip bowl of water, an empty food bowl and a chew toy sat next to it. A rope toy peeked out from under the refrigerator.

Sabrina returned to the living room wearing a more reasonable pair of black shoes with cork wedges. "Better?"

"Perfect." And he meant it. Her shiny dark hair, her expressive eyes, the dress—she looked like she should be on a magazine cover. And yet she'd stood up to a bully with a tire iron. There was more to Sabrina than met the eye, although what met the eye was rather spectacular.

"Here, let me fix your tie." She stepped up and reached for the knot.

"I tried to tie it from an internet video, but it's harder than it looks."

"Video, huh?" She laughed and retied the tie, deftly flipping the ends around each other and pulling them through. "This is a Windsor knot. It was probably named after the Duke of Windsor because he preferred a wide knot in his ties. It works best with a spread collar like yours."

"I didn't know there was more than one way to tie a tie," Leith admitted.

"Four-in-hand. Half Windsor. Probably more I don't know about. I worked in the menswear department for a while during college." Sabrina snugged the knot up against his shirt and straightened his collar. "Take a look."

He checked his tie in the mirror. A perfectly triangular knot filled the space under his collar. "Nice. And you said you didn't know how to tie a bowline."

"Until you taught me, I didn't even know there was such a thing as a bowline. But now I can tie a tent line like an expert." She picked up the dog, whispered a few loving words and put him into the kitchen, pushing the box back into place. "I don't know why I bother. When I used a smaller box, he jumped over it. He can't jump this one, but he can apparently move it by bouncing against it."

"Does he get into trouble while you're gone?"

"Not really. He's housebroken. He dug in the trash once but hasn't damaged anything."

"There's not a lot here to damage." As the

words left Leith's mouth, he realized how rude that sounded. "I mean, if he gets out, it's probably okay."

"Yeah," she said, and grinned. "I know. I don't usually go with minimalist decor, but I could only bring what would fit in my car, so I sold all my furniture before I came."

"Didn't Orson's give you a moving allowance?"

She grimaced. "They did, but unfortunately, most of that went toward a new transmission so my car would make it up the highway."

"Wasn't the car covered under warranty?"

She laughed. "Not since I've owned it."

"Transmissions are usually good for a hundred thousand miles or so."

"Well, then, I guess mine was overdue. I have a hundred sixty-five on it now."

"And everyone gives me a hard time over the Land Cruiser. It's only at one-thirty." Based on her clothes and her former residence, he'd expected a late-model luxury car. "I'm surprised they allowed you to drive it in Scottsdale."

She turned to take a key from a bowl on the countertop. "What are you talking about?"

"Your car. I didn't think they allowed vehicles over three years old in Scottsdale."

Sabrina crossed her arms and glared at

him. "Okay, enough. Number one. I didn't live in Scottsdale. I worked there. And as it happened, I usually took the light rail in to work, but I doubt anyone noticed or cared how old my car was. Number two—what's your problem with Scottsdale, anyway? It's a nice place. Have you ever even been there?"

"Yes, I've been there. I lived there, in fact, for three hundred and fifteen days."

"Three hundred and fifteen?" Sabrina raised her eyebrows. "I suppose you kept track by scratching marks onto the wall of your cell?"

"Something like that."

"Seriously, you lived in Scottsdale? When?"

"It was my senior year of high school. My mom is a massage therapist. One of her clients here was opening a new spa in Scottsdale, and convinced my mother to come down and help her get it started. I tried to get my parents to let me stay in Anchorage. My dad still had his business, so he was up here half the time anyway, but Mom wouldn't go for it. She dragged my sister and me down to Arizona with her. I hated it."

"Why?"

"It was just… I don't know. Wrong. Fake. No snow. No salmon. I didn't fit in at school. Wrong clothes. Wrong car."

"Wrong attitude."

"What?"

"Wrong attitude. It's no wonder you didn't make friends. If someone came to your school in Anchorage, complaining about how boring Alaska was because it didn't have outlet malls or their favorite restaurant chains, would you want to be their friend?"

He considered. "Probably not."

"It sounds like to me you were looking for an excuse to be unhappy. If you'd tried to fit in, you might have found things to like in Scottsdale."

"Is that what you're doing?"

"What?"

"Trying to fit in? Looking for things to like?"

"Yes, that's exactly what I'm doing. And you know what? I do like it. I like seeing the mountains every day when I drive to work. I like walking the dog before bedtime and meeting people still out working in their gardens. I like my coworkers."

"You like living in an empty apartment?"

"It's fine. No use spending a lot of money on furniture until I'm sure where I'll land. I was able to pick up this stuff at a thrift store once I arrived."

He looked again at the chair, with its curved legs, shield-shaped back and patterned cush-

ion. "That's a nice chair. I'm surprised someone gave it up."

"Thanks. It looks a lot better with a coat of
paint and a new seat."

"Wow. You did that?"

"Mmm-hmm. I like to paint and upholster."

"Speaking of painting." He nodded toward
the front wall with only the edges painted.
"What's the deal here?"

"The landlord offered me a break on rent
if I'd shampoo the carpet and paint the walls.
As you can see, it's been a slow process."

"It looks great." He went closer to the walls
she'd completed. "Not a single smear. I painted
my bathroom last year and spent more time
cleaning up my mistakes than painting. You're
really good."

"I told you. You should have traded for
painting instead of this wedding."

He grinned. "Maybe I should have, but it's
too late now. Are you ready to go?"

"I am." She gathered a tiny purse and a
deep blue shawl from the top of her kitchen
counter. "Bye, pup. Be a good boy while I'm
gone."

Leith waited while she locked the door.
"That's his name? Pup?"

"No. I'm not naming him, because I'm not
keeping him."

"How long ago did you bring him home?"

"Last Monday evening. It's been super-busy at work this week, and the private shelter where I want to take him has odd hours. I'll take him next week."

"Uh-huh." Leith didn't argue, but he knew. The bed, the toys and the loving way she'd interacted with the dog gave her away. She might tell herself it was only temporary, but all the signs were there. That dog wasn't going anywhere.

SABRINA WASN'T SURE what she'd expected a reindeer farm to look like, but this wasn't it. They parked in front of a rambling farmhouse, painted a crisp white with green shutters. From the parking lot, she could see a big red barn set against the backdrop of snowcapped mountains. A bunch of animals, presumably reindeer, milled around inside a fence. Beyond that was a newer-looking metal barn.

Leith had been right about the shoes. The gravel parking area would have done a number on the leather heels of the stilettos she'd been wearing. Whenever she wore the Bianchis she'd found tucked away in a consignment store, she felt like a runway model. At first. It usually took about an hour of standing before the pain outweighed the pleasure. She could stand all day in these ankle-tie espadrilles with a medium wedge.

A woman wearing black pants and a crisp tuxedo shirt stepped out onto the porch. "Hey, Leith, how are you?" She set the clipboard she was holding on a chair and hurried over to hug him. "It's been too long."

"I'm good. Sabrina, this is my friend Marissa. She and Chris own the farm. They got married here, what, a year ago?"

"Almost. There's been so much going on around here, but we need to get together. We'll have to plan something soon. Hi, Sabrina. Welcome to the reindeer farm."

"Thank you."

"Leith, go on inside. Zack, Erik and Sam are already here. Ryan can show you where they are." She retrieved her clipboard. "Sabrina, I was just about to go check the barn, to make sure the flowers are set up. Would you like to come?"

"I would. I know barn weddings are trending, but I've never been to one." With a wave at Leith, Sabrina followed Marissa across an open area toward the barn.

"That's a fabulous dress." Marissa glanced over it as they walked. "It's designer, isn't it?"

"Actually, this one is my own design."

"I love it. I've never met a designer before. Do any of the stores here carry your clothes?"

"I'm not a professional designer. I took some design classes in college but went into merchandising instead."

"Do you work for one of the big department stores?"

"No, I'm working for Orson Outfitters in their management training program." Sabrina decided it was time to change the subject before her sad story of layoffs and job hunting came up. "How about you? How does someone become a reindeer farmer?"

"I grew up here. My aunt and uncle established the farm, and last year Chris and I took over operation. I'm also a wildlife biologist, so I'm only a part-time reindeer farmer."

"Wildlife biologist. So you, what? Study the animals?"

"Exactly. Right now, I'm involved in a bear study part-time. Chris and I have been putting a lot of time into fixing up the reindeer farm. I've been selected for a full-time position to study caribou populations starting in the fall, so we're trying to get as much accomplished this summer as we can."

As they got closer, Sabrina could see a few graceful deer heads with huge antlers poking over the top of the pen. It was a unique setting. "Do you do a lot of weddings?"

"Actually, this is the first. After we had our own wedding here, a few people asked about renting the barn for weddings and parties. We needed more room anyway, so we decided to build a new barn for the animals and convert the old one. Since I'll be working full-time after this summer, I'm hoping to get this wedding thing organized to the point the rest of the family can take over."

That sounded like a huge project. Sabrina looked around. "How many people are coming?"

"About seventy. We're using the field near the highway for parking, and my uncle Oliver will ferry people back and forth in the reindeer cart." Marissa glanced at her watch. "Unfortunately, one of the groomsmen forgot his tie, so Oliver volunteered to drive into town to get it. Chris is on the phone, trying to fix some last-minute problem with the band, and my aunt Becky is supervising the caterers. That leaves me to get the reindeer harnessed and hitched up once I've checked on the flowers." Marissa pushed a huge sliding door to one side.

They stepped inside. White tablecloths topped round tables scattered through the area, with hand-lettered place cards at every spot. A row of flower baskets and one larger arrangement of roses and baby's breath lined up across a rectangular table along one wall. A punch bowl and the wedding cake were set up in the corner.

An arched candelabrum decorated with flowers divided the table area from rows of folding chairs, which faced a raised platform at the end of the barn. Twin pillars with floral arrangements of daisies, peonies and delphiniums rested on the platform. Overhead, sheer ribbons in shades of pink and burgundy were draped over a center beam and fanned out to the sides to create almost a floating-ceiling effect. Lights twinkled between the ribbons.

"Oh, no! They set it up backward, and they didn't put out the centerpieces. It's right here on the plan." Marissa snatched a piece of paper from a table near the door and pointed to the detailed diagram. "That's clearly labeled north. Besides, who would put the wedding arch at the back?" Marissa rubbed her forehead. "I don't have time for this."

"Why don't you let me set up the flowers while you do whatever you do with the reindeer?" Sabrina offered.

Marissa eyed her, clearly tempted. "Are you sure?"

"All I have to do is follow the plan, right?"

"Right."

"Okay, then. You go do your reindeer thing and I'll handle the flowers." When Marissa hesitated, she added, "I've done dozens of store displays. I'll be careful. I promise."

Marissa gave a relieved smile. "You're a lifesaver. Thank you."

A boy about the age of Leith's niece galloped through the door, almost knocking over a table. "Aunt Becky says I can help you with the reindeer if I promise not to get dirty."

Marissa grabbed the table to steady it. "Careful, Ryan. Say hello to Sabrina. She's our first guest."

"Oh!" He stood at attention and offered his hand. "Hello. Welcome to the reindeer farm." After Sabrina returned his greeting and shook his hand, he turned to Marissa. "Was that right?"

Marissa grinned. "Perfect. Sabrina is going to help us by doing the flowers while we harness the reindeer."

"But you said the guests don't work."

"I'm sort of a special guest who came early to help out," Sabrina explained. "I'm with one of the groomsmen."

"Oh. Okay. See ya later." The boy grabbed

Marissa's hand. "Who's gonna pull the wagon? Belle?"

"Yes, and I was thinking we might try Tannenbaum in as a wheeler today." She waved at Sabrina as they walked out the door. "Do you think he'll behave?"

"Yeah," the boy said. "Uncle Oliver says his training is going real good."

"You mean 'well.'"

"Well what?" Their voices faded as they moved away.

A rose head rested on the floor near the table. Ryan must have knocked it off. With a little adjustment, the arrangement looked fine, though, so no harm done. Sabrina set the damaged flower on the table to dispose of later. She checked the plan and went to work, moving the candle arch to the platform in the front and the two arrangements behind the chairs, where people would pass between them as they walked up the aisle. Humming as she worked, she straightened blossoms and fluffed bows until the arrangements were perfect.

The baskets for the dining tables were either white daisies trimmed with pink ribbon, or pink flowers with white ribbons. After consulting the plan again, Sabrina arranged them so the colors were evenly distributed through the room and moved a more elaborate arrangement to the long table in one corner, where the cake was set up. She studied the effect. Nice, but the proportions weren't quite right. The flowers needed more visual weight to offset the punch bowl.

She looked around for something to use as a pedestal, but her eye fell on the damaged flower. Perfect. She stripped the pink petals from the rose head and scattered them around the floral arrangement on the snowy tablecloth. There. Instant romance.

"Oh." Marissa had come in while she was busy. "That wasn't on the plan."

"No, but one of the roses had dropped, so I thought I'd scatter the petals. I can brush them away if you don't like it."

"No, don't. It looks good." Marissa gave her a sheepish smile. "Sorry. I tend to get a little weird when my plans don't go right. Chris is always giving me a hard time about sweating the small stuff. Honestly, it's a huge improvement. Thank you."

"You're welcome, and I understand. I know what it's like when plans go off-track. Is everything else coming together?"

"I think so. The food is coming along nicely. Oliver is back with the tie and has the parking signs set up. Chris seems to be on top of the musician problem."

Ryan ran inside again. "Oliver says I can ride along and help drive the reindeer if it's okay with you."

"That's fine, as long as you remember to be polite to the guests."

"Okay." The boy hugged Marissa then turned and ran out of the barn. "She said yes!"

"Ryan is your son?"

Marissa beamed. "Yes, he is. The adoption was finalized two months ago, so Chris and I are officially Ryan's mom and dad."

"With all it entails." A smiling man with reddish-brown hair and beard walked into the barn and slid his arm around Marissa's waist. "Last crisis solved. I got through to a friend in Eagle River, and a new amp is on the way to replace the one the musicians dropped from the back of their truck." He offered a hand to Sabrina. "Hi, I'm Chris."

She shook hands. "Sabrina."

"I thought so. Leith said to find the pretty girl with flowers on her skirt. I'm supposed to ask if you'll come show the other guys the knot you used for Leith's tie. What's it called?"

"A Windsor knot."

"That's the one." He shook his head. "The

group includes three survival experts and an engineer. I was a sailor. Between us, we probably know how to tie a hundred different knots, but that's not one of them. Good thing you're here."

"Isn't it?" Marissa said. "She fixed the flowers, too. We may have to put Sabrina on staff as a wedding troubleshooter."

"Just glad I can help." Sabrina picked up her clutch and tucked it under her arm. "Where do I find these guys with ties?"

Chris took her to a bedroom in the farmhouse, where Leith waited along with three more men in identical suits, including Erik, the tall guy she remembered from the company team-builder. He looked surprised to see her. "Oh, hey, it's Explo—umph." A sharp blow from Leith's elbow interrupted him.

Leith stepped toward her. "This is Sabrina, my date. Sabrina, you probably remember Erik. This is Zack, the groom, who also works with us at Learn & Live. And this is Sam, who was on the same hockey team as Zack and me in middle school." Sam was the only one besides Leith whose tie was tied, although the knot was smaller. Erik's tie hung loose around his neck, and Zack held his in his hand, staring down at it as if he'd never seen one before.

"It's nice to meet you, Sabrina." Sam stepped forward. "Leith says you're the tie expert."

She laughed. "I wouldn't say 'expert,' but I promise I won't blow it up." She glanced out of the corner of her eye at Erik, who hid a grin. "Here, let me show you a Windsor knot."

"Can I video this?" Chris asked. "For future weddings?"

"Sure." Sabrina took the tie from Zack and stood in front of the mirror, demonstrating step by step as the groomsmen followed along. When she'd finished, she gave the tie back to Zack to slip over his head and tightened the knot. "There you go. Windsor knots are best for spread collars. You'll want a smaller knot like a four-in-hand for a button-down."

"Four-in-hand." Chris made a note. "I'll look into that one. Maybe print instructions."

"Good idea. Anything else I can help you with while I'm here?" Sabrina noticed the corsage box on the table. "You know how to attach your boutonnieres?"

"Well, now that you mention it…" Zack shrugged.

Sabrina laughed and reached for the white rose. "Hold still."

LEITH LOOSENED THE knot Sabrina had so carefully crafted in his tie and relaxed into his chair.

The wedding had gone off without a hitch. For dinner, they'd been seated at a table with Volta and Emma; Sam, his wife, Dana, and their toddler, Griffon; and two of the bride's aunts, identical twins Virginia and Georgia. They must have been some of the problem relatives the bride had to separate from the rest of the family. One of them, Leith wasn't sure which, had spent most of the dinner sneezing and blaming the barn for her hay fever, while the other kept insisting it was all psychosomatic. Since Leith could detect no sign of hay and the whole place had obviously received a recent coat of paint, he tended to side with the second aunt, although he wasn't silly enough to get in the middle of what was obviously a long-running debate.

During dinner, Chris and Marissa had cleared the chairs from the wedding end of the barn, creating a dance floor. The aunts watched the band set up and decided, based on the musicians' hair, that the music wouldn't be to their liking. They'd left early, to everyone's relief.

Emma was all giggles and excitement this evening, wearing her "flower" dress that flared out when she twirled, as she'd demonstrated for Sabrina several times. Leith wasn't sure what to make of Emma's sudden desire to wear dresses and look pretty. He was a lot more comfortable with the tomboy he'd always known who liked to stomp in puddles and catch frogs. While the aunts were dominating the conversation with their bickering, Emma had been entertaining Griffon by making goofy faces.

"Eww, something stinks," Emma announced now.

"And that's my cue. Come on, son. Let's go find a place to change you." Sam grabbed a diaper bag from the back of Dana's chair, lifted Griffon from her lap and bent to kiss his wife. Leith suppressed a groan. All this huggy-kissy wedding stuff was getting to him.

"I'll go with you," Volta told Sam. "I need to find the ladies' room."

Sabrina was talking to Dana about her move to Alaska when the music changed, and Emma jumped to her feet. "I know this one! Come on, Sabrina. You and Dana have to dance with me." Emma grabbed Sabrina with one hand and Dana with the other to tug them toward the dance floor.

Sabrina tossed a grin over her shoulder as she allowed herself to be dragged away. Leith waved. Yet another reason he was glad he'd brought Sabrina today. Otherwise he would probably be Emma's designated dance partner for the "Macarena." Leith watched Emma put her hands behind her head with exaggerated drama. Sabrina was laughing, but she never missed a beat. Turned out dancing was another thing she did well. Not that he was surprised.

When they'd entered the barn at the start of the wedding, Sabrina had been sitting between Emma and Volta. From the smugness of her smile, he suspected Volta had shared some embarrassing tidbit of his childhood history, and Sabrina planned to hold it in reserve for the next time she thought he needed a lesson in humility.

She'd already given him a few lessons. Like the one about his disastrous senior year of high school in Scottsdale. He'd fought the move from the moment his mother mentioned it and taken the typical teenage attitude of "you can drag me here, but you can't make me like it." And his resentment over moving away from his friends had ensured he didn't make any new ones. He hadn't even tried to fit in.

Sabrina, on the other hand, was doing everything in her power to fit into her new life, and he had to admire that. But that admiration was mixed with misgivings. Nicole had appeared to fit into his life, at first. When they met, she'd been in her outdoor-girl stage, eager to camp and hike with him and post the pictures on the internet. That should have been his first clue, that the hike itself seemed secondary to getting the picture. They'd been dating about a year when she'd decided it was time for Leith to propose.

She'd stage-managed it all, sending him links to various theatrical proposals, along with her ring size and pictures of her favorite rings. Eventually, he took the hint. He took her camping and proposed to her on the beach at sunrise at Clam Gulch. When she'd realized what was happening, she'd insisted on reenacting the proposal after she'd brushed her hair, done her makeup and set up a camera to "capture the moment." Of course, the sunrise was long gone by then. She'd never quite forgiven him for that.

Her next phase was Nicole the Bride. Wedding planning had taken a full year. After the wedding, it was her domestic-goddess phase, with her never-ending list of home projects that ate up all his days off. Fortunately, that one only lasted two years or so. Once she found the job at the bank, Nicole decided upper management was what she was meant to be, which eventually led to the out-of-state MBA, where she became Nicole the Two-Timing Cheater. And now she was getting married again to some poor sap, and she expected Leith to sign papers pretending their marriage had never happened.

Mercifully, the song ended before Leith could fall further into that pit of regrets. Sabrina dropped into the chair beside him. "Whew. Emma's wearing me out."

"Would you like me to get you something to drink?" Leith offered.

She looked over. "It's a long line. May I just have a drink of yours?"

"Sure." He handed her the bottle and watched her take a swallow. He would have expected, assuming she drank beer at all, that she would demand a glass. But then, she surprised him at every turn.

An attractive older woman stopped at the table and put her hand on Dana's shoulder. "Ursula!" Dana jumped up and gave her a hug. "Sam's been wondering what happened to you."

"We saw him on the way in. The Seward Highway shut down for a while. A motor home rolled and blocked the northbound lanes. They'd dragged it off the road when we went by. It was a mess, but they're reporting the driver is in stable condition, so that's good news."

"That is good." Dana turned to the table. "Everyone, this is Ursula, Sam's auntie."

After they'd all exchanged greetings, Ursula smiled at Emma. "I wonder if you'd like to come over and meet my goddaughter, Rory. She's about your age."

Emma jumped up. "Where is she?"

Ursula pointed to a table across the room. "Over there, with my husband."

Sabrina glanced over and then did a double take. "Your husband looks exactly like one of my favorite authors, R. D. Macleod."

Ursula smiled. "Come on over and I'll introduce you."

"It's really him?" Sabrina turned to Leith. "Do you mind if I leave you for a minute?"

"Of course not. Go ahead."

Leith watched Sabrina, even prettier than usual with her cheeks flushed and eyes opened wide in the excitement of meeting a celebrity. While they chatted, Sam returned and made his way to their table, where Ursula held out her arms for the baby.

Volta came back to Leith, carrying two bottles—one beer and one water. She set the beer in front of him and slid into the other chair. "Cheer up. They're married now. Your part is done. You can relax and enjoy the party."

"Thanks." He took a sip. "You're not indulging?"

"I'm on call later, remember?" She looked around. "Where's Sabrina?"

He pointed across the room. "Meeting her favorite author."

"Oh. I met him on the way in. I'd heard R. D. Macleod moved to Alaska, but I didn't realize he'd married Sam's auntie Ursula until just now when Sam introduced us. He seems like a good guy. Said to call him Mac." They both watched as Sabrina favored the author with that dazzling smile.

"You're still okay with taking Emma tonight? She could probably spend the night with her friend Hannah if you and Sabrina have other plans…" She waited, as though she expected him to confess they were planning to elope that evening.

"Emma's fine with me." He took another pull from his beer.

"I was talking with Sabrina earlier. I like her."

Leith nodded, not paying much attention. When the music changed to an old Chuck Berry tune, Sabrina joined Emma and her new friend on the dance floor. Her skirt swirled around her as she demonstrated to the girls how to do the twist.

"Emma likes her, too. Are you taking her anywhere next weekend?" Volta asked.

"Who? Emma?"

"Duh, who were we talking about? Sabrina."

"Why? Do you need me for something next weekend?"

"No, I'm just curious. This is the first second date you've had in a while."

Leith raised an eyebrow. "I don't need you to keep track of my dating history."

"I've just been worried about you. After Nicole—"

"I don't want to talk about Nicole." And he sure didn't want to talk about the annulment papers sitting in his desk drawer. "Why don't you concentrate on your own love life? Which hasn't been particularly active, from what I can see."

"It's different for me. I'm a mother."

"So?"

"So, Emma needs my full attention right now. I don't have time to date."

"But you have time to interfere with my dating life."

"Yes." His sister grinned. "That hardly takes any time at all."

He spotted Carson out there with his wife, doing a pretty mean twist. Then he noticed another dancer on the floor and frowned. The bride's younger brother had worked his way closer to Sabrina and was eyeing her with interest. Leith didn't know him well, but well enough to know he didn't want him anywhere near Sabrina. The song was winding down.

"Excuse me." Ignoring Volta's questioning gaze, Leith made his way to the dance floor just as the band shifted to a slow song. The little girls giggled and ran toward the punch bowl, leaving Sabrina unattended. The guy had moved closer and was talking to her, his head close to her ear. Leith stepped up and took her elbow. "I believe this is my dance."

Sabrina tilted her head up at him. "It is?"

"Yes. Remember? You promised you'd dance the first slow song with me."

"O-kay." She turned back to the stranger. "Sorry. I guess—"

"That's okay. I'll catch up with you later."

"Not if I can help it," Leith muttered under his breath as he took Sabrina into his arms to dance.

She looked up at him with amused eyes. "I don't remember you asking me to save this dance."

"No, but you don't want to dance with that guy."

"Oh?" She raised her eyebrows. "I thought I just had to appear as your date for the wedding. I didn't realize you got to run off potential dance partners."

"Hey, if you want to dance with him—"

"What? You'll chase him down for me?"

"I doubt I'd have to do that." He looked over her shoulder. "He's watching you right now, waiting for an opportunity to swoop in." He danced them in a partial circle. "He's the bride's brother. At a prewedding party, I saw him get slapped and have a drink thrown in his face in two separate incidents, but if you want me to step aside—"

"Don't you dare." Sabrina moved a little closer. "Is he still watching?"

"Yep."

"Kiss me."

"What?"

"Just for show. So he'll think we're together."

Leith's eyes drifted to her soft pink lips. "Well, if you insist." As they continued to sway to the music, he pulled her closer, tilted his head and pressed his lips to hers. He intended the kiss to be brief, but once he felt her lips under his, he didn't want to stop. She slid a hand behind his head and threaded her fingers into his hair. When he finally broke the kiss, he'd forgotten where he was.

"Is he still watching?" she whispered.

"Who?"

"The guy."

Leith looked over. The bride's brother had wandered over to the bar and was chatting up one of the bridesmaids. "Yeah, still watching. Let's try this one more time." And he slanted another kiss on her warm lips.

The song ended, and a fast number started, but Leith was so caught up in that kiss he didn't notice until someone bumped into them. Sabrina stepped back and laughed. "Okay. I think I'm safe. Let's get some punch." She grabbed his hand and pulled him toward the table at the back of the room.

Marissa and Chris were there, refilling the punch bowl. Marissa smiled at Sabrina. "Hi, again. Are you having fun?"

"It's a great wedding. I think you've got a winning venue here."

"I'm glad you think so."

Sam wandered over. "Say, I heard the early king run has made it to Spot Creek. My shift on the slope starts next Friday, so I wondered if anyone's interested in getting together for a campout one night this week?"

"Ryan would love that," Marissa said. "I have to work Monday and Tuesday, but I don't think we have anything Wednesday or Thursday. Do we?" she asked Chris.

"Assuming Oliver and Becky don't mind feeding the animals," Chris answered.

"They won't. You know Oliver loves filling in." Marissa turned to Sabrina. "Are you guys interested?"

"We, uh… That is, Leith and I—"

"Would love to come," Leith interrupted before Sabrina could spill the beans that they weren't really dating. If Marissa knew, she'd probably tell Volta, and she'd commence matchmaking once again. "That is, if it fits Sabrina's schedule. I'm doing a workshop next weekend, so I can get off midweek."

Sabrina checked the calendar on her phone. "Well, I have Wednesday and Friday off, but I could probably trade shifts."

"Sounds good," Sam said. "I'll send everybody the details. They're saying it's the strongest run in years." He collected two cups of punch and carried them away.

Once they were alone, Sabrina whispered, "You want me to camp with you and your friends?"

"I thought you might enjoy actually camping out overnight. If you'd rather not, I can tell them your schedule changed or something, but I thought it might be fun. I have all the equipment we need."

"Well, more camping experience couldn't hurt."

"Exactly."

"So what do I have to do to earn this lesson? Do you have any more weddings lined up?"

"I'm sure I'll think of something. In the meantime, would you like to dance again?"

CHAPTER SEVEN

THE SUNNY WEATHER lasted through the weekend. Sabrina took the dog for a walk in the morning and had a fleeting temptation to call in sick and spend the day outdoors, but, of course, she would never do anything to jeopardize her job. If she could convince Walter to recommend her for the management track, this job meant security. And security was what she craved.

She filled the dog's water bowl, made sure his favorite toys were available and shut her closet door. She'd learned her lesson Saturday night, when she'd come home from the wedding to discover one of her Bianchis lying in the middle of the living-room floor. Tooth marks spiraled around the leather of the heel, creating a pattern of piercings that almost looked intentional. She was annoyed, of course, but the outrage she would normally have felt at the vandalism inflicted on a pair of exquisite shoes just wasn't there.

Maybe this practical Alaska attitude was

rubbing off on her. Even secondhand, the Bianchis cost far more than she should have spent on a single pair of shoes, and as a result, she'd felt obligated to wear them whenever they fit the occasion. Now she would never again have to endure their torture for the sake of fashion.

Or maybe she'd just been in too good of a mood to let it be spoiled by something as silly as a pair of shoes. She'd had a great time at the wedding. The setting was glorious, the food was delicious, and Leith's friends and sister were a lot of fun. Almost as much fun as his niece. Sabrina had enjoyed dancing with Leith, and she had enjoyed his kisses. A lot.

Of course, he wasn't serious. He'd only kissed her to warn off that guy who was hitting on all the women. But if that was how Leith kissed when he wasn't serious, she had to wonder what it would be like to be kissed by him when he was. Possibly spontaneous combustion.

Those kisses were both the highlight of the evening and a source of worry. Because if she wasn't careful, she could easily fall for Leith. He was capable, and funny, and the way he interacted with his niece was adorable. But Sabrina couldn't let herself get sidetracked.

She had one goal: to make the management program. Nothing was going to get in the way of that. Certainly not a few kisses.

Maybe she shouldn't have accepted the invitation to go camping with him and the others this coming week. She didn't want to give him the wrong idea about their relationship. But his friends were so much fun, and she did need more camping experience.

A glance at the clock on the stove reminded her she needed to go if she expected to get to work on time. She grabbed her bag, which was hanging beside her vest next to the door. She'd noticed last week that on clear summer days, the sunshine warmed the tall western-facing windows at the front of the store and fooled the thermostat into revving up the air conditioner so that her department at the back of the store, under the air vent, was freezing. She grabbed the vest, too.

Once she arrived at work, she left her purse in her employee locker, slipped the fleece vest on over her Orson Outfitters polo and headed to her department, where she found Autumn hanging up a new shipment of T-shirts.

"Hey, Sabrina. Can I take lunch now? My boyfriend is meeting me."

"Sure."

"Nice vest."

"Thanks."

Autumn looked around. "You'd better take it off, though, before Walter sees you."

"Why?"

"He hates it when employees wear stuff from the competition. That's probably a Caribou Pass, isn't it?"

"No." Sabrina laughed. She'd seen the Caribou Pass catalog while she was comparing Orson's products to their competitors. "Two hundred dollars for a vest is a little out of my price range. It's ours. I just fixed it up a little."

"Cool. When I get back, you'll have to show me what you did."

While Autumn was out, Sabrina finished unboxing the T-shirts and helped a customer choose a jacket. Another woman browsed a little but drifted away without buying. About ten minutes before Autumn was due back from lunch, Walter stopped by. "Sabrina, someone called in sick in the camping department. Would you be willing to fill in for a little while?"

"Sure." She moved out from behind the rack she'd been straightening.

Walter frowned. "What are you wearing?"

"A fleece vest. It's always a little chilly back here under the vent. It's one of ours," she assured him quickly. "I just tweaked it a little."

"The fabric on the pockets looks familiar."

"It's a dog scarf from our pet department. See, I just combined two of our products into one."

"Uh-huh. You might want to lose the vest before you go to the camping department so you won't, uh, confuse the customers."

"Sure, okay. I'll get right to it."

"Good. They're swamped over there." He didn't say they weren't swamped here, but his glance around the department made it clear that was what he was thinking. Her displays had created a modest increase in sales, but clothing was still an afterthought at Orson Outfitters.

Sabrina dropped off her vest in her locker and hurried to camping, pinning her name tag on as she went. How was she going to convince Walter she was management material when she was tucked away in the back of the store, hidden from customers?

Tim and two other employees were already assisting customers when she arrived. She waved and hurried to a woman tapping her foot near Tim. "Hi. How can I help you?"

"I'm looking for those toothbrushes with toothpaste in the handle."

"Yes, I saw those right over here." Sabrina led her to the travel toiletries, then directed another guy who was looking for camping guides to the correct department. She turned to find a mother with two school-age kids waiting.

"We're just starting out camping, and we need all the basics. My brother gave us his old tent. What else do we need?"

A cold flash of panic shot through Sabrina's chest. This woman and her kids were going out into the wilderness and they were depending on Sabrina to make sure they were properly equipped. One day of simulated camping was not enough preparation. She looked around, hoping to hand her over to one of the other employees in camping, but they were all occupied with other customers.

Sabrina smiled at her. "Okay, let's get started. You'll need to cook, so let's take a look at the camp stoves." Sabrina managed to bluff her way through stove selection, mostly by reading the boxes. She had no idea which stove was best suited for the woman but steered her toward the one that looked the most like Leith's. They picked out folding pans, dinnerware, metal mugs and cute little salt-and-pepper holders that screwed together.

"Oh, and a matchbox," Sabrina said, remembering the one Leith had given her. "It will keep your matches dry."

"What about sleeping bags?" the woman asked.

"Right." Since they didn't spend the night, Sabrina's only experience with sleeping bags during her lesson with Leith involved stuffing one into a sack. "Right over here."

"So, do we want down, or are these bags with synthetic insulation easier to wash?"

"Eww, orange. Can we get the blue one, Mom?" the girl asked.

"I like the orange one," her brother said.

"How warm are these bags? Is it better to go heavier than you think you'll need?"

"I'm, uh, not sure." Sabrina noticed that the department supervisor was just finishing with his customer. "Tim, could you come over here, please? This family has some questions about sleeping bags."

Tim took over. "These are our most popular midweight bags. We have summer-weight, but in Alaska they're more for cabin or RV camping rather than tents. You'll want sleeping pads as well to insulate you from the ground."

They seemed to be in good hands, so Sabrina excused herself and looked for the next customer who needed help. Instead, she saw Walter standing at the edge of the department, his arms crossed. His mustache drooped over his mouth, but he clearly wasn't smiling. Sabrina gave a little wave and hurried over to a guy browsing the freeze-dried foods.

Great. Between the vest and her ignorance on sleeping bags, she'd created a bad impression with the one person who stood between her and a secure job. She clearly needed more hands-on experience in camping...the sooner the better. It sounded like Leith's invitation couldn't have come at a better time.

THAT EVENING, Sabrina trudged down the stairs to her apartment, debating the relative merits of going for a run versus eating a quart of peanut-butter-and-chocolate ice cream for dinner. In addition to Walter watching her flounder in the camping department, a carton of hiking pants had arrived with water damage, and one of her employees called in sick at the last minute, so Sabrina had to cover both the sales floor and the paperwork over the damaged order. Not that there was a lot of traffic in her department—yet another depressing thought.

Her mood took a U-turn when she opened the door to find the little dog wagging his tail at her as though she was the most wonderful person on the planet. He danced on his back legs until she reached down and gave his ears a rub. As soon as she straightened up, he ran to the leash hanging beside the door and stood there, looking expectant.

"Okay, we'll go. Just let me change into some running clothes." The dog followed as she moved from the bathroom to the bedroom to the kitchen for a drink of water, never letting more than a foot separate them. She was snapping the leash onto his collar when her phone rang.

The area code looked vaguely familiar, but she didn't recognize the number. Probably someone wanting to sell her a time-share or offering to refinance her nonexistent home loan. She let it go to voice mail.

Forty minutes later, she and the dog returned, both feeling pleasantly tired and more than a little hungry. She gave the dog his kibble and decided to be virtuous and dine on a green salad with boiled eggs. And then maybe a few spoonfuls of ice cream because she'd earned it.

As she set her phone on the counter, she noticed someone had left a voice mail. Maybe not a spam caller, then. She listened to the message.

"Hi. Um, Sabrina, this is Misty, and I, like, need to talk with you. It's about Dad. Your dad, I mean. Anyway, please call me back."

Misty? She didn't know anyone by that

name. And why would anyone be calling about her father? He'd walked out of her life eighteen years ago, and now, according to her mother, he was dead.

Dead. Sabrina had avoided thinking about her father's death, just as she'd always avoided thinking about the way he'd abandoned her and her mom. Nothing positive came from dwelling on loss. It was more important to move forward.

She closed her eyes for a moment and remembered the day when her daddy had carried her on his shoulders across a parking lot so the pavement wouldn't burn her feet through the thin soles of her shoes. And when they went out for ice cream, he'd given her the cherry from his sundae, too. Now that man was gone, forever. And she'd never have an opportunity to ask him why he'd stopped loving her.

She blew out a long, slow breath. It didn't matter anyway. The call was probably a scam. *Hello, you've inherited a million dollars. Just give me your account number and the password, and I'll transfer it right over.* Like she'd fall for that, especially in a message from someone who didn't even leave a last name or business title.

Sabrina put the eggs on to boil and started

grating a carrot for her salad. There was something odd about the call, though. The caller had seemed nervous, not like someone who'd read the same script over a hundred times. And how would they have gotten her cell-phone number?

She thought about it while she finished preparing and ate her salad. It was no use—her curiosity wouldn't allow her to enjoy her ice cream until she'd cleared up this mystery. She found the number and dialed.

"Sabrina?"

"Yes, this is Sabrina. Am I speaking to Misty?"

"Yes." Sabrina waited for the spiel, but Misty didn't say anything else.

"The Misty who left a message on my phone about an hour ago?"

"Yes, right. I, um… That is, I'm your sister."

Sabrina paused. "My sister?" She didn't have a sister. Or maybe she did. Maybe her father had a whole brood of kids after he deserted her.

"Well, half sister. I found a picture of you, after Dad died. You knew he died, right?"

"Yes, I heard," Sabrina admitted slowly.

"It was so weird. He was sitting on the couch and watching TV and I was, like, listening to my tunes when he stood up and left. I thought he was going to the bathroom or something. Later I got up to go to my room and there he was in the hall, where he'd, like, collapsed. I called 911, but when they got there they said he was already dead. His aorta burst."

"Wow. I'm so sorry."

"Yeah. I felt bad because I didn't hear him fall, because of the earbuds, but they told me it probably wouldn't have made any difference anyway. It's weird, not having him here, you know?"

Sabrina did know, or at least she knew how weird it had been for her. And it had only gotten weirder when the bank foreclosed on the house. But that wasn't Misty's problem. "I'm sorry," Sabrina repeated.

Misty took a deep breath. "Well, anyway, when I was helping Mom go through some of his stuff after the funeral, I found this picture of you and Dad, and I made her tell me who you were. I kind of knew Dad had been married before he married my mom, but I never knew he had a daughter."

"You didn't?" Sabrina assumed she didn't know about Misty because she wasn't in touch with her dad. It hadn't occurred to her that her father wouldn't have told Misty about her.

"No, they never told me. At first, when I

found the picture, Mom said you were just a neighbor kid who lived near them when they lived in Arizona before they moved to Tacoma, but on the back of the picture it said, 'Daddy and Sabrina, age nine,' so I knew she was lying."

"Does she lie a lot?"

"Oh, yeah, all the time." Misty's answer was matter-of-fact. "Not usually about big things like this, but you know, if she forgets to pay a bill she says it must have been lost in the mail, or she'd tell Dad she got something on sale for fifty bucks when it was really two hundred. Stuff like that."

"I see." This was the woman Sabrina's father had deserted them for? A habitual liar?

"I found out Dad had been married before because my grandma said something once about Mom being his second wife, but my mom shushed her. She told me Grandma was getting senile or something, but I knew she wasn't. Anyway, I found the picture and I know about you now, so Mom can't lie to me anymore. I've always wanted a sister."

"How did you get my number?"

"It wasn't easy." Misty sounded proud of herself. "My friend Junie's mom is into all that genealogy stuff, so Junie helped me find the marriage record with your mom's name on it, and we saw that she had another marriage license not that long ago, so we knew her new name, and her husband's name. He had a landline listed, so I called her and she gave me your number. I asked her not to tell you because I wanted to surprise you."

Well, that worked. Sabrina couldn't believe her mother didn't tell her to expect a call from a sister she never knew existed.

"I wanted to call you right away, but my mom made me help her clean out Dad's whole closet and stuff, and then I had to go to this college-orientation thing."

"How old are you?"

"I'm eighteen. I start college at Seattle Pacific this fall."

Eighteen. It was a little over eighteen years ago that Sabrina's dad left them. So his second wife must have already been pregnant when he decided to bail on his first wife. Sabrina couldn't decide if that made it better or worse.

Misty rattled on. "See, I was thinking Junie and I could tell our moms that we're taking a road trip to Vegas. They won't like it, but since we're both eighteen we can talk them into letting us go. Really, though, we'll drive to Phoenix and I'll get to meet you. Won't that be great?"

Sabrina wasn't sure how great it would be.

Not that it was Misty's fault, but Dad had abandoned Sabrina and her mother in favor of Misty and hers. And apparently, he'd stuck this marriage out. Why would Sabrina want to meet the daughter who had replaced her?

"Actually, I'm not in Phoenix anymore. I'm working in Anchorage," Sabrina reported, happy to have the built-in excuse.

"Anchorage, Alaska? That's so cool! I want to see Alaska. How long does it take to drive to Alaska from Seattle?"

"Oh, weeks." It was a slight exaggeration, but it was a long way. "And you'd have to drive through Canada. You'd need a passport." *Please don't let her have a passport.*

"Oh." Misty sounded so deflated, Sabrina felt like she had to throw her a bone.

"But flights from Alaska usually stop through Seattle. Maybe, sometime, we can get together there."

"Yes! Call me anytime and I'll come meet you at the airport or whatever, 'cause I really do want to meet you. Send me your picture, okay? And I'll send mine."

"Sure, I'll do that. Thanks for calling, Misty."

After letting Misty gush a little more, Sabrina was able to end the call. She set the phone on the table and stared blankly at the wall. She had a sister. A sister with whom she shared a father, but Sabrina had only had him for the first twelve years of her life, whereas he'd been there for Misty until he died.

And yes, it was sad that he'd died, and especially that Misty found him, but a tiny part of Sabrina couldn't help but feel that karma had finally caught up with the man who had abandoned his family. Did that make her a bad person?

Her phone chimed, and a photo of Misty appeared on her screen. Her hair was the same reddish-brown shade as their father's. Misty must have gotten the blue eyes from her mother, but they were exactly the same shape as Sabrina's. And they had the same arch to their eyebrows and the same chin. They did look like sisters.

It occurred to Sabrina that if everything went as planned and she ended up with the Orson Outfitters management job, she would be living in the same city as her half sister. Maybe, once she'd gotten used to the idea, Sabrina would want to spend time with her.

It might be fun to have a sibling. Maybe they could window-shop together, or eat junk food and watch sad movies, or whatever bonding thing sisters did. Maybe Misty would be proud to tell her friends she had a sister who worked for Orson Outfitters at their headquarters downtown. Or maybe not. But if Sabrina didn't find a way to impress Walter and get that job, it would be a moot point.

CHAPTER EIGHT

By Wednesday morning, Sabrina was ready for a break. She'd stayed late at the store yesterday, adding women's clothes and accessories to the displays in the camping and fishing departments, after getting permission from their department managers. She had to increase sales in her assigned department if she was going to convince Walter she was management material, since she sure wasn't impressing him with her outdoor savvy.

Today, however, was the camping trip, a chance to learn more about the outdoor lifestyle and get away from the stress of the store at the same time.

Sabrina was putting her hair into a ponytail when the doorbell rang. The dog barked once and ran back and forth between her and the door as though she could possibly have missed hearing the doorbell in this little apartment. She grabbed her backpack and opened the door to Leith. "Come on in while I get my stuff."

He stepped inside and crouched down to run his hand over the dog's head. "I see he's still here."

"Yeah," Sabrina admitted. "Every time I tried to take him to the shelter, he'd give me that look." The dog tilted his head and gazed up at her, tail wagging. "Yes, that's the look. I finally gave in and sent a pet deposit to my landlord. We went to the vet yesterday for shots and a dog license."

The dog shook his head and jingled the tags on his collar as though showing them off. Leith laughed and straightened, glancing around the apartment. "You've finished painting. It looks good. And you have a new chair."

Sabrina looked over at the wicker chair she'd painted the same deep red as the other chair. "I found it at a garage sale. Turns out there's not enough room in my lap for a computer and a dog, so I needed a bigger chair. Once I sew a new cushion for it, I think it will look nice."

"It already does."

Leith picked up Sabrina's backpack. "I've got all the equipment. What else do you need?"

"Just the dog's stuff. It's okay if I bring him, isn't it?"

"Sure. Everybody will bring their dogs."

She scooped up a tote with dog food, water and bowls inside and tucked the dog bed under her arm. "Can you grab that leash on the hook behind you, please?"

Leith snapped it to the dog's collar and chuckled. "She's bringing a cushion on a camping trip. You are one lucky dog."

"Does poor Tal have to sleep in the dirt?"

"Well, no. She sleeps in the tent with me. But she doesn't get a mattress." He picked up the dog and followed Sabrina outside, waiting while she locked up. "So now that he's yours, what did you decide to name him?"

"The vet asked, too, but I haven't found the perfect name yet. I was considering Terrance."

"Terrance?"

"After Alexander Terrance. He designs a lot of those gowns you see celebrities wearing on the red carpet."

"I don't know." Leith studied the little dog with tufts of hair sticking out at random angles. "He doesn't look like a red-carpet kind of dog to me."

"Yeah, maybe not. Do you have any suggestions?"

"Hmm." He set the dog on the ground and allowed Terrance to trot toward the car, tugging on the leash to try to hurry Leith along. "I'd call you...Eagle Bait."

Sabrina slapped Leith's shoulder with the pillow. "Hey, that's my dog you're talking about."

"Well, he's not much bigger than a rabbit, just the right size for an eagle snack."

"You're kidding, right?"

"Mostly."

"Mostly?" She stopped walking.

He shrugged. "There was a famous incident many years ago, where an eagle snatched a Chihuahua at a gas station in Valdez." She must have looked horrified, because he hurried to reassure her. "It's one of those struck-by-lightning things. The odds of an eagle getting your dog must be at least a million to one. Not to say you should let him wander unaccompanied in the wilderness, but he'll be fine."

"You're sure? Because I'm not taking him if he's in any danger."

"I'm sure. Come on. Let's introduce him to Tal."

"Oh, I forgot he'd need to ride with Tal. Will they be okay together?"

"Let's find out. I'll put her on a leash and we'll let them sniff each other."

Tal hopped out of the car and wagged a

greeting. Sabrina's dog, in typical terrier fashion, approached her stiff-legged, all bluster and ego. Tal dropped her chest to the ground in a play bow. When the little dog sniffed her, she wagged madly. Apparently her scent reassured him because he dropped some of his attitude and allowed Tal to lick his head.

Leith smiled. "Yeah, they'll be fine."

Sabrina laughed as the little dog closed his eyes and squirmed like a kid getting his face washed. "He thinks he's such a tough guy, but he has a soft heart. Kind of like Humphrey Bogart in *Casablanca*. What do you think of Humphrey for a name?"

"Humphrey," Leith said, trying it out. "Hey, dog, what do you think? Are you a Humphrey?"

The terrier wriggled away from Tal and cocked his head at Leith with a puzzled expression on his face. Then he sneezed.

"I don't know," Leith told Sabrina. "He may be allergic to that name."

"We'll keep thinking."

Leith loaded the dogs and wrenched open the passenger door for Sabrina. He waved a hand toward her old blue compact parked in the corner of the lot. "Car running okay?"

"So far, so good."

He closed the door behind her and went

around to the driver's seat. "By the way, Emma got wind that I was taking you camping and invited herself along. You don't mind, do you?"

"Of course not. Emma's adorable."

"Good because I said yes. We're picking her up on the way."

Sabrina laughed. "You're really close to your family, aren't you?"

"Yeah. We're all pretty tight."

Sabrina thought about the phone call. "I recently discovered a new family member myself."

"Oh?"

"A half sister. My dad died recently, and it turns out he had another daughter."

"Wait. What? You didn't know you had a sister?"

Sabrina shook her head. "My dad left when I was twelve. I never saw him again."

His eyebrows drew together. "Never?"

"No. The whole thing was…" She shook her head. It was too complicated to get into, and besides, she had no desire to drag down the mood on their camping trip. "Anyway, it turns out my sister didn't know about me, either, until she was going through his things. She called and said she wants to meet me."

He glanced over at her. "How do you feel about that?"

Sabrina thought about it. "I don't know. I'm all over the place. My dad left my mom for hers, and I resent that."

"That's understandable."

"But my sister wasn't even born at the time, so it's not her fault." She looked out the window at a planter overflowing with golden nasturtiums before she continued. "I kind of like the idea of a sister. I don't have much family. And Misty seems nice."

"Misty, huh?"

"Yeah." Sabrina smiled. "She's already been texting me and sending funny photos."

"So are you going to meet with her?"

"I haven't decided yet. I guess I'll play it by ear."

Leith nodded, a thoughtful expression on his face. At the next stoplight, he turned into Volta's neighborhood, but he drove past her street.

"Where are we going?" Sabrina asked.

"Volta's working today. Emma's at my folks' house."

"Oh." Sabrina's first thought was to dig out a mirror and check her hair and makeup. But why should she be nervous about meeting his parents? It wasn't as though she and Leith were together.

A few blocks down, Leith made a right turn, followed a winding street to the end and parked in front of a two-story painted a restful shade of blue-gray. "We might as well bring the dogs in. Mom won't let us go until she's greeted Tal."

Sabrina gathered her dog in her arms and followed Leith and Tal up the steps to the front porch. He opened the door without knocking and held it for her. Sabrina stepped inside to find herself in a tiled entryway with a staircase on one side and an archway into a living room on the other. It was a tranquil room, with soft yellow walls and a minimum of furniture. The only accessories visible were three pillows on the sofa and a potted palm near the window. Over the sofa hung a large abstract painting that reminded Sabrina of a desert landscape. A knotted rug in shades of gold, russet and deep red covered the living-room floor, and in the center of the rug, a woman with silvery highlights running through her dark hair sat cross-legged, her eyes closed.

Tal ran past Sabrina to sit on the rug directly in front of her, silently gazing at the woman. After a moment, she opened her eyes, smiled at the dog and rose to her feet in one graceful motion. She stroked Tal's head and turned toward them. "Hello. You must be Sabrina. I've heard so much about you."

Sabrina flashed a questioning glance at Leith, who shrugged. His mother laughed. "Not from this one. He never tells me anything. But Volta and Emma told me they'd met you at the wedding. I'm Dawn Jordan."

"Sabrina Bell."

"It's nice to meet you, Sabrina." She leaned forward to pet Sabrina's dog. "Hello, sweetie."

Behind them, Emma came dashing down the stairs, her purple duffel thumping on each step and a fishing pole in her hand. "I'm ready to go fishing, Uncle Leith. We're gonna catch a really big one, right?"

"That's the plan."

She dropped her things when she reached the bottom of the stairs and ran toward Leith. He caught her up and swung around to deposit her on her feet in the living room.

She giggled. "Hi, Sabrina." Emma spotted the dog in Sabrina's arms and squealed. "She's so cute! Is she yours? What's her name?"

"It's a boy dog, and I haven't named him yet," Sabrina explained.

"You should name him Cutie McMuffin."

Leith laughed. "How could he show his face in the dog park with a name like that?"

Emma considered. "Maybe it would be better for a girl dog." She looked up at Sabrina. "Do you have your fishing pole?"

"Oh, uh, I don't think—"

Before Sabrina could formulate an answer, Leith grabbed Emma's duffel bag and pole. "Is this everything?"

"No. I still have my sleeping bag and Rufus up in my room. I'll get them." Emma started up the steps.

"Why are you bringing Rufus on a camping trip?" Leith called after her.

Emma didn't pause in her mission. "He wants to come."

Dawn laughed. "You can't argue with that logic."

"Who's Rufus?" Sabrina asked.

"Emma's stuffed dog. Leith gave it to her, and she never goes anywhere without it." Tal nudged Dawn's hand and she tickled under the dog's chin. "I hope you don't mind Emma tagging along."

"I love having Emma along. She's great."

"We all think so." Dawn gave Leith a hug. "You keep this son of mine in line, okay?"

As if Sabrina had any influence over Leith. But apparently Leith was keeping up the charade that they were dating, so she went along with it. "I'll try."

After double-checking that Emma had everything she needed and admonishing her to listen to her uncle, Dawn hugged her granddaughter goodbye and Emma climbed into her seat in the Land Cruiser. The dogs went in after her. Emma stroked their heads and talked to them while Leith drove toward the Seward Highway.

Just before they left town, Leith pulled into a grocery-store lot and parked under the shade of a tree. "We'll need ice for the ice chests, and I want to pick up some trail mix and fruit."

"And gummy bears?" Emma prodded.

"Maybe a few gummy bears, if you don't tell Grandma." He winked at her. "Mom doesn't do candy," he explained to Sabrina.

Sabrina glanced into the back seat, where the two dogs were sleeping beside Emma's booster seat. Sabrina's little dog was curled up against Tal's neck. When Emma unbuckled and slid out of the truck, the terrier jumped up and tried to follow, but Tal put a paw over him and restrained him until Leith had shut the door. He wiggled loose and ran to the window, where he pressed his feet against the glass, so he could bark out of the crack at the top.

"We'll be right back," Sabrina assured the dog, but she could hear him carrying on as she followed Leith and Emma across the parking lot. She felt like a traitor for leaving him behind, even if it was only for a few minutes. Once she passed a van and was out of sight, though, the barking stopped, which made her feel a little better.

Inside the store, Leith steered them toward the customer-service desk. "Before we look for gummy bears, we need to get Sabrina a fishing license."

Sabrina slowed her steps. "Why do I need a fishing license?"

"Uh, to fish? That's the whole point of this outing."

"I thought we were camping."

"We are. We're camping at Spot Creek, so we can fish for kings. Let me guess. You've never been fishing."

"Doesn't it involve putting worms on hooks?" She wrinkled her nose. "I'm not so thrilled about worms."

"Then you're in luck, because the area we're fishing requires artificial bait. People come from all over the world to fish in Alaska. Come on—give it a try. My treat."

"Fishing is fun," Emma assured her. "Uncle

Leith will do all the yucky stuff with the guts and everything."

"Is that right?" Sabrina asked Leith.

"If that's what it takes to convince you, I'll give you the no-guts Emma treatment. It's pretty special. Everyone else has to process their own fish."

"I don't know." Camping was one thing, but fishing sounded complicated.

"You have to at least try fishing while you're in Alaska, and this is one of the best spots for beginners. It's a relatively small river with a wide gravel bank, so you don't even have to wade or use a boat. Besides, if you fish it will give you something to talk about next week at the store and you can impress everyone with your 'outdoorsy-ness.'"

She smiled at the silly word, but what he said was true. Fishing stories and salmon recipes were some of the main topics of conversation in the break room. "Okay. I'll try it."

They approached the desk. "She'll need a nonresident fishing license."

"For one, three, seven or fourteen days? Or annual?"

"Annual," Leith declared at exactly the same time Sabrina stated, "One day."

"Annual is a better deal."

"I said I'd try it once. I don't even have fishing equipment."

"I have plenty."

"Yeah, but…" Sabrina looked over at Emma, who was busy inspecting the impulse items near the register. She whispered, "You and I aren't, you know—together."

"Fine." Leith frowned and turned to the clerk. "Three-day. And a king stamp."

"What's a king stamp?" Sabrina asked, while the clerk was fetching the necessary forms.

"A special license for king salmon."

"Oh." They'd mentioned kings at the wedding. Just how many kinds of salmon were there, anyway? Cheap and nutritious, canned salmon had been a staple for Sabrina and her mom when money was tight, which was pretty much all the time. They'd always bought the pink instead of red because it cost less, but she didn't realize there were other types. She'd never heard of king salmon. But then, there were lots of things in Alaska that Sabrina had never heard of.

She filled out the forms. When the clerk told her the total cost, she gulped, but reached for her wallet. Before she could find it in her bag, Leith pulled his out. "I said it's my treat."

"But—"

He swiped his card before she could pull hers out. "It's all part of the how-to-be-outdoorsy package we agreed on."

"I think you've already fulfilled the conditions of our exchange."

"Then consider this a bonus." He picked up the license and tucked it into his shirt pocket. "Come on, Emma. Let's find the gummy bears."

Sabrina followed more slowly. It was nice of Leith to pay for the license, but it left her feeling uncomfortable. She didn't like to be in anyone's debt. Going as his guest to a wedding where she'd had a wonderful time wasn't much of a sacrifice. Somehow, she was going to find a way to pay him back for all he'd done.

Once they'd picked up the groceries and Leith had stashed the ice and fruit in an ice chest in the back, they pulled onto the highway. It wasn't long before they'd passed a marsh Leith said was a bird refuge and reached the ocean.

Sabrina watched out the window as they drove the narrow ribbon of road squished between the mountain and the sea on their way to the Kenai Peninsula. Across the water, snowcapped mountains glinted in the sunlight. They rounded a corner and passed the blue-and-yellow cars of an Alaska Railroad train, rumbling along the tracks beside the highway.

Up ahead, she could make out a few figures scattered across the water. "Are those people?"

Leith glanced at the water. "Paddleboarders. They're there to take advantage of the bore tide this morning."

"Bore tide?"

"Yeah. Because the water comes from a wide bay into a shallow inlet, Turnagain Arm has some of the highest tides in the world. When the tide turns, it can sometimes create almost a wall of water pushing along the surface. They call it a bore tide. We're almost to Beluga Point. If you want, we can stop and watch."

"I'd like that."

The figures grew bigger as they got closer, and now Sabrina could make out the shapes of people in wetsuits standing or crouched on surfboards. Before long, Leith pulled into a parking lot with several other cars. A group of people had gathered on the point of land jutting into the ocean.

When the car stopped, Tal and Sabrina's dog jumped up and looked expectant. Before he turned off the key, Leith rolled down the windows a crack. "Sorry, dogs. Too many people for you here. We won't be long. Stay."

Tal sighed and lay down on the back seat, but Sabrina's dog was determined not to be left behind again. Before Sabrina had even unbuckled her seat belt, he'd jumped over the seat into her lap, and was staring up at her and wagging his tail.

"Are you sure they'll be okay in here? In Phoenix, they're always warning you how dangerous it is to leave kids or dogs alone in cars in the sun."

"Yeah, but it's sixty-five degrees and partly cloudy here, and we'll only be gone ten or fifteen minutes."

"Okay." Sabrina scratched the little dog behind his ears while Leith got Emma out of the car and shut the door. "I know you want to go, but you need to stay here with Tal." She picked up the dog and set him in the back seat, but before she could turn and open the door, he was in her lap again.

Leith scooped him up and set him on the floor behind the seats. "Stay." Immediately, the dog scooted under the seat and popped out between Sabrina's feet. Leith laughed. "I think I figured out what breed he is. I believe you have one of those boomerang terriers."

"You are a boomerang." Sabrina lifted the dog onto her lap.

"You should call him Boomer," Emma offered.

"Are you a Boomer?" The dog reared onto his back legs and tickled her chin with his tongue. "You like that, huh? Boomer it is, then."

Leith collected a leash and handed it to Sabrina. "I think the only way you're going to keep him in the car is to tie him."

She looked at the leash, and then at the eager eyes watching her. "Or I could just carry him. You said we won't be long."

"You shouldn't reward a dog for misbehaving."

"He's not really misbehaving. He just doesn't know any better."

"You need to teach him basic commands, like 'stay.'"

"Yeah, yeah. I only just decided to keep him. Give us time." She smiled down at the dog. "Besides, he's so cute. How can you say no to that face? He's irresistible."

"That is going to be one spoiled dog," Leith declared. "Okay, bring him. Tal, we'll be back soon."

Tal gave a little whimper, but she stayed where she was. Sabrina pulled on a windbreaker and tucked Boomer inside, only his head poking out above the zipper. Leith looked at them and shook his head, but he was smiling.

The three of them joined the other people on the point, looking out over the water. On the far side, mountains seemed to rise straight up. In the distance, Sabrina could see what appeared to be a white line across the water, moving toward them at a rapid clip. The water behind the line was a churning gray-blue, pushing the wave against the calmer water. The paddleboarders were positioning themselves in readiness.

"Here it comes!" Emma pointed.

Within five minutes, the white line had caught up to them. It really was a wall of water, a wave eight or ten feet tall flowing across the top. It reached the first paddleboarder, who caught the wave and let it carry him forward. One by one, the others grabbed the wave. One of them missed. His body sagged in disappointment as the wave and his buddies were carried far ahead and up the inlet.

Sabrina turned to Leith. "That was incredible. I went to the beach in California once and saw some big waves, but I've never seen a single wave like that."

"I'm not surprised. There are only a few places in the world with bore tides."

"Then I'm really glad we got to see it. Thanks for stopping."

"You're welcome. We'd better get back on the road, though. I told the others we'd meet them at the campground."

As they passed a car, a mini schnauzer jumped against the window and barked. Emma jumped, and then giggled. Boomer wiggled free and leaped out of Sabrina's coat, dashing toward the car and barking. The schnauzer squirmed through the opening at the top of the window and launched himself onto the parking lot.

Leith tried to grab Boomer but missed, and both dogs dashed under a nearby SUV. Sabrina ran around to catch them when they came out on the far side, but they stayed underneath. She crouched down. Leith was looking from the other side, with Emma beside him calling, "Here, doggies!"

The dogs ignored her, busy sniffing each other. Leith flattened himself against the ground. "Emma, stay right here. If the dogs run toward you, try to stop them but do not chase them in the parking lot. Understand?"

Emma nodded. Leith crawled on his belly under the SUV. Boomer saw him coming and ducked away, but Sabrina snagged the dog when he got within reach. Leith was able to grab the schnauzer. Holding on to the dog, he was squirming out from under the car when a woman ran up. "What are you doing with my dog?"

Leith bumped his head on the frame. "Ouch." He pushed free and handed over the dog. "Here."

Sabrina rushed around the car to stand beside Emma and Leith. "I'm sorry. This was my fault. My dog got loose and yours jumped out of your car to chase him. Leith was rescuing them."

"You should keep your dog under control," the woman said.

"Yes. I will. I'm sorry." Sabrina refrained from pointing out again that the other dog had escaped as well. Under her hands, Sabrina could feel Boomer's muscles quivering, and a low rumble escaped from his throat. Leith didn't say anything, but his raised eyebrow screamed "I told you so."

They made their way back to Leith's car. Once they were all safely inside, Sabrina asked Leith, "Is your head okay?"

"I'm fine. I didn't hit it that hard."

"Good." Sabrina sighed. "Okay, you're right. Boomer does need to learn better manners.

How do I go about teaching him to obey like Tal does?"

Leith rubbed his forehead and glanced back at the terrier, now innocently resting next to Emma. "I'd suggest an obedience class, or if you can't fit that into your schedule, I have a book on basic training techniques I could lend you. I have to tell you, though, he'll probably never be as obedient as Tal. It's in their nature for German shepherds to respect authority. It's a terrier's nature to thwart it."

"That's okay. Boomer doesn't need to be perfect, just learn enough to be safe." She smiled at the dog. "Because we don't want you run over or getting carried away by eagles, do we?"

Boomer sniffed as if to say he wasn't afraid of any eagle. Tal licked his ear and encouraged him to curl up between her front legs. She rested her chin on top of him.

Leith seemed surprised. "I've never seen Tal this affectionate with another dog before."

"I told you. Boomer's irresistible."

He smiled. "Apparently Tal agrees."

By the time they arrived at the campground, the others had staked out adjoining campsites and were busy unloading the camping gear. A couple of tents and a pop-up trailer were set up on the other side of the campground, but it didn't look too busy. Emma jumped out and danced in a circle. "We're here!"

Sabrina climbed out of Leith's truck, suddenly shy, but Marissa hurried over to greet her. "Hey, so glad you made it." She bent down to pet the dog cradled in Sabrina's arms. "Who's this?"

"This, we've just decided, is Boomer."

"Just decided?"

"Yes. I wasn't sure I was going to keep him, so I didn't name him until today. I hope it's okay that I brought him."

"Of course it is. Ryan's corgi, Donner, is here somewhere and Sam might bring his Lab, Kimmik. Sam and Dana are leaving Griffon with Ursula, though, so they might leave the dog, too. Dana's excited because this is her first chance to catch a king salmon. Last summer she was nine months pregnant during this run. Have you been king fishing before?"

"No."

"I think you'll like it. King fishing can be a little slow, but it's superexciting when you catch one. The downside is the limit of one fish, so once you get your king, you're through. If you get one today, though, you can still try for grayling or dollies tomorrow."

"Grayling or dollies." Sabrina repeated the

words and nodded as though they meant something. She was going to have to corner Leith and quiz him on what exactly was so special about king salmon.

"Nice vest. Is that a new style? I'll have to come to the store and look."

"Uh, no. It's the same basic vest they've always had. I just added some curved seaming and some trim."

"I like it. You should tell them to make all their vests like that."

"Well, maybe if I make the management team, I'll have the chance to do that."

Sabrina snapped Boomer's leash in place and allowed Emma to take him to meet Ryan and Donner. Leith started to unload the camping equipment, and she hurried to help, eager to see if she remembered the skills Leith had taught her. "Do you want mc to set up the tent here?"

"Here's good, but this one sets up differently. Since we're car camping, I thought I'd bring the cabin tent, so we could use cots instead of sleeping mats."

"Oh." A different tent meant she'd look stupid in front of Leith's friends, with him showing her how to set it up in baby steps. Which was exactly why she hadn't been all that eager to try fishing. She was getting tired of being the helpless one all the time.

But it didn't turn out like that. Leith set up the tent without much fanfare, just asking her to hold a pole in place or hand him a stake now and then. Together, they set up cots inside and carried in sleeping bags, spreading Emma's purple bag on the center cot. By the time they'd finished, Sam and Dana had arrived and were setting up their camp.

Leith looked at his watch. "It's been about an hour since the tide came in. Let's gear up." He opened one of the plastic tubes he'd unloaded and pulled out some fishing rods.

Rivers had tides? And if they did, what did that have to do with fishing? Marissa must have noticed Sabrina's puzzled expression because she stepped closer. "The salmon spend their first year in fresh water, but then they migrate to the ocean and live there for several years. Now they're returning to the place they were hatched to spawn. They like to get a boost from the tides to start them swimming up the river. We're likely to see a surge of salmon coming by here about an hour after the tide turns."

"Oh, that's right. You said you're a wildlife biologist."

"Yeah. I did a presentation on salmon life

cycles in an elementary school last month. Sorry if I'm lecturing."

"No, I like learning about things like this. So, the salmon hatch in the river, but they live in the ocean. Then they come back to the rivers to lay their eggs every year? Sort of like sea turtles?"

"Not exactly. Sea turtles lay their eggs on the beach and return to the ocean. Spawning is the end of a salmon's life cycle."

"They die? But that's so sad."

"I don't know. It's a natural cycle. Salmon have an amazingly strong instinct to return home. They swim against the current, leap over cascades and brave people fishing and bears to get to the spawning grounds."

"Bears?" And Sabrina had been worried about eagles.

"Sure. Salmon are grizzlies' favorite food."

"How do the salmon know where they're supposed to go?"

"They have an amazing sense of smell, and they imprint the river they grow up in. At the fish hatchery in Valdez, you can see them all pooled up, trying to swim up a two-inch pipe to get inside where they were hatched. I think it must be a huge victory for them to reach their spawning grounds. They've lived a full life and accomplished their purpose."

Sabrina smiled at her. "You really like your job, don't you?"

"I do. If spawning is a salmon's purpose, studying wildlife is mine. That and my family."

"Sabrina," Leith called. "Do you want to come over here with Emma and Ryan? I'm about to give the fishing safety talk."

Marissa laughed. "You'd better go. Leith won't trust you with his fishing tackle until you've had—" she formed quotation marks with her fingers "—The Talk."

Sabrina joined the kids to listen to Leith. Just like in the first-aid class, he was funny and energetic, but made his points clear. "I know face piercing is in fashion, but you do *not* want it done with a fishhook." He held a gaudy green lure up next to his cheek. "See, as a fashion accessory, it's a total bust."

The group laughed, but then focused again as Leith continued. Once they were properly instructed in safety, Leith handed out fishing rods and assigned them to their spots along the creek, with Ryan just downstream from Chris and Emma and her far enough apart so they weren't in danger from each other. The other adults were already at work farther up the river, fishing lines arching over their heads before they stretched out and landed in the water.

Before she tried fishing, Sabrina tied Boomer to a tree within sight of the riverbank. The other two dogs were loose, but they seemed inclined to stick close to the group. Sabrina wasn't at all sure Boomer wouldn't take off into the woods on a whim, so she decided not to take any chances.

Her phone chimed. Misty had sent two photos of herself. In one she wore a retro sundress with a full skirt in a cherry print, in the other white jeans and a fuchsia cold-shoulder top. Sisterly input needed. Date tonight. Which one?

Sabrina had to smile at the thought of a little sister who wanted her advice. Where are you going?

Pizza & Movie.

The dress. And a sweater so you don't freeze in the movie.

Cool. Thnx.

Have fun.

She put away her phone and bent down to give Boomer an ear rub before she went to fish. But the moment she stepped away, leaving him tied, Boomer expressed his dissatisfaction. Loudly. Sabrina pretended to ignore him, turning her back and picking up her fishing rod, but that didn't discourage him from barking and whining as though she was deserting him forever.

She'd just about decided to go back and get him when he stopped making noise. She turned to see Tal had joined him and was licking his head. After a moment, Tal flopped on the ground and Boomer curled up between her paws for a nap. She rested her big head beside him. After a moment Donner wandered over and lay down nearby.

Now that the dogs were settled, Sabrina picked up her rod. She looked over to watch Leith help Emma untangle some leaves from her line. The sun shone down on his broad shoulders and his blue eyes sparkled when he smiled at something Emma said. He was so good with his niece, and with Ryan, too. He'd make a good dad, someday.

Sabrina liked kids, but she wasn't sure she wanted to be someone's mother, to have another person totally dependent on her. At least not until she had a secure job and was positive she could support a family on her own because you could never be sure about marriage.

"Hey, are you going to fish or just admire the view?" Leith called.

"I don't know. It's a nice view."

He threw back his head and laughed. "Better fish. You can't eat scenery."

It wasn't the scenery she'd been referring to, but Leith didn't need to know that. She tried casting the shiny green lure into the river, the way Leith had shown them. It took a few tries, but before long Sabrina got the hang of casting and slowly reeling in the line, allowing the lure to wiggle and jerk like a minnow. Even though there was no sign of any salmon on her line, Sabrina decided she rather liked fishing. The sunshine felt warm on her back, and the air smelled fresh and clean.

Across the river, a group of black-and-white ducks paddled along. The repetitive motion of casting the line out and reeling it in was soothing, like knitting or enjoying a rocking chair. They'd been fishing for almost an hour when Emma squealed, "I think I've got a fish!"

Leith, who had been fishing just upstream between Emma and Ryan, set down his pole and hurried over. "You're right. Reel it in, slowly. Keep your tip up. That's right. Good job." He continued to coach her until she'd successfully brought the fish close to the shoreline, where he could scoop it up in a net. He called out, "Emma's got the first catch of the day. A nice little jack." He pulled a measuring tape from his vest. "It's fourteen inches. The regs say if it's under twenty, it doesn't count toward your one-king limit. That means you can keep on fishing, while I take care of this one."

Leith carried the fish toward camp, presumably to clean it. Not long after that, Dana's pole arched sharply. "Fish on!" Sabrina stopped fishing to watch. This one seemed to take a lot longer to get it close to the shoreline. Sam reached down with the net and held up the fish. It must have been close to three feet long. Now Sabrina understood why they called them kings. They were enormous.

Chris moved closer to check out the fish, blocking Sabrina's view for a moment. When he moved again, they were hooking something into the fish's mouth. Chris held it at arm's length, the fish dangling. "Thirty-three pounds. Nice."

"Not bad for your first king." Sam kissed his wife. "Congratulations."

Dana beamed. "Grilled salmon for supper. I'll go start a fire while the rest of you fish."

After another hour of fishing, Chris and Leith had pulled two more huge fish from the water. Leith went off with the salmon, saying something about cleaning them and starting coals while Chris stayed with the kids. He returned a little while later. Ryan had hooked one, but much to his disappointment, his line broke before he could reel it in. Leith came to stand close to Sabrina. "How's it going?"

"Well, I haven't caught a fish, but my arm muscles have gotten a good workout." She cast once more and had started reeling it in when she felt a sharp tug on the line. "Hey, I might have one!"

She reeled it in slowly, trying to follow Leith's instructions. "Easy. Turn its head upstream. Now bring it closer." Sabrina reeled in part of the line, but with a sudden jerk, the reel started spinning outward.

"Oh, no."

"That's okay. Just play the fish. You might have to let him wear himself out a little. Let him run a bit and then bring him in."

The fish ran several times before Sabrina was able to work it even close to the shoreline. She could see it, looking like the shadow of a whale in the water a few feet out. It changed direction suddenly. "Don't let him get into the current," Leith advised, but before Sabrina could react, the fish darted and the line snapped, shooting backward and slapping Leith in the face.

"Cielos!" Sabrina threw down the pole and ran to him. "Are you all right?" A red mark slashed across his cheek.

"I'm fine. Fortunately, the fish took the lure with him, so I only got the line."

"I'm so sorry."

"It's my fault." Leith rubbed his cheek. "I wasn't following my own advice about standing too close. No harm done."

"I've got one and it's a giant!" Ryan shouted. The arch of his fishing rod seemed to back up his assertion. This time Chris and Marissa gave advice and helped him play the fish, while the rest of the group watched and cheered. It probably took thirty minutes, but finally Chris netted it and pulled it out. It was huge, or at least it seemed that way to Sabrina.

They pulled it out of the net and onto the bank. The fish gave a sudden thrash and managed to flip itself into the river. In that instant, Chris launched himself into the water, tackling the fish like a rugby player. "I've got it. Get the net."

Sam grabbed the net and waded in, easing the net beneath Chris, who held on until he was sure the fish was safely caught. Together they dragged the fish from the water once again, this time farther from the bank.

Ryan ran over and, heedless of Chris's soaking wet clothes, wrapped his arms around him. "Thanks, Dad."

Chris grinned from ear to ear. "Are you ready to weigh this monster?"

"Yeah!"

The salmon weighed in at thirty-two pounds, and Ryan couldn't have been more thrilled. After that, they all decided to call it a day.

Back at camp, Dana already had a fire going, and was brushing olive oil over the biggest salmon fillet Sabrina had ever seen.

"We've got the vegetables covered, from Becky's garden," Marissa said. "Leith, you said you had dessert?"

"We do," he answered. "Sabrina and I will just get it in the Dutch oven, and it can cook while we eat."

Sabrina and I. It felt nice to be part of a team. Sabrina passed off Boomer's leash to Emma. Leith had pulled out a big cast-iron pot and was rubbing the inside with a butter wrapper. "How can I help?"

"When I was cleaning out my freezer to

make room for fish, I found a bunch of blueberries from last year. Can you get them from the ice chest? And you'll find the other ingredients in that box."

She found the gallon bag of berries, cake mix, cinnamon, pecans and sugar. Meanwhile, he'd arranged smoking coals in the firepit. Sabrina set the ingredients on a folding table. "Are we making a cake on the campfire?"

"No, it's more of a cobbler, and we're using charcoal. I started the coals earlier, and they're hot now. Go ahead and add the ingredients to the blueberries in that bag."

Sabrina followed his instructions, and they soon had the cobbler mixed and the Dutch oven nestled onto a bed of coals with more coals on the lid.

Leith held his hand about seven inches over the coals and slowly counted to six before jerking it away. "Rule of thumb—if you can leave your hand this close for six seconds, the coals are medium-hot. Based on my experience, it will take about twenty-five minutes to cook this cobbler."

"I'll set my phone alarm. No chance the cobbler will explode in the meantime, right?"

Leith grinned. "Nope. If the steam builds

up, it can escape around the lid. No explosions tonight." He gathered up the tongs and wrappers.

Sabrina returned the phone to her pocket. "You know, if you ever get tired of this survival trainer gig, you should audition for the Cooking Channel."

Leith laughed. "Yeah, I'll send in my résumé as soon as we get back. I'm sure they'll be calling right away."

If he sent in a video, they probably would. Especially if he smiled like that. Even the mark on his cheek from her fishing line didn't detract from his appeal.

She smiled back at him. He stopped what he was doing and met her eyes. And held them.

"Dinner's ready," someone called, breaking the spell.

Leith set his tongs on one of the flat stones beside the firepit. "Our mess kit is over there. Could you help Emma with her plate, please?"

Sabrina blinked. "Sure." She gathered the plates and utensils and took a set to Emma.

Marissa dished up glazed salmon and grilled asparagus. "There's salad and rolls on the picnic table."

They all gathered around the campfire, sitting in folding chairs or on ice chests. Sabrina took a bite of salmon. "Oh, this is good. This is really good. Can I get the recipe?"

"It's just olive oil, salt and dill. The reason it tastes so good is because the salmon is so fresh. It will never be as good again as it is the first day out of the river."

Conversation died while the hungry fishermen enjoyed their dinner. Most of them went back for second helpings until everything was gone. Sabrina's phone chirped. "Oops. That's the cobbler."

"Perfect timing," Chris said.

The cobbler was a little dark around the edges, but it looked done. Sabrina dished it out to everyone before trying some herself. It wasn't Abuelita's famous apple empanadas, but the blueberries were bursting with flavor and the rich, sweet crust was almost scone-like.

Once everyone had pitched in to clean up, Sabrina and Emma brushed their teeth and change into sweats for bed. One of the guys threw more logs on the fire, and everyone gathered in a circle around it. The sun hadn't set, but it was far in the northwest, casting long shadows across the camp. Sabrina settled into a big folding chair, with Boomer on her lap. Emma wandered over beside Sabrina's chair and yawned.

"Sleepy?"

"No," Emma insisted, stifling another yawn as she stroked the dog.

Sabrina scooted to one side. "Here, sit with us and keep me warm."

Emma snuggled into the big folding chair with Sabrina. Boomer laid his head on her leg. Tal walked over, gave Boomer a sniff and lay down on the ground with her head on Sabrina's foot.

Leith settled on an ice chest next to them with his guitar. He strummed a few chords, adjusted a couple of tuning pegs and riffed a short section of "Classical Gas." Sabrina watched in wonder as his fingers flew over the strings, but no one else seemed surprised.

After a moment he looked up. "Requests?"

Emma immediately shouted, "'The Lady Who Swallowed the Fly.'"

Leith chuckled. "You always want that one."

"It's funny."

"Okay." He strummed an intro and began singing in a strong, clear baritone. Emma jumped in, as did the rest of the group. Sabrina wasn't familiar with the song, but she soon caught on enough to sing along on the chorus. Ryan could hardly sing for laughing at the silly lyrics.

Leith played a few songs the kids knew, which led to "Yellow Submarine" and some other Beatles tunes. The sky grew darker and Emma was soon too sleepy to sing, but she still cuddled with the dog and listened. Leith smiled as he sang and played. Then Marissa suggested "And I Love Her," and Leith's expression went flat. Chris and Sam exchanged a look Sabrina couldn't quite decipher.

Marissa didn't seem to understand the undercurrent, either. She leaned forward. "If you don't know that one—"

"I do." Leith strummed a chord, sang a few words and paused. He put his hand over the strings to still them. "Actually, maybe I don't remember. How about this?" He launched into "American Pie," and Sabrina hurried to join in, hoping to smooth over whatever was bothering him. After a moment the others sang, too.

At the end of the song, Leith looked over at Emma, who had all but fallen asleep on Sabrina's lap. "Bedtime, I think." He set his guitar on the ground and reached for the case.

Sabrina watched him pack his guitar away.

He'd been having such a good time until Marissa had suggested that song. Sabrina wished she knew how to help, how to banish whatever memory the song had summoned and bring back his good mood, but she and Leith really weren't on those terms. Sadly.

CHAPTER NINE

EVERYONE STARTED GATHERING up their things and dispersing to their tents. Sam doused the fire. Leith felt a little guilty, breaking up the group when everyone had been having a good time, but he couldn't get into the music anymore tonight. Not after Marissa had suggested that song. Not that it was her fault. She didn't have any way of knowing what the song represented. It was Leith's fault for letting memories of the past get to him. And he hated that they still had the power to do that.

Emma was curled half in Sabrina's lap, with her hand resting on that little dog. Leith normally wasn't a fan of lapdogs, but he rather liked Boomer. Sabrina smoothed Emma's hair back from her forehead. It had to be crowded with all three of them in the same chair, but they looked quite comfortable, cuddled up together.

He lifted Emma from Sabrina's lap and carried her to the tent. Sabrina and the dogs followed. He tucked Emma inside her bag. "Where's Rufus?" she murmured.

"I'll get him." Leith pulled the stuffed toy from her duffel. When he folded down the side of the sleeping bag to hand Emma the dog, Boomer jumped in beside her.

"Boomer, come here," Sabrina said, in her soft voice. Of course, the dog paid no attention. Instead he turned in three circles and curled up against Emma's ribs.

Emma hugged him. "I want Boomer to sleep with me, too."

Leith looked at Sabrina. "Okay with you?"

"Sure, if Emma doesn't mind."

Emma snuggled farther into the bag. "Good night, Uncle Leith. Good night, Sabrina."

"Good night, sweetie." Sabrina dropped a kiss on her forehead. "Sleep tight." Boomer looked up at Sabrina and Leith could have sworn he winked before he gave a happy sigh and closed his eyes. Tal stretched out on the floor under Emma's cot. Leith tucked the sleeping bag up under Emma's chin, gave Tal a pat and followed Sabrina outside.

He zipped the netting shut and picked up his guitar case to stash in the car. It was just a song. He shouldn't let it ruin the evening. He slammed the liftgate closed and leaned against the car, looking up at the dusky sky that passed for night this time of year. A few filmy clouds floated around a milky almost-full moon. The blinking light of an airplane passed in front of it.

A few moments later, Sabrina walked over and leaned against the car beside him. "Whatcha looking at?"

"Nothing really. Just taking a moment, you know?"

"Yeah." She closed her eyes and breathed in. "It smells so good here. Woody and natural and clean."

"In another few weeks, it will smell like old fish."

She laughed. "I guess we came at the right time, then. Say, when I was bartering for your survival-expert services, you didn't tell me you're also a guitar hero. Where did you learn to play like that?"

He shrugged. "I took a few lessons early on. During the time I was stuck in Arizona, I spent a lot of time in my room. Practice makes perfect, I guess."

"Well, count me impressed."

He chuckled. "Must not take much to impress you."

"You'd be surprised." She leaned a little closer and laid a hand on his arm. "What was the deal with that one song?"

Her hand was warm against the skin of his forearm. Should he tell her? "It's just not a favorite of mine…anymore."

"Anymore?"

It had been a favorite. That was why, when Nicole was deep into picking out bridesmaid dresses and flower arrangements, he'd suggested it. The surprising part was that she'd taken his suggestion, but maybe that was because she didn't really care about music. "I… That is, someone sang that song at my wedding."

"Oh." Sabrina was probably sorry she'd asked. "How long were you married?"

"Five years. It didn't end well."

"What went wrong?"

"I don't know." Well, he did but he wasn't sure how deeply he wanted to get into it with Sabrina. "We were probably too young, but she wanted to get married and I wanted to keep her happy. At first, it seemed like we had a lot in common. We did a lot of camping and hiking while we were dating, but she sort of lost interest later. In that stuff." Leith thought of that guy he'd caught her cheating with. "And in me."

Sabrina gave his arm a little squeeze. A few moments passed and she said, "You know, I sometimes think having things in common is overrated."

Overrated? Leith looked to see if Sabrina was joking, but she seemed serious. "What do you mean?"

"Superficial things, at least. My parents seemed to have a lot in common. He was focused on his business. She worked for him. After they married and I was born, she stopped working but she devoted her time to supporting him, like giving dinner parties for his business associates. She even chose her exercise classes based on who was in them so she could network for him." Sabrina paused and licked her lip. "And then, when his business went bankrupt, my father took off and left both of us behind. I guess we were just part of the old life he was leaving."

"What a…" Leith bit back the word he'd been about to say. He'd assumed, when Sabrina had talked about her sister earlier, that her parents' animosity toward one another was what kept Sabrina from her father, but this was far worse. He could understand the man wanting to start over in a new place after his business failed, but how could he just abandon his wife and daughter? Leith hated that Emma's dad had died before she was born, but it must have been so much worse for Sabrina, knowing her father had chosen to leave her. "I'm sorry that happened to you."

"Thanks." A loose strand of hair blew across her face. She slid the elastic from her ponytail and gathered her hair to redo it. "But I didn't bring it up so you'd feel sorry for me. I'm just using them as an example of a couple who seemed to have things in common. Now, my grandparents, my mother's parents, weren't at all alike."

The strand escaped again. Sabrina gave up and removed the hair tie, letting her hair fall loose onto her shoulders. "Grandy was a retired salesman—one of those people who knew everybody. He was on every committee and organization, and never missed an opportunity to socialize. Abuelita was a homebody who filled her days cooking and reading books. But they adored each other."

Leith was still steaming, thinking about how it must have hurt Sabrina when her father disappeared from her life, but if she didn't want to talk about it, he wouldn't push. "Abuelita?" he asked.

Sabrina smiled. "'Little Grandmother.' She said that's what she called her grandmother, and that's what I should call her."

"So you're saying opposites attract?"

"I'm saying the things they had in common went deeper than favorite foods or taste in music. They both valued home and family. They were faithful to each other, and they respected each other. She admired his way with people, and he admired her ability to hold them together to weather any storm."

Leith considered her words. "You may be right. Maybe the problem with my marriage was that we went into it with different expectations. I thought it was forever. I've come to believe she hadn't thought much past the wedding."

Sabrina didn't say anything, but she moved a little closer. After a moment, Leith continued. "She wants an annulment. A do-over. As if those five years of marriage never happened." As if all the time and effort he'd put into trying to make her happy counted for nothing.

"An annulment? Why?"

"She's engaged again. Apparently, her fiancé's brother is a priest, and they want to marry in a big ceremony in his church. And they can't do that if she's divorced."

"You don't seem too enthralled with the idea."

"Nope."

Sabrina paused. "Do you still love her?"

He scoffed. "No. She took care of that when she used me and threw me away."

"What do you mean 'used you'?"

"She enrolled in an MBA program in Seattle because it allowed her to spend time with some guy she'd met through her job, while I stayed here and worked to pay her tuition. I'm convinced she had no intention of ever coming back to Alaska. Or to me."

"Wow."

"It's bad enough that she cheated on me, but now she wants to pretend we were never married. That I never existed in her life. I took those vows seriously, even if she didn't." He puffed out a breath. "I guess that's why I'm not in a big hurry to make things easier for her by granting her that annulment."

"Hmm, I can't say I would be, either." She shook her head. "Marriage is like rolling dice. You just never know what's going to turn up."

"So it's all a matter of luck?"

"I don't know. Chris and Marissa seem really happy. And so do Sam and Dana. But so did my parents. At least I thought so. But I was a kid. What did I know?" She tilted back her head and stared up at the moon. "When it comes down to it, the only person you can depend on is yourself."

Ten minutes ago, Leith would have agreed

with her, but seeing the pensive expression on her face changed his mind. "What about those grandparents you mentioned? Can't you count on them?"

"They're gone. My mom's still alive." She smiled. "I love her, but she's never exactly been a rock in my life."

You can count on me. Leith almost said it aloud, before he realized it was untrue. Once her assignment ended, she'd either be moving to Seattle as part of the management team, or looking for another job somewhere else. Either way she was out of Alaska, and out of his life. But he wanted to be able to say it, because someone as strong and smart and giving as Sabrina deserved to have someone she could count on to be there when she needed a friend. And maybe he could be that, at least for now.

"While you're here, in Alaska, you can count on me."

"On you?"

"As a friend."

"A friend?" She sounded as though she wasn't familiar with the term.

"Yeah, a friend. You know. People you like, who you enjoy spending time with. Who will pick you up when you have to leave your car at the shop or take care of your dog while you're out of town or tell you when you're about to marry the wrong person." He probably shouldn't have said that last part, but Sabrina just smiled.

"Did your friends do that?"

"A couple of them did. Wish I'd listened."

"And you want to be my friend."

"Yes, I do."

"All right, then. Friends it is." She smiled up at him, her dark eyes shining, and he was suddenly overcome with an unfriendlike urge. He touched her face, stroking his finger over the wondrously smooth skin of her cheek. Her eyes grew wider.

His eyes traveled to lips that were no longer smiling, but soft and waiting. He bent to kiss her, stopping just an inch away, where he could feel her breath on his mouth, giving her time to pull away if that was what she wanted. Instead, she reached up to slide her arms around his neck and pull him closer.

He'd thought the kisses at the wedding were amazing, but they were nothing compared to kissing Sabrina under the moon. He slid his fingers into that dark cloud of hair, which smelled of ripe fruit and sunlight, with a smoky overtone from the campfire. His new favorite scent.

She drew back just far enough to look up

at him, a half smile on those luscious lips. "Is this how you greet all your friends?"

"No. Just the ones whose hair smells like strawberries." And he kissed her once again, bringing her close against him as he explored those soft lips.

The sound of log hitting log, as someone stacked their remaining firewood, reminded Leith that they weren't alone in the campground. They were in the shadow of the car, but it wasn't dark enough to hide them from anyone passing by on the way to the campground facilities, and he didn't want this kiss to become a topic of conversation among his friends. Reluctantly, he released Sabrina and took a step back.

Odd, because when they were pretend-dating, he'd had no compunction about kissing her in public, but this was different. This meant something—he wasn't sure exactly what—but until he was sure, he didn't want anyone else butting in.

"Leith?" She'd tilted her head to watch him as if she couldn't quite figure him out. Well, that made two of them.

He touched her cheek once more before turning toward the tent. "We'd better get some sleep if you're going to catch that king tomorrow."

"Okay."

Emma was sleeping soundly when they slipped inside the tent. Boomer raised his head, but seemed content to stay where he was on Emma's pillow. Sabrina crawled into her sleeping bag, and whispered, "Good night, Leith."

"Good night." His cot was maybe four feet away from hers on the other side of Emma's, but after holding Sabrina in his arms, it felt like a canyon between them. Judging by her even breathing, Sabrina dropped off almost instantly, but it was a long time before Leith got any sleep that night.

THE NEXT MORNING, Sabrina woke to the sound of a couple of birds squabbling. She peeked through the screen window on her side of the tent to see a raven with what looked like a piece of bacon in his mouth, and another trying to grab it. Sunlight turned some of their feathers from black to iridescent blue. The first bird turned his head and flew away, with the second in hot pursuit.

Boomer's dog tags jingled, and Emma sat up, yawning. "I'm hungry."

To Sabrina's surprise, Leith seemed to have slept through the whole thing. He lay on his side, bundled in his sleeping bag. She whispered to Emma, "Let's go find breakfast."

They tiptoed out of the tent, along with the dogs. The other tents were quiet, but through the trees, Sabrina could see people at the river. They must have already eaten and gone to fish. Sabrina dug through the food chest for something quick and easy. Paper packets caught her eye. "How about oatmeal?"

"What kind?"

"Um, apple-cinnamon or blueberry."

"Blueberry!"

"Great." Sabrina handed Boomer's leash to Emma. "Why don't you take Boomer, while I cook?"

"Okay. We'll go for a walk."

"Only around the campground where I can see you, okay?"

Emma gave a little eye roll but agreed. "Come on, Boomer."

Sabrina carefully followed the steps Leith had taught her to light the camp stove, surprised to find it worked on the first try. She found a folding silicone-sided pan like the ones from the team-builder, snapped it into shape and used it to bring water to a boil. While she was waiting, she found a French press and a package of coffee.

The water boiled. Sabrina had just finished

stirring it into the instant oatmeal and making coffee when the flap of the tent opened and Leith stepped out, unshaven and with the worst case of bedhead Sabrina had ever seen. He was adorable. She smiled at him. "Good morning."

"Morning." He yawned. "Can't believe I slept so late. Is that coffee I smell?"

"It is."

He accepted a mug from her and noticed the camp stove. "You did all this?"

"Well, if by 'all this' you mean I boiled water, then yes." She waved to Emma. "Breakfast is ready."

He took a sip of coffee. "This is good. You're a quick study."

"Thank you. I've discovered a new side to my personality. Wilderness woman."

"Oh, yeah? And what do you think of her?"

"I like her. She takes me places I'd never have thought to go."

Emma and Boomer came dashing into camp. Sabrina handed her a bowl of oatmeal and a spoon, and poured Boomer a bowl of kibble. They both dug in. Sabrina turned to Leith. "Oatmeal? I still have some hot water left."

"Sure. Thanks."

She stirred up a packet for him and sat in

the chair beside his to eat her own breakfast. Instant oatmeal had never tasted so good.

"Uncle Leith, are you almost ready? The others are already fishing, and I haven't caught a big one like Ryan did yet."

"Give me a few minutes to finish my breakfast, shortcake. I'm running a little behind this morning."

"Hey! A ptarmigan." Emma dropped her bowl and ran after a plump little bird that sounded like a chicken on fast-forward as it scurried along the ground. Boomer bounded beside her. The bird burst into flight and disappeared into the woods.

"Stay where I can see you," Leith called.

Emma skidded to a stop at the edge of the forest. She waved to let him know she'd heard and turned to patrol the perimeter of the campground, eyes peeled for more wildlife.

Leith smiled and turned to Sabrina. "And how about you? Are you up for more fishing?"

Sabrina turned to him. "Sure."

"Even though you didn't catch anything yesterday?"

"Even though. In fact, maybe I liked it better that way. I just enjoyed practicing my casting and being beside the water. Although it was exciting when Ryan's fish almost got away and Chris had to tackle it."

"Yeah." Leith laughed. "That's the first time I've ever seen a man wrestle a king out of the river with his bare hands. If Chris wasn't already Ryan's hero, he would be after that."

Sabrina finished her oatmeal and carried her bowl and Emma's to wash in the leftover hot water. "Marissa told me that once the salmon get all the way up the river to where they were hatched, they lay their eggs and die. It seems kind of sad."

"It's just their natural life cycle."

"I suppose. Marissa said that returning to spawn was a salmon's purpose."

"I never really thought about it, but I suppose she's right. Their instinct drives them to complete their purpose."

"Do you believe that's true of people, too? That we're driven to complete our purpose?"

"Maybe. I know I'm happier when I feel like I'm accomplishing something."

"It seems like you like your job."

"I do. I didn't start out doing this. When I got out of high school, I trained as an emergency medical technician. I worked up at Prudhoe Bay."

"That sounds rewarding."

"It was and it wasn't. I was helping people, which I liked. I even used the paddles once to jump-start a guy's heart. That was a little more excitement than he'd expected."

"Wow. That's way up in the Arctic Circle, right?"

"Right. I mainly handled minor injuries and illnesses. If anyone was very sick or hurt, I stabilized them until they could be airlifted back to Anchorage. That's what Volta does. She transports patients by plane or helicopter."

"Did you work together?"

"No. When she was certified, I was back in college for my degree in outdoor recreation."

"What made you choose that? I mean, I know you like the outdoors, but you'd already started a different career."

"That's why Learn & Live is such a great fit for me. As an EMT, I would come into the situation when everything had already gone wrong and I tried to keep it from getting worse. At Learn & Live, I can train people how to take care of themselves so that hopefully they'll never need to be rescued."

"Not as much glory, though."

"I don't need glory. Most days, when I wake up in the morning and think about the coming day at work, I can't wait to get started. That's how I know it's right."

"You're lucky. Not everyone gets that kind of satisfaction from their job."

"You're right. I am lucky. Most people work because they need to put food on the table, and there's nothing wrong with that. You mentioned a purpose before. I think for most people, their purpose is to take care of and provide for their families, and their job is a way to do that. I'm just one of the fortunate people whose job provides a lot of satisfaction as well as a paycheck."

Sabrina thought about that. She'd been lucky as well. She'd enjoyed her job as a buyer. She loved keeping up with fashion, searching out the clothes that her store's customers would enjoy. She'd once dreamed of designing those clothes, but discovering wonderful designs was rewarding, too, and it brought a steady paycheck. Until that paycheck disappeared.

A sudden squeal and barking drew their attention to Emma. Something brown shot past her. A rabbit, heading directly toward their campsite. In her excitement, Emma dropped the leash and Boomer took off after the rabbit. Tal jumped up.

"Sit," Leith commanded.

Tal sat, but she quivered in eagerness. The rabbit ran through the campsite with Boomer right behind it. His leash caught on the leg of Emma's folding chair and knocked it over, sending Tal scurrying out of the way.

Leith stepped on the end of the leash and brought the terrier to a halt. "Boomer, that hare is bigger than you. What would you do if you caught it?" Boomer barked, as if annoyed he'd been caught, and Sabrina laughed.

Emma ran up and scooped up Boomer's leash. "That was a snowshoe hare, right, Uncle Leith?"

"That's right, kiddo." He picked up his cup and swallowed the last of his coffee. "Let's clean up camp so you can fish." It wasn't long before they joined the others at the river. Ryan waved, but didn't leave the spot where he was casting into the water.

"How come Ryan still gets to fish?" Emma asked. "He already got his king."

"I'm sure they've rigged him up with a six-weight line and spinner for trout or grayling. You just worry about catching your own king, okay?"

"I caught the first fish, anyway. And today I'm gonna get one even bigger than Ryan's."

"It's a matter of luck what fish decides to take your lure. Fishing isn't a competition. Right, Sabrina?"

"You're the expert."

"Exactly." He winked at her. "Now, ladies, let's see you catch some fish."

"We will." Emma cast her lure into the river. Judging by the look on her face, she didn't intend to leave the river without one.

Sabrina was happy just to be out in the sunshine, enjoying the day, but since Leith had gone to all the trouble to buy her a fishing license and rig up a rod for her, she moved downstream a little ways and tossed out her line.

Since Leith had already caught his king, he took charge of Boomer while they fished. Tal tagged along, never letting the terrier out of her sight. She'd apparently appointed herself Boomer's bodyguard. Having enjoyed one rabbit chase that morning, Boomer was intent on checking the area for wildlife.

"Uncle Leith! I got one. Hurry!" Emma struggled, but she must have hooked something big because the line was feeding out rapidly.

"Set the brake," Leith called.

Sabrina dropped her pole and hurried over to help. Emma pushed on the brake. The sudden force jerked the pole from her hands. Sabrina lunged into the river and managed to grab it, but ended up on her knees, up to her waist in the cold water, struggling to hang on to the rod with both hands. Leith ran toward them, but must have hit a slick spot because he disappeared below the surface of the river and popped up several feet downstream, laughing.

Everyone came running. Chris took the pole from Sabrina and moved over while Marissa held out a hand to assist her out of the river. Leith shook the water from his hair and waded onto the bank. Meanwhile, Dana quickly got Emma into position to put her hands on the rod and help Chris play her fish. Ryan shouted encouragement. It took a good twenty minutes, but eventually Chris and Emma worked the fish to the shoreline, where Leith could net it.

"Emma, I think you may have the record," he told her.

Sam brought the scale. "Thirty-six pounds. Biggest one yet."

"Yay!" Emma jumped up and down in excitement. "Take my picture."

The king was practically as big as Emma, so wet but proud Uncle Leith stood beside her supporting the fish's weight while Emma beamed toward the camera. Sabrina snapped several shots, glad she'd invested in a waterproof phone case. "Great photos. They should put these on tourism websites."

"Let's take a picture with everybody." Emma beamed.

"Great idea," Marissa said. "I'll get my tripod."

Sabrina shivered as a breeze cut through her wet jeans. Leith noticed. "Give us a minute to change first, okay?"

"Sure. You and Sabrina get into dry clothes while I get the camera set up."

Leith took Sabrina's hand and led her toward the tent. "Thanks for grabbing Emma's pole for her. Sorry you had to get wet."

"I'm not sorry." Sabrina laughed. "It was an adventure, and Emma is thrilled with her fish."

"You still have time to catch yours before we have to break camp."

Sabrina shook her head. "This may sound silly, but I don't really want to catch one. I kind of like the idea of my king going on and laying eggs. You know, fulfilling its purpose."

He squeezed her hand. "There's nothing silly about it."

"I hope you don't mind that I wasted the fishing license."

"Did you enjoy your time on the river?"

"I really did."

He smiled. "Then it wasn't wasted." They

reached the tent, and Leith gestured for her to go in and change first.

"I had a great time." Sabrina slipped inside, peeled off her wet jeans and tugged on a pair of yoga pants. She stepped out and spread her jeans over a chair to dry. "Especially watching Emma. She has so much determination."

"She's determined, all right. Good thing you saved her fish, or she'd probably insist we stay here until she caught one, even if it took all summer." Leith took his turn to change.

Once he was dressed, they returned to the shoreline, where Marissa had set up a camera on her tripod.

They all moved in close, with Ryan and Emma in the center front with the dogs and everyone clustered behind and around them. Marissa set the timer and hurried to join the group. The camera flashed and clicked off a series of photos.

Marissa went to flick through the shots. "Aw, these are great. Come look."

Sabrina peered at the camera screen. The last picture caught her facing toward the river and Leith looking over at her with an odd expression on his face. Sort of warm and soft and… Sabrina was probably imagining it. "These are great. Will you send me copies?" she asked Marissa.

"Sure."

Everyone crowded around to look. Leith slipped an arm around Sabrina's shoulders. She looked up at him, and he smiled. And there on the shoreline, amid the chatter and laughter, Sabrina felt something she hadn't felt in a very long time. A sense of belonging.

CHAPTER TEN

LEITH TOOK EMMA home first. When they arrived, Volta was kneeling in the front yard, digging dandelions out from the lawn. Emma jumped out and ran to tell her mom all about fishing. "I got two. The first one was a little one. Uncle Leith said it was a jack. Ryan got a big king, and Chris had to jump in the river because it almost got away, but I caught a king the next day and mine was even bigger. Sabrina and Uncle Leith got wet and we brought lots of fish home and can we have my fish for supper tonight? Please?" Emma finally stopped to breathe.

Volta hugged her daughter. "That's great. Yes, we can cook your fish for supper." She turned to Leith and Sabrina, who were digging Emma's things from the back of the car. "You guys want to stay for dinner?"

"I wish I could," Sabrina said, "but I have to do laundry and a few other chores before I head in to work tomorrow. But thanks for the offer."

"Maybe another day." Leith opened the ice chest and pulled out several gallon bags of fish. "Here's Emma's haul."

"Wow, Emma. Look at all that fish. We have a lot of vacuum-packing to do this evening."

"Can I press the buttons?"

"Sure. Did you thank Leith and Sabrina for letting you tag along on this fishing trip?"

"Thanks, Uncle Leith. Thanks, Sabrina," Emma obediently sang out, and gave them both hugs. "I had fun."

"Me, too. I'm glad you convinced me to fish," Sabrina told her.

"See you later, shortcake." Leith waved and climbed into the Land Cruiser.

Sabrina waved, too, as they drove away. She pulled the elastic from her hair and shook it loose, running her fingers through it. "That was so much fun."

"I'm glad you think so." Leith glanced over. He wasn't ready for his time with her to end. "Do you really have to do laundry?"

"I really do. Otherwise I would have stayed. I like your sister."

"Yeah, I like her, too, but I was kind of wondering if you'd like to have dinner with me this evening. But if you're too busy..."

Sabrina twisted her mouth to one side as

she thought. "I really do need to go to the Laundromat, but—" She paused for a few seconds. "This is the part where you try to convince me no one will notice if I dig my work polo out of the hamper and wear it to work."

Leith laughed at the idea of Sabrina wearing a crumpled shirt anywhere. "I have a solution if you like Thai?"

"I love Thai."

"There's a great restaurant not far from my house. Let's call ahead for takeout, and you can bring your laundry to my house to wash while we eat."

"You're brilliant."

"What can I say?" He handed her his phone. "Here, go ahead and order. There's a menu in the glove compartment."

She opened the door to reveal a stack of take-out menus. "Wow. I gather if it's not over a campfire, you don't cook."

"Not often," he admitted. "It seems kind of pointless to cook for one. Easier just to get takeout."

"Hmm." Sabrina found the menu and studied it. "The red pineapple curry sounds good."

"It's hot," Leith warned.

"That's how I like it. What are you having?"

"Pad thai, spicy."

"Excellent choice." She called in the order, hanging up just before they pulled into the parking lot of her apartment. "They said twenty minutes. Come on in while I grab a quick shower and change."

"You look fine." In fact, she looked much better than fine, with the fitted green vest and cloud of dark hair waving over her shoulders. With or without makeup, she was gorgeous. But he shouldn't be thinking about things like that. Kissing her last night had been a mistake. They needed to stay in the friend zone.

"I need a shower. I must smell like river and mosquito repellent."

"That's my favorite perfume."

She laughed. "Still…"

"All right." Leith got her backpack from the back while she unloaded the dog's things. He followed her into her apartment.

Sabrina unsnapped Boomer's leash and headed toward the back. "Make yourself at home. Water and sodas in the refrigerator. I'll only be five minutes."

He'd heard that one before, usually about half an hour before Nicole declared herself ready to go. Resigned, he opened the refrigerator door. A jug of water and a carton of milk rested on the top shelf. He took out the water and opened a cabinet door, looking for a glass.

The one nearest the sink held four glasses: one tall and thin, one short and round, a stemmed wineglass and a faceted juice glass. Obviously, Sabrina didn't plan on much company. He poured water into the tallest glass and sat in the wooden chair in the living room.

A sketch pad rested on the table beside him. Curious, he flipped up the cover to find a sketch of the vest Sabrina was wearing. On the second page was a jacket, black with thin red lines running along the seams and lining the collar. A fishing shirt, not too different from the one he wore but colored a soft purple and curved like a woman's body, was next.

Sabrina came into the living room carrying a laundry basket. "I'm ready."

He looked at his watch. "Four minutes, forty-five seconds. Impressive."

She laughed. "Maybe I should go back for lipstick."

"Not necessary." Her full lips were naturally rosy. And they'd be a lot rosier if he kissed them. Which was a bad idea if he planned to keep their relationship in the friend arena. He turned another page. "What's all this?"

"Oh, just doodles."

"They're more than that. Even I can see you put some effort into these. They're good."

"Thanks." She shrugged. "I had a couple

of ideas for Orson's women's wear. I thought maybe if I make the management team, I could bring up the possibility of making a line that was a little more stylish, more like the expensive brands."

"Would they cost more to manufacture?"

"Not a lot. Orson already uses quality fabrics and manufacturing techniques. A lot of women would pay a little more for clothes that look good on them, even for camping."

He'd noticed Marissa and Dana asking about her vest. "You may be onto something. The takeout should be ready by the time we get there. Are you?"

"Do you mind if Boomer comes?"

Leith looked down at his dog, who was lying quietly at his feet, her tail sweeping from side to side, while the terrier tugged on her ear. "Tal would never forgive me if he didn't."

It took a little over thirty minutes to collect dinner and drive to Leith's house. He parked in the garage and led Sabrina in through the kitchen door, glad he'd taken the time yesterday to straighten up a little before going camping.

Sabrina swept her gaze over the all-white kitchen and dining alcove. "Wow. Look at all that counter space. And two ovens. But I must admit, I'm surprised. This is a very nice kitchen, but it doesn't look like you."

"It's not. The previous owners did this. I always feel like I'm in an operating room."

"It is a little sterile. Have you considered painting the walls a different color?"

"Yeah. In fact," he admitted, "I bought paint. But I painted the bathroom first, and that was so tedious I've been putting off tackling this room."

"I'll do it."

"What? No. It's a huge job."

"It's not so big. Other than the dining area, most of the wall is covered with cabinets."

"No way." Having Sabrina over for a meal was just a date, but having her paint his kitchen seemed to cross a line. Like she belonged here in his house, in his life. And after his experience with Nicole, he wasn't letting anyone get that close again. Especially not someone who wasn't staying.

Sabrina ran a hand over the texture on the wall. "Come on. I owe you for all you've done for me."

"I told you, we're friends. Friends don't keep score of who owes who a favor."

"Any relationship where one person is always giving and the other taking doesn't last long. Please, I want to do this for you. What color paint did you choose?"

Leith set the take-out bag on the table. "Why don't you start your laundry while I unload the car, and then we can eat before it gets cold. We'll discuss paint later, okay?"

"Okay. Dinner first." The little smile she gave him made it clear she wasn't going to let it go. Maybe she was right. Friends helped each other. Really, painting a wall wasn't such an intimate thing. He wouldn't think twice about hiring a painter, so why did it seem like a big deal to let Sabrina do it?

He grabbed the mail and stuffed it into his pocket before carrying the leftover camp food to the kitchen. He could unload the equipment later. Meanwhile, Sabrina carried her laundry basket inside, and he showed her the laundry room off the kitchen. She stuffed a load into the washer while he set the table. While he filled glasses with ice water, Sabrina opened the take-out cartons. The aroma of sesame oil, spices and peppers wafted across the kitchen.

They filled their plates, sharing the food between them. Ignoring the fork he'd set beside her plate, Sabrina unwrapped the chopsticks the restaurant had provided. She took a bite of pad thai. "Mmm." She chewed and swallowed. "That is spicy. So good." She tried the curry and rice.

Leith watched her, fascinated with her dexterity with chopsticks and the expression of bliss when she tasted the spicy food. She smiled at him. "Aren't you going to eat?"

"Yeah." He took a bite, reveling in the burst of flavor with a tinge of pain. "Extra spicy tonight."

"It's perfect. I expected Alaska to be all about seafood, but I've seen all sorts of ethnic restaurants and little grocery stores."

"A friend of mine teaches social studies, and he says his is the most diverse high school in America."

"I wonder why so many different people wind up in Anchorage, of all places. I mean, you have to come here. You don't just happen to be driving through on your way somewhere else."

"Probably the same as you. Job opportunities. But then they live here awhile, make friends, put down roots. In the winter, they see the snow-covered mountains turn pink in the alpenglow, and in summer they watch the goslings grow up in neighborhood lakes. It becomes home."

"You love it."

"I do."

"Even in winter?"

"Especially in winter. No, that's not true. I love fishing and camping in the summer, and that's when we teach most of our outdoor classes. But winter in the woods is beautiful. Anchorage has miles of trails. I ski and bike."

"Bike? In winter?"

"We use fat tire bikes. They have wide, soft tires that don't sink into the snow."

She shook her head. "You Alaskans are a special breed. You must be born with anti-freeze in your veins."

"Maybe. Mostly it's just a matter of the right clothes and equipment."

"We're starting to get in some of our fall and winter inventory at the store. The thermal underwear selection is astounding. Poly-propylene, bamboo, silk—I had no idea there were so many variations."

He grinned. "Didn't carry a lot of thermal underwear at Cutterbee's?"

"Not much. Plenty of silk lingerie, but that's a whole different thing."

"I'll bet." He could picture the type of under-wear she was talking about. Better if he didn't, though. Sweat was beading on his forehead and he wasn't sure it was all due to the cap-saicin in the pepper. "I'm getting more water. Want some?"

"Sure. Thanks."

They ate until Leith couldn't take any more heat. He got out some plastic containers and remembered he hadn't seen a lot of food besides yogurt and eggs in Sabrina's refrigerator. "Want to take some of this home for tomorrow?"

"No, thanks. If I ate like this every day, I'd have to buy a whole new wardrobe." She licked the last bit of curry from her chopstick. "Although it might be worth it. Oh, my wash cycle is probably done. I'll put the clothes in the dryer before I help clean up."

"I can do it."

She waved him away, then disappeared into the laundry room and returned a few minutes later. Leith had already started washing the plates, so she picked up a dish towel and dried. It felt good. Companionable. It was nice to share dinner with someone who was capable of conversing and wasn't covered in fur.

Once she'd put away the last glass, she turned to him. "Okay, about that painting. When can I start?" He started to shake his head, but she interrupted. "Are you afraid I'll mess it up?"

"No. I've seen what you did at your apartment. It looks great."

"Okay, are you afraid you won't like the color you chose?"

Not really, but it made for a decent excuse. "Right. I'd hate for you to go to all that trouble if it turns out to be a bad color."

"Show me."

Fine. He fetched a bucket of paint, along with a sample card, from the closet in the laundry room. "It's called Caramel Delight, whatever that means. It looks tan to me. It was that or Spruce Tree, and I decided this was the safer choice."

"I agree. Deep green would look great, but that's a lot of drama to live with every day." She examined the sample. "This isn't really caramel-colored, though. Caramel is more golden, whereas this has some red undertones, which is even better. I think you'll really like the way this warms up your kitchen."

The paint had been sitting in the closet for six months, but now that Sabrina had described it, he was suddenly eager to see it on the walls. "I have a workshop to teach this weekend, and quite a few things next week. I'm not sure when I can get to it."

"I'm off Tuesday. Is there any reason I can't come and paint while you work?"

"You really want to paint on your day off?"

"Yes. I like painting. And I want to do something for you. You've taught me so much, and it's really helped at work."

"Okay, you've talked me into it. I'll show you where the spare key is hidden, and you can let yourself in."

"Yes!" She stepped forward and hugged him. "You won't be sorry."

He allowed himself a brief hug in return before stepping away from her. If she kept hugging him like that, it was going to be very difficult to keep this relationship on a just-friends basis. And if he couldn't manage that, he had a feeling he was going to be very sorry indeed.

SABRINA ARRIVED AT work the next day forty minutes before the store was scheduled to open. A steady drizzle made her especially thankful for the stellar weather they'd enjoyed on the camping trip. She greeted the security guard, who let her in the door. Unfortunately, Walter was standing next to the front registers talking to a woman, and because of the cold, Sabrina was wearing the offending vest again. Maybe she could sneak by without Walter spotting her.

"Sabrina," he called, and waved her over.

Well, so much for that thought. She smiled and headed in that direction. The woman with him looked familiar, but Sabrina couldn't immediately place her.

"Sabrina, you remember Kate Simonton."

Oh, one of the upper managers Sabrina had met during the interview process. At headquarters, Kate had her hair up and wore a business suit. Today, she still looked businesslike, but in tailored slacks and a silk shirt with low-heeled pumps.

"Of course I remember." What was she doing here? Did it have anything to do with Sabrina's internship? "It's good to see you again, Ms. Simonton."

"Kate, please. I'm glad to see you, too. Walter tells me you're managing women's wear for now."

"Yes." Sabrina tried to think of something brilliant to say concerning her job, but nothing came to mind. "I am."

Kate tilted her head. "That vest."

"It's one of ours." Sabrina hastened to assure her, pointing to the double-*O* logo on the zipper pull. "I just did a few alterations. I plan to leave it in my locker before customers come in."

"Let me see the back." Kate made a twirling motion with her finger and Sabrina obediently turned in a slow circle.

"I like it. What kind of fabric did you use for the accents?"

"Microfiber. It's from a dog scarf from the pet department."

Kate laughed. "Very creative. What other alterations have you come up with?"

"Um, this is the only piece where I've made major design changes. The rest are just fitting alterations." Sabrina paused, and then decided to go for it. "I've sketched a few other design ideas for outdoor wear."

"I'd like to see them."

"I'm afraid I left them at home."

"That's okay. Bring them tomorrow."

"Tomorrow?"

"Since Kate's in town, I've scheduled an afternoon meeting with all the department heads tomorrow at my house," Walter said. "I'm just about to send out a memo. The rain is supposed to clear up, so we'll do a potluck cookout in the yard for dinner."

"Sounds great," Sabrina said, wondering what in the world a potluck cookout entailed.

"You can bring dessert." Walter smiled at her as though he'd given her a gift. Maybe he had. At least he hadn't mentioned anything about beans.

"I'll look forward to it. I'd better get to work. I'll see you tomorrow, Kate." Sabrina made her escape. She probably should have hung around and schmoozed a bit, but even after all she'd learned from Leith, hanging out with Walter was a risk. The more she said, the more likely her ignorance of camping and outdoor activities would be exposed. Even worse if it happened in front of Kate, who, if Sabrina recalled correctly, was a vice president.

Sabrina stashed her vest in her locker, pinned her name tag to her polo and hurried to her department to make sure it was in good shape, just in case Kate wandered by. To her relief, Autumn had left everything neat and organized. Sabrina decided to make a couple of changes on the end-of-rack displays to showcase a new shipment of plaid shirts.

The displays seemed to be helping. Sales of women's wear were up almost 20 percent since she'd taken charge of the department. Darn it, that was what she should have mentioned to Kate. Well, maybe tomorrow she'd have a chance.

Dessert. She could make brownies at home. Abuelita's recipe was always a hit. Or she could make the dessert Leith had shown her. She didn't have any wild blueberries in the freezer, but she could pick up some peaches. Assuming Walter's backyard had a firepit, she could wow everyone with her outdoor cooking skills.

She layered a red T-shirt under a blue-and-white plaid shirt with a tiny red stripe and stepped back to look. It needed something else. She hung a navy cap from the end of the hanging rack above it. Better.

Just after the lights flashed, signaling the store was opening, Sabrina turned to see Walter and Kate passing by on the way to his office. Kate gave her a thumbs-up. Sabrina's spirits soared. If the vice president liked what she'd done, that had to be good for her prospects. She just had to make sure she kept the positive vibe going at the meeting tomorrow.

Her cell vibrated in her pocket. A new email with official notification of the meeting and cookout. Good thing she'd scheduled Autumn to cover the department tomorrow afternoon. Sabrina had planned to do paperwork, but it could wait. She sidled over to the camping department. "Hey, Tim, did you hear about the meeting tomorrow?"

He patted the cell phone in his pocket. "I just got the email. I'm grilling."

"So, you've done this before?"

"Sure. Walter has these all the time, especially when someone from headquarters drops in. It gives him a chance to show off the equipment."

"They drop in a lot?"

"Oh, yeah. Especially during salmon season. They usually tack on a fishing trip to their official business."

"Ah. Well, I was thinking about doing a dessert in a Dutch oven. Will there be a firepit or something?"

"Sure, sure. Walter's backyard is practically a campground. He buys charcoal by the ton, so just bring the Dutch oven and ingredients. I'll show you where everything is tomorrow."

"That would be super. Thanks, Tim."

"No problem."

On her way back to her department, Sabrina passed a display of Dutch ovens. The price made her flinch. As much as she hated to be further in his debt, she'd have to borrow Leith's. But at least she'd convinced him to let her paint his kitchen, which would help even up the score. Sabrina wandered back to her department, where a woman and her teenage daughter were exclaiming over the new plaid shirts. Sabrina hurried over to make the sale.

LEITH WAS RUNNING late that morning. He grabbed a granola bar and an apple from the bowl on his countertop, knocking off yesterday's mail as he reached for it. He picked up the mail off the floor, noticing for the first time the hand-addressed envelope. He knew that looping handwriting. Nicole—no doubt inquiring about why he hadn't returned the annulment papers. Well, he didn't have time to get into it right now. He tucked the envelope in his back pocket and ran out the door, forgetting the apple in the process.

Two hours later, he called a fifteen-minute break in the class he was teaching at one of the big office buildings downtown. Between his growling stomach and the letter in his pocket, he'd had a hard time concentrating on emergency-response training. He invested in a candy bar from the vending machine in the employee break room and decided to take a walk around the block while he ate it, both to clear his head and to avoid running into students who might try to start a conversation.

Ordinarily, he welcomed student questions and comments, but today he needed a moment alone, because this unread letter was looming over him like one of those Road Runner traps that Wile E. Coyote was always setting. Once he'd turned the corner and was sure no one from class was following, he tore open the envelope.

Typical Nicole. Why hadn't he gotten off

his butt and mailed the papers? The wedding was only six months away, and she and her fiancé had already spent a fortune on deposits, etc., etc. It hadn't even occurred to her that he might not want to sign the papers. She expected him to give her whatever she asked for, just as he always had. But they weren't married anymore, and her happiness was no longer his responsibility. Maybe it never had been.

Sabrina was right—a relationship where one person did all the giving and the other all the taking was doomed. Sabrina might be right about a lot of things. He'd taught her about woodcraft, but she'd taught him about life. About adaptability. About passing judgment. He cringed at his early assessment of her, that she was empty-headed and used her looks to get by. She was smart and hardworking and eager to learn. She deserved that management position. Even if it was in Seattle. Even if it took her away from him.

His phone vibrated. As if thinking about her had summoned her, Sabrina had texted, asking if she could borrow his Dutch oven for some job thing tomorrow. She could stop by his house after work to pick it up, if that was all right with him.

It was. And for some reason, knowing that

he was going to see Sabrina lifted his spirits. And that made him wonder: Was it this letter that had him off his game, or was it the thought that in a couple of months, Sabrina would be going away for good? He looked at his watch, and realized he had three minutes to get back to the classroom. He'd have to figure out the answer to that question some other time.

CHAPTER ELEVEN

WALTER'S HOUSE WAS something of a surprise. If asked, Sabrina would have guessed Walter lived in a log cabin with antler chandeliers and rustic furniture. Instead, she pulled up in front of a silver-gray contemporary home punctuated with soaring half gables and unusually shaped windows.

She was met at the door by a smiling blonde woman dressed in pressed linen slacks and a fine-gauge cotton sweater—Sabrina thought she might well have been a model in her younger days. Walter's wife, Mallory, as she insisted Sabrina call her, had to be at least five inches taller than her husband.

She took the container of ice cream Sabrina gave her to stash in her freezer and led Sabrina through the house toward a vast wall of windows facing across the inlet toward Mount Susitna. A long dining table with fourteen Scandinavian-style chairs anchored one end of the room. Pale polished wood made up the center of the table, with an inlaid pattern of darker wood and turquoise forming a border. Chairs and couches clustered around a towering stacked-stone fireplace at the other end. Walter, Kate, Tim and the head of the fishing department were already chatting at the dining table. Just after Sabrina joined them, Amy from the shoe department arrived, carrying her baby in a car seat.

Walter came around and held out a finger for the baby to grasp. "Look at you, little William. You're growing up fast. Mom must be feeding you well. Amy, I appreciate you interrupting your maternity leave to come in today."

"No problem. I wanted to hear what Kate has to tell us. Thanks for letting me bring William."

"I'm looking forward to getting to spend time with this handsome young man while you do your business," Mallory said.

Sabrina joined the others in oohing and aahing over the baby. He was adorable, with his chubby cheeks and big eyes. Once all the staff had arrived, Walter pushed a button and shades descended, closing off the view and darkening the room so that Kate could project her slides on the far wall of the dining area. Mallory entertained the baby in the living room while they met.

They spent a couple of hours going over how sales stacked up between stores within the Orson Outfitters' umbrella, and how those sales compared with their competitors. Numbers were swimming in Sabrina's head, but it looked like the Anchorage store was once again on pace as the sales leader. According to Kate, Orson's was holding their own against the competition, but management would like to do better. "We're considering a few changes in the inventory mix."

"What kind of changes?" Amy asked.

"That's still in discussion. Once we've made the decision, we'll be sure to get the word out."

"But what sorts of things are you looking at? Adding new departments or lines of inventory, or taking some away?"

"We're always working on finding the right mix to give our customers what they want. That's all I can say for now."

The department heads exchanged nervous glances, but it was clear Kate wasn't giving out any more information. Walter stood. "Thank you, Kate, for an informative presentation. What say we all adjourn to the backyard and make some dinner?"

Tension eased as everyone gathered their equipment and ingredients and filed down the stairs and out into Walter and Mallory's yard. Tim started up a pile of coals in the enormous grill built into a river-rock wall at the edge of the expansive deck. Most of the other supervisors clustered around the tables, preparing their own contributions to the feast. Sabrina watched Tim light the coals, and then duplicated his activities in the firepit in the center of the yard, surrounded by a circular patio of paving stones.

Leith had given her detailed instructions last night on how many coals she'd need, how to know when they were ready and how to stack them evenly on the Dutch oven. He'd seemed almost as eager as she was that the recipe turn out well. She paused, thinking about her visit last night. He'd been in an odd mood, glad to see her and yet it almost seemed as though part of him was somewhere else. But then, when it was time to go, he'd kissed her. He'd said it was for luck.

Just where did she stand with Leith? At first it was a simple barter, and exchange of favors. Then he'd invited her along on the fishing trip and declared his friendship. But almost immediately after saying they were friends, he'd kissed her. Maybe he'd meant it to be a friendly kiss, but if it had been on a Thai menu, there would be five hot peppers beside it. She pulled out the Dutch oven and removed the lid. Right now, she needed to concentrate on impressing her boss, not mooning over the meaning of kisses.

While waiting for the coals to heat, Sabrina peeled the peaches and arranged them with the other cobbler ingredients in the Dutch oven just as Leith had shown her. Walter, Mallory, Kate and Amy were relaxing in chairs on the patio not far away, looking off toward the water. Walter bounced William in his lap, chuckling as the baby grabbed at his mustache.

"Sabrina, did you bring those sketches you mentioned?" Kate asked.

"I did." Sabrina pulled the sketch pad from the box with her cooking tools and handed it to Kate. "Give me just a minute to get this cobbler cooking, and I'll be over to answer any questions."

Once the coals were covered with gray ash, Sabrina used tongs to make a bed of coals with half the briquettes, arranging the other half on top. Leith said to check it in twenty-five minutes. She noted the time on her watch and went to join the group, where Kate, Mallory and Amy had their heads together and were examining her sketches with interest.

Kate looked up. "Pull up a chair, Sabrina.

I want to know more about this jacket. What fabric did you have in mind?"

"I was thinking a textured fleece outer layer, very soft, with a quilted nylon lining."

"I like a slick lining in a jacket," Mallory commented. "It's easier to get on and off. Are there pockets?"

"Yes—six in all." Sabrina showed them where the pockets fit into the design and continued to discuss the details of another sketch or two. Meanwhile Walter played with the baby, who was now tugging on the end of one of his bolo strings.

"May I borrow these?" Kate asked. "I'll make copies and return them to you tomorrow."

"Sure, that's fine." Sabrina wasn't sure exactly what Kate had in mind for her ideas, but her interest had to be a good sign. Maybe this could help Sabrina stand out among the management candidates.

Sabrina glanced over at Walter. The baby had turned away from him and was staring toward the group of women, his eyes wide and panicky. His lips seemed paler, almost blue. Blue lips?

Sabrina jumped up and reached for the baby. "He's choking!" She put him over her knee, the way Leith had instructed in the first-aid class, and tapped her hand against his back. Nothing happened.

Amy and the others had jumped up, too, and were surrounding her. "Don't hurt him," Amy begged.

"I won't, but he can't breathe." Sabrina gave the baby another whack, not too hard but hard enough to jar him. Something flew out of his mouth, and he gasped, then sucked in a big breath and let out a wail.

Amy snatched him up and hugged him tight, murmuring assurances even while tears streamed from her eyes. "You're okay now, William. It's going to be fine. You're good now. Mommy's got you."

Walter reached down to pick up the silver tip from his bolo tie from the pavement. "I'm so sorry, Amy. I had no idea it was loose."

"It's my fault. I should have been paying closer attention." Amy rubbed her hand up and down the baby's back. William let out another whimper or two and then stuck a thumb in his mouth and snuggled against his mother.

"Should we take him to the hospital?" Walter asked.

Amy gazed down at the baby, stroking his head. "No, I don't think that's necessary. He seems fine now."

"I'm just glad Sabrina was here and knew

what to do," Mallory said in a soothing voice. She asked Sabrina, "Where did you learn that?"

"In a first-aid class."

Walter grabbed her hand and shook it. "Thank you. It might be a good idea for all of us to have a refresher. I'll schedule some classes at the store for the employees. What class did you take?"

"Well, I didn't actually take the class. I was more of a volunteer assistant. Leith Jordan taught it."

"Leith Jordan. From Learn & Live?" Walter asked.

"Yes."

"I didn't realize you and Leith…" Fortunately, his words trailed off before Sabrina had to explain her relationship to Leith. Because if she didn't understand it herself, how could she explain it to someone else?

"I better take William home now," Amy said.

"Of course. I'll drive you." Walter hurried to her side. "I can take a cab home." He continued to apologize as they walked toward the house.

"Uh, is everything okay over here?" Tim had left the grill and come to join the group.

"It is now," Kate said. "Thanks to Sabrina's

quick thinking. The baby was choking, but she knew what to do."

"Wow. I didn't realize. That's great, Sabrina. But I thought I should point out that whatever's in the Dutch oven is burning."

"Cielos!" Sabrina rushed over to the firepit, where smoke was escaping around the rim of the Dutch oven. She pushed the coals off the top and used a thick hot pad to lift the pot off the other coals and set it on the pavers. When she opened the lid, a thick cloud of black smoke poured out and then cleared to reveal a charred mess. "Oh, no. It's ruined."

"It doesn't matter. We still have the ice cream for dessert," Mallory said.

"Don't worry about it." Kate rested a hand on Sabrina's arm. "Once, years ago, I accidentally set a can of chili too close to the fire and someone knocked it in without me noticing. Half an hour later, it exploded. Made a huge mess. I was so embarrassed."

Sabrina gave her a wry smile. "I know exactly how that feels."

"RAIN THURSDAY AND FRIDAY, but clearing by midnight, and the weekend looks clear and sunny. Stay tuned for the fishing report." Leith adjusted the volume on his radio and stopped his car to allow a Canada goose, followed by a row of goslings, to cross the road to the park near his house.

"Hop to it, folks. I need to get home."

That morning, even before he'd left for work, Sabrina had arrived carrying his Dutch oven, a paintbrush and her little dog, which, of course, made Tal happy. In fact, when Leith tried to take Tal to work with him as he usually did, she'd looked so disheartened he'd decided to let her stay home with Boomer and Sabrina. Sabrina had assured him she'd have the kitchen done by the end of his workday. She might have already left.

Once the geese were all safely across the road, he drove the last three blocks. Sabrina's car sat in his driveway. His heart gave a little extra beat of excitement.

Now that he was here, he hesitated to go inside. Sabrina said she wanted to paint the kitchen because she was his friend. He'd said much the same. And yet the feelings she stirred in him didn't feel like something he'd feel for a friend.

Maybe if he quit kissing her, he could get these feelings straightened out. Kissing her was stupid and he knew it, and yet when he looked at those rosy lips smiling at him, he kept forgetting all the reasons kissing was a bad idea. Like the fact that she didn't belong in Alaska.

That she was leaving as soon as her assignment was up. That all they had in common was a fondness for Thai food and a soft spot for dogs.

She stepped outside onto the porch and raised her hand to shade her eyes. "Leith, you're home!"

"Hi." He felt the corners of his mouth tugging upward. How could he stay ambivalent with such a greeting? He hustled over to the porch. "How's it going?"

"You'll see. Come inside, but don't look yet." Her excitement practically crackled.

The second he stepped inside his living room, the scent of cumin and chili reached him. His stomach perked up. "What's cooking?"

"Abuelita's chicken enchiladas. Come on." She took his hand and tugged him toward the kitchen, but stopped just before they reached the doorway. "Close your eyes."

"Really?"

"Come on. Please?"

He sighed and closed his eyes. She led him into the kitchen and stopped. "Okay, you can look."

He opened his eyes. The wall color looked great, transforming the kitchen from chemistry-lab bland to a place he'd enjoy spending time. But she hadn't stopped there. She'd put a curtain with a green leafy pattern across the top of the window in front of the sink and hung dish towels in a similar shade of green on the oven door. A cutting board with a pile of something green and leafy rested on the countertop, next to a copper cylinder that held a collection of wooden spoons, and something was different about the cabinets. On closer examination, he realized she'd replaced the white knobs with square copper ones. A pot simmered on the stove, and a plate of chocolate cookies rested on his table, which was set for two with place mats that matched the curtain.

"Wow."

"Do you like it?"

"It's amazing. How did you have time to do all this in one day?"

"It didn't take that long to paint, so I had time left over for decorating and cooking."

"I can't believe it's my kitchen. How much do I owe you for all the extra stuff?"

She waved him away. "It hardly cost anything. I made the valance and place mats from a fabric remnant, and I found the cabinet pulls and copper canister at a garage sale when I was walking Boomer last Sunday. They'd just remodeled their kitchen and were selling the old things for next to nothing."

"You know, when I first met you, I would

never have believed you would go within a square mile of a garage sale or a thrift store."

She laughed. "That's kind of the point. You don't want your secondhand items to look like secondhand items. Unless they're antiques, of course."

"I can't believe you painted the whole kitchen, cooked and sewed curtains and place mats all in one day."

"I didn't sew today, silly. I did those Sunday night. Do you like the color?"

"I like everything." Leith stared at the transformed kitchen. "This is one of the nicest things anyone has ever done for me." He pulled her into a hug. "Thank you."

"You're welcome." She hugged him back and then stepped away. "Oh, I almost forgot my other surprise. Look what Tal taught Boomer. Boomer, sit." Sabrina spoke with authority. Tal sat. Boomer didn't.

"Boomer, sit." Still no response. Sabrina bent down closer to the dog. "Come on, Boomer. You're making me look bad. Sit."

Tal reached out a paw and nudged Boomer. He looked up at her and then sat, his mouth open in a doggie grin as if it was all a hilarious joke.

"Good boy." She beamed at Leith. "There, see?"

"I do." He did see, a lot more than a contrary little dog. Leith saw a woman who would stand up to a bully to protect a dog she didn't even know. A quick learner who cheerfully adapted to different situations. A giver, happiest when she was spreading happiness to others. He saw a woman he could build a life with. Just his luck he'd finally found the perfect woman, and her time with him came with an expiration date.

"Is something wrong?" He must have frowned because Sabrina was staring at him with a concerned look on her face.

"No, of course not. I was just thinking of something I forgot to do at work, but I'll take care of it tomorrow. Nice sit, Boomer."

Sabrina stepped over to stir something on the stove. "Are you hungry?"

"I'm starved." He leaned over the pot and sniffed. "What do you have there?"

"Frijoles. To go with the enchiladas."

"Another of your *abuelita*'s recipes?"

"Mmm-hmm. She was a wonderful cook."

Leith believed it, if this dinner was any indication. The enchiladas were cheesy and spicy, and the cilantro-flavored beans made a perfect complement. Leith wolfed down a full plate and went back for more. "This is so good. But speaking of recipes, how did your peach cobbler turn out?"

"That's an odd story, actually." Sabrina explained how the cobbler had burned while they were all concentrating on the baby. "I was so thankful I'd been to your class and knew what to do."

"Is the baby okay now?"

"He was fine once he spit out that silver tip from Walter's bolo. I think it shook Walter up more than the baby. Of course, Amy was upset, but she seemed to settle down when the baby did, although I bet she won't be letting anyone hold her baby until she's done a wardrobe check from now on."

"And this was all in front of the vice president from Seattle?"

"Yes. Kate was great. Very calm, which I think calmed everyone else down."

"You realize now you're a shoo-in for that management position. Every time the vice president hears your name, her first thought will be how you handled that situation."

She seemed startled at the idea. "You think so?"

"How could she not? I'm proud of you."

"You are?"

"Of course I am. You probably saved that baby's life."

She shrugged, making light of her accomplishment. "I'm sure one of the others would have noticed and acted if I hadn't."

"Still, you're the one who reacted."

"I wouldn't have known what to do if it hadn't been a part of your class. If I get the job, you'll get part of the credit."

Leith had mixed feelings about that thought. On one hand, Sabrina was hardworking and resourceful, and she deserved that job. On the other, it stung a little to think that the skills he'd taught her were the very things that would take her away from him. "I'm just glad it all worked out."

"Cookie?" Sabrina offered the plate.

"Thanks." Leith bit into the chocolate cookie, and blinked. A faint kick of hot pepper and cinnamon mingled with the rich chocolate. Wow. He took another bite.

They might seem like ordinary chocolate cookies, but the complex combination of sugar and spices was different from anything he'd ever tasted before. It reminded him of a nursery rhyme he'd seen in one of Emma's picture books. *Sugar and spice and everything nice.*

Kind of like Sabrina herself.

She was going to win that job in management. But was there any possibility she might turn it down? There had to be other jobs in

Anchorage for someone as smart and hard-working as Sabrina. Maybe he needed to give her a reason to stay.

He smiled at her. "I love the cookies. What are they called?"

"I've seen different names, but Abuelita called them Diablo cookies."

"They're delicious. You've worked really hard today. What time do you get off tomorrow?"

"Around six. Why?"

"Because I'd like to take you to dinner downtown."

"You don't have to do that. I enjoyed decorating your kitchen."

"And I'd enjoy taking you out for dinner. Someplace nice. May I pick you up at six thirty?"

"Someplace nice, hmm? Sounds great. But Boomer will need a walk and I'll need a little time to get ready. Is seven thirty too late?"

"Seven thirty it is." Leith gave an inner nod of satisfaction. Step one of his campaign to show Sabrina all the advantages of living in Anchorage was now in place.

CHAPTER TWELVE

SABRINA RAN A brush through her hair, sweeping it up into a high ponytail. She and Leith were meeting at a park for a picnic breakfast before work this morning. Rain threatened, but there were picnic shelters at the park, and she didn't want to miss a chance to spend time with him. They'd been getting together almost every day since she'd painted his kitchen.

Suddenly, Leith had transformed into some sort of Anchorage cheerleader and tour guide. It started with an elaborate meal in a downtown restaurant. Within the next couple of days, he'd taken her to a symphony concert at the PAC, a summer-league baseball game and the Alaska Native Heritage Center. And she'd enjoyed them all, especially the Native Heritage Center with all the outdoor exhibits featuring different sorts of traditional Native homes. They'd also had a blast taking Emma to the children's science museum downtown and walking through the botanical gardens.

Since then, they'd been hiking, biking and fishing, and just last weekend, they'd toured the art galleries downtown during the First Friday art walk. Sabrina had sent Misty a photo of herself next to a statue of a salmon decoupaged with sheet music, entitled "Sockeye in D Minor."

Sabrina had to admit, with her focus firmly on the job, she'd all but ignored the cultural opportunities Anchorage had to offer. It was an interesting and unique city and she'd loved every minute of the time she spent exploring it with Leith. But that was the problem.

She was enjoying Leith's company way too much. The more time she spent with him, the more she wanted. He was attentive, and fun, and those kisses… She smiled to herself. They called them good-night kisses, but in Leith's case they made it very hard to say good-night. It was going to be torture when the time came to say goodbye.

She paused, brush still in her hand. She should really insert a little distance between them. Wean herself away from him, so that when her stint in Alaska was over, it wouldn't hurt so much. Kind of like when she first started running. On day one, she'd only been able to run about two blocks without stopping. But each day she'd go a little farther, until the day came when she'd finished a half marathon. She needed to prepare because the day was coming when she was going to have to make a life for herself that didn't include Leith.

She set down the hairbrush and prepared to go, grabbing the rain jacket she'd worn out in the drizzle when she walked the dog earlier. "Okay, Boomer, I've refilled your water bowl and set your bed under the window where the sun puddle will be if the sky clears. We'll take a run when I get home. I have to go now. I'm meeting Leith."

When she said Leith's name, Boomer wagged his tail. When the time came to move, Boomer was going to miss Leith and Tal almost as much as she was. How had a man she'd only gotten to know recently become so important in her life?

Boomer rubbed against her ankle and sat down, staring up at her in adoration. The little dog had had no qualms about devoting himself to her almost from the first moment they'd met, even when she was still planning to take him to a shelter. He didn't worry about somedays or broken hearts.

Maybe she should take a tip from her dog and live in the moment. Sure, it was going to hurt when it ended, but she and Leith were here now, and it would be stupid to give up something good today because it wouldn't always be there. That would be like never tasting a hot-fudge sundae because you couldn't eat one every day.

She reached down to give Boomer a rub. "You're a smart boy, Boomer. Be good while I'm gone."

Just before she stepped outside, the rain started in earnest. She slipped on her rain jacket and headed for the car. The rain didn't matter. She was on her way to meet Leith. It was going to be a beautiful day.

THE NEXT THURSDAY was a short workday for Sabrina. Leith taught a class that morning, but called to propose an afternoon hike up one of the Chugach Mountains. Sabrina agreed.

They were halfway up the mountain when Sabrina realized this trail was as challenging as the one she'd hiked during the Orson team-builder, and yet she wasn't struggling. Her heart and lungs were getting a workout, but they had plenty of reserve left. A number of hiking trips, even small ones, had made a huge difference in her conditioning.

Thirty minutes later, they encountered a steep section of trail skirting a huge boulder. Leith climbed up first, and then reached down. Sabrina lifted Boomer and passed him to Leith, with Tal scrambling up beside him. Once the dogs were set, she took Leith's hand and let him help her up. He didn't immediately let go of her hand.

"Doing okay?"

"Just fine."

He smiled that magnetic smile of his and leaned forward to brush a kiss across her lips. "Good, because we're almost to the top."

He led the way along the trail, but suddenly stopped. Sabrina leaned around him to see what he was looking at. Up ahead, the trail ran along a ledge on the edge of the mountain, beside a sheer wall. He turned around to face her. "Sorry, I forgot about this part of the trail. We can turn back here."

Cielos, that stupid fear of heights was holding her back again. And not just her. She eyed the ledge. "I hate to stop when we're so close."

Leith shrugged. "It doesn't matter. The hike is the main thing."

"But you talked about the view from the top." The ledge wasn't that narrow, maybe four feet wide. "How long does the trail run along the ledge?"

"Just around this corner. Maybe six feet."

Could she make it? She licked her bottom lip. "I really hate this—this being afraid."

She pushed back her shoulders. "I'm going to do it."

"Are you sure? You don't have to prove anything to me."

"I just want to face my fears."

"Want me to walk beside you?"

Not a chance. If she was going on that ledge, she didn't want anyone near enough to jostle her. "No, thanks. I plan on hugging the wall." Boomer looked up at her, no doubt wondering about the holdup. She picked him up and handed him to Leith. "Here. You hold Boomer, so he doesn't decide to dangle over the edge just to terrify me."

"Okay." Leith held the dog against his chest and commanded Tal to stay. "Shall I go first?"

She nodded, her mouth too dry to speak. He walked onto the ledge a few steps and stopped to wait. She took a deep breath. She could do this. She stepped forward, determinedly looking at the point where the trail met the wall and away from the overhang. She took another step. And another, her hand pressed firmly against the wall beside her. Her heart pounded, but she was halfway there.

She rounded the corner. Something moved in her peripheral vision. She turned her head to see a raven flash past, and her eye traveled from the bird, past the edge of the overhang, to the sheer drop-off below. She froze.

"You're okay." The words seemed to come from far away. "Just walk toward me. It's only a couple more steps."

"I— I can't." She could only stare at the space below.

"Yes, you can." The sound of her own blood pounded in her ears, but Leith's voice came through, calm, soothing. "Look at me."

Slowly, she dragged her gaze away from the ledge and toward him.

"Do you trust me?" Those blue eyes. She locked onto them.

She opened her mouth, but only a squeak came out.

He smiled at her. "Sabrina, do you trust me?"

She swallowed. "Yes. I trust you."

"Good." He reached out. "Take my hand."

She couldn't. What if her panic dragged them both over the edge? "If I fall, I might take you with me."

"I won't let you fall. Now, take my hand."

She measured his expression and saw no censure, no disappointment. Just patience and understanding. Slowly, she reached out and grasped his hand, and suddenly it was easy, almost as though he was sharing his strength.

She took a step, and then another, and after three more quick steps, they were past the ledge to the main trail. A few steps more, and they were well away from the ledge. Leith stopped and handed her the dog.

Boomer licked her face, making her laugh. She smiled at Leith. "Whew. Thank you. I'm not sure how I'm going to get back down, but I'm glad you were there."

"There's another trail we can take down. I would have used it to go up if I'd remembered about the ledge."

"That's okay. I did it!"

Leith called, "Tal, you can come now."

Tal trotted along the ledge without hesitation and came to press her nose to Sabrina's hand reassuringly. Sabrina stroked her head. "You're a good girl, Tal." She clipped Boomer's leash onto his collar to make sure he didn't decide to wander back to the drop-off, and took a deep breath. "Okay, let's finish this climb."

LEITH KEPT A close eye on Sabrina for the rest of the hike, but as they reached the summit, she seemed to have forgotten her panic. She'd worried him there for a minute, but she'd done well, taking control of her fears. Sabrina was no quitter.

They stood well back from the edge on the

flat mountaintop and looked out over the Anchorage bowl. Sabrina slipped an arm around his waist. "Wow. You weren't kidding about the view."

"Told you." He squeezed her shoulders. Boomer scampered over to sit on Sabrina's foot and Tal leaned against her leg. Just like him, they wanted to be as close to Sabrina as possible.

They stood together, looking out over the city and across the water. Shadows from the clouds painted ever-changing patterns on the rugged landscape. Across the inlet, the windmills on Fire Island turned slowly in the breeze.

He took a water bottle from his pack and offered it to Sabrina. When she tilted back her head to drink, the graceful lines of her throat reminded him of a swan. Wow—since when did he notice things like that? He knew, of course. He'd started noticing about the same time he'd realized how important Sabrina was in his life. About the time he'd realized he loved her.

He hadn't told her yet. He didn't want to risk scaring her away, not until he could show her how good they were together, how good life could be here. He was hoping that, like so many people he knew who came for a visit and stayed for a lifetime, Sabrina would fall in love with Alaska. And, if he was lucky, fall in love with him.

Sabrina took a long drink and then handed it back to him. While he drank, she pulled a folding dog bowl from her pack, so he could pour water for Tal and Boomer. The dogs lapped it up and collapsed in a sunny spot in front of a rock. Sabrina climbed on top of the rock and sat, her legs dangling. Leith went to stand beside her. "More water?"

"I'm good, thanks." She raised her hands above her head in a stretch and tilted her face to the sun. "It's just so beautiful up here."

"It's always been one of my favorite spots."

Sabrina's phone rang. "Huh. I'd have thought we'd be out of cell-phone range up here. I guess it's because we're so high." She pulled the phone from her backpack. "Oh, it's an old friend I haven't talked to in months. Do you mind if I take it?"

"No—go ahead."

"Thanks." She swiped the phone. "Hi, Andrea."

He ambled a few yards away to give her some privacy. When he looked back, Sabrina was talking fast, gesturing with her free hand as though the person on the other end could see. Then she stopped to listen, wide-eyed.

When she finally hung up the phone, she was staring toward Mount Susitna, but he had a feeling she wasn't seeing the Alaska scenery anymore.

He walked over to her. "Everything all right?"

Slowly she turned to look at him and smiled. "Yeah. That was my college roommate, Andrea. We were in the same major. She lives in Savannah now." Sabrina slid down from the rock to stand in front of him. "She was telling me she heard there's an opening for a buyer with McCormick and Sons."

Leith swallowed. "In Georgia?"

"No, no. McCormick's is a regional department store, privately owned, headquartered in Scottsdale. Ever since I decided to go into fashion merchandising, working for them has been my dream job."

Leith's heart struck a double beat, but he kept his voice calm. "Your dream job? Why, in particular?"

"Well, first of all, it's very upscale. Beautiful fabrics, amazing designs. But mostly because they're a great place to work. They pay well, they have excellent benefits and they care about the welfare of their employees, and vice versa. It's almost impossible to get on with them because nobody ever leaves, but one of their senior buyers just retired."

"They're looking for someone to step in and fill that position?" Leith wasn't sure what a senior buyer was, but Sabrina probably wasn't old enough to qualify.

"No, they'll fill it from within, and everyone will step up a level. The opening will be for someone with five years of experience. At least, that's what Andrea says. She heard it from a friend of a friend who works in HR there. The position's not listed yet, but it will be tomorrow or the next day. I was just short of five years when my old employer went belly-up, but I had some intern experience during college. If I were to send in my résumé—"

"You might get a head start," Leith said, finishing for her and trying to sound enthusiastic. "But what about your commitment to Orson Outfitters?"

"Yeah. I would hate to bail on them," Sabrina answered slowly. "Especially Walter. But they're only taking half the candidates, anyway, and some of them are MBAs or people with management experience. There's no guarantee I'll be chosen for the management team. But there's even less chance I'd be chosen for the McCormick job." She sighed. "I probably wouldn't even get an interview. Maybe I should just forget it."

Leith hated seeing the spark of excitement leave her eyes. "You should try. You're hardworking, talented and enthusiastic. Who could be a better candidate than you?"

"You think it's worth applying?"

"Nobody ever gives motivational speeches about how they gave up before they ever started."

She laughed. "No, I suppose they don't."

"If this is really your dream…" Leith left the sentence unfinished.

"I should go for it." Sabrina nodded decisively. "You're right. Thanks for the pep talk."

Leith tried to ignore the selfish part of him that had been hoping she would declare she had a new dream. One that kept her here, with him. But why would she? They'd both understood, from their first meeting, that this was temporary. That she would be going away. How could she even know he wanted her to stay?

He should tell her. "Sabrina, I—"

"You really—" Sabrina said at the same instant. They both paused.

"Go ahead. What were you saying?" Leith asked.

"I was just going to say it means a lot that

you have faith in me. You're the best friend I've ever had." She put her arms around him and hugged him.

He pulled her close. How could holding her feel so good and hurt so much at the same time? She felt solid enough in his arms, but her heart was already drifting far away to some high-fashion store in Scottsdale. And if she went, she just might take his heart along, too.

She smiled up at him. "What were you going to say?"

He shook his head. "Nothing important. Just that I hope you get whatever it takes to make you happy."

CHAPTER THIRTEEN

"SABRINA, WAKE UP. The mountain is out."

Sabrina yawned, reluctant to leave the cozy warmth of her borrowed sleeping bag. After the hike last week, she and Leith had decided to spend their days off in Denali National Park. They'd driven up after work the day before and set up camp.

She opened her eyes. *The mountain is out?* What…? Oh, *the* mountain, Denali. It had been shrouded in clouds when they arrived yesterday evening. She shimmied out of the sleeping bag, threw a fleece jacket over the yoga pants and T-shirt she'd slept in, shoved her feet into shoes and hurried outside.

The shimmering white peaks jutted far, far into the blue sky above them. A few wispy clouds clustered like a tutu about halfway down the mountain. Leith was ready with a cup of coffee. "What do you think?"

"That may be the most beautiful sight I've ever seen this early in the morning." Sabrina sipped the coffee. "Thank you."

"For what?"

She smiled at him. "For the coffee. For bringing me here. For being you. Pick one."

"In that case, you're welcome." He gazed up at the sky. "Looks like it's going to be a beautiful day. We've got reservations for the first bus into the park this morning, so we'd better get moving." Leith bent to light the camp stove.

"Okay." Sabrina reached into the gear bag for a folding silicone-sided skillet and popped the ridges into place. She handed him the skillet to preheat while she gathered bacon and eggs from the ice chest. They'd camped together often enough now to have developed routines.

"I'll start cooking while you get ready," Leith offered. "There's warm water in that pan."

"Thanks." Sabrina used the water to wash her face before disappearing into the tent to change into hiking pants and a long-sleeved T-shirt under her vest.

She'd applied for that job with McCormick eight days ago but hadn't heard anything back yet. In the meantime, this visit to Denali was just the distraction she needed. She was brushing her hair into a ponytail when the aroma of cooking bacon permeated the tent and drew her back outside.

"Mmm, is there any better smell in the world than the combination of bacon and forest?" she asked.

Leith used tongs to flip the last piece of bacon. "Not many. It's almost done."

"Here, I'll finish and scramble the eggs while you get dressed."

"You just want the first piece of bacon."

"True. But I promise to save you some."

"You'd better." He stood, but instead of going into the tent, he brushed a kiss across her lips. "Good morning."

"Good morning to you." She kissed him back.

"I'm glad you were able to rearrange your schedule, so we could see Denali together."

"Me, too." She gazed into the brilliant blue of his eyes, deciding whether to kiss him once more until she noticed the smoke. "*Cielos!* The bacon's burning!"

She grabbed the skillet off the stove and scraped the bacon to a plate, while Leith chuckled.

"Hey, you shouldn't be laughing. This is your fault."

He held up his hands. "I regret nothing.

There's more bacon in the package. Do we need to start over?"

"Nah. One piece is charred but most of it is okay." She made a shooing motion. "Go. Get dressed. New safety rule—no more kisses until the eggs are done and the stove is off."

"So now you're the safety-and-survival expert?"

"Somebody has to be." She turned her back and cracked an egg into the skillet but looked over her shoulder to flash a smile before continuing her task.

It was a memorable day. They stopped at several of the stations along the way, took a couple of short hikes and enjoyed a picnic at Wonder Lake. While they were eating, a furry face appeared, peeking around a rock.

"Is it an arctic fox?" Sabrina whispered. "It looks like the picture in the visitor center, but it's not all white."

"It's in the process of changing from summer gray to winter white."

"He doesn't seem afraid of us. I wish I could give him a bite."

Leith shook his head. "You saw the sign about feeding the wild animals."

"I know. I'll follow the rules. Even if he is cute."

Denali towered over them the entire ride, although by midday, the top was once again veiled by clouds. Late in the day, they were almost back to the campground when the driver stopped the bus and pointed toward his left. "Grizzlies. A sow and three cubs."

Sabrina pressed her face to the window to watch the back end of an enormous furry animal not terribly far off the road. Dirt and rocks flew, as the bear ripped them from the hillside. "Look, Leith. She's digging."

"I see." Leith leaned beside her to train the telephoto lens of his camera toward the bears.

Three cubs were watching their mom, but when the bus stopped, it caught their attention. Two of the cubs stood on their back legs to better inspect the vehicle. The sound of shutter clicks echoed through the bus, as the bears posed. The mother bear glanced over her shoulder and went back to digging, giving the bus no more mind than she would a bird flying by.

Once they were back at the visitor center, Leith and Sabrina decided to eat at one of the lodges rather than cook at camp. They had just settled into a booth when Sabrina's phone beeped.

"Ah, we must be back in cell-phone range."

She checked the message. "Volta says the dogs are fine and Emma's keeping them entertained."

"I'm sure she is," Leith said. "I need to wash up. Go ahead and order me the western burger if you don't mind, with sweet-potato fries."

"Jalapeños and guacamole. Yum. I'll have that, too." When the waiter arrived, Sabrina placed the orders. Since Leith was still gone, she pulled up a photo of Denali and sent it to Mama. Misty had texted a picture of herself pushing a cart piled high with boxes into a college dorm room. Sabrina smiled. She sent a thumbs-up and wished her sister luck with her classes.

She glanced at her email inbox and sucked in a breath. McCormick and Sons. She opened the email and was still reading it when Leith returned.

"What's so fascinating?" he asked as he slid into the booth. "Did you post your picture of the fox?"

"They want to interview me." Sabrina bounced in her seat. "They said my references were outstanding, and they're very interested. Can you believe it?"

"Wow." Leith didn't seem nearly as excited as she would have thought.

Maybe she hadn't been clear. "McCormick and Sons. They want to fly me down to interview for the job as buyer."

"Yes, I got that. Are you going to do it?"

"Of course I'm going to do it. This is exactly what I was hoping for when I applied." She frowned at his expression. "Why are you looking at me like I spit in your burger?"

"I was hoping..." He stopped.

"What were you hoping?"

"I was hoping you might change your mind."

"About the job?"

He nodded.

"But you're the one who said I should apply."

"I know." He looked down at the table.

"So why—?" Suddenly, she realized the truth. "You thought they'd turn me down. That you were safe acting like a supportive friend and encouraging me because there wasn't actually a ghost of a chance I'd get the job."

"That's not true. I know you're talented."

"Then why did you encourage me to apply for a job and then hope I wouldn't take it?"

"I just thought, maybe, if we spent enough

time together, had enough fun, that you'd decide you wanted to stay here."

"Here? In Alaska?"

"Yes."

"But that was never the plan. I don't have a job in Alaska, only a temporary assignment. I spent five months unemployed before I took this job. I can't just quit and hope. There's no security in that."

Before Leith could answer, the waiter appeared and set plates in front of each of them. "Anything else I can get you?"

"We're fine. Thank you," Leith said through tight lips. As soon as the waiter was out of sight, he spoke. "Walter likes you. I'm sure—"

"What? That he'd hire me as a salesclerk? I had that job in high school. That's not why I went to college. This position with McCormick is exactly what I've been working toward."

"Why? Why, exactly, is this your dream job? I mean, I realize you get to travel and shop for pretty clothes, but what's so special about McCormick and Sons?"

"I explained that. They hire the best, and they keep them. Once you're part of the team there, you're set for life. That's what I want."

The waiter returned and set a bottle of

ketchup on the table. "I thought you might need this. Is everything else all right?"

Sabrina looked down at her untouched plate. Everything was far from all right, but there wasn't much the waiter could do about it. "It's fine, thanks."

Once he left, Leith shook some ketchup onto his plate, dipped a fry in it and then set the fry back on his plate without tasting it. "Okay, I get it. This job is important to you. Alaska isn't. I'm not." His gaze seemed to go right through her. "You've made your priorities very clear."

"Leith—"

He shook his head. "Don't try to let me down easy."

"You are important to me. If I move somewhere else, that doesn't mean we can't stay in touch."

"No." He met her eyes and didn't waver. "If you go on this interview, we're done."

"But that's stupid. I probably won't even get this job."

"But you want it. You want to be somewhere else. And I can't be with someone who doesn't want to be with me." His mouth formed a grim line. "I've been there before, and I won't do it again."

"Leith, please."

He shook his head. "Eat your burger. I'll take you home tonight. Or, anyway, back to your apartment in Anchorage. You'll have to get home on your own."

CHAPTER FOURTEEN

SABRINA PULLED UP to the gate and rolled down the car window. Instantly a blast of Arizona heat penetrated the air-conditioned interior of the rental car. She leaned out to punch in the code her mother had given her, and the gate swung open. A few minutes later, she pulled into a circular drive and stopped in the sparse shade of a palm tree.

She removed her suitcase from the back seat, turned toward the tile-roofed house and took a breath of the parched air, so different from the soft crispness of an Alaskan summer morning. Just as she reached the porch, one of the heavy oak doors swung open and her mother rushed outside.

"Sabrina!" Mama threw her arms around her. "You're finally here."

Sabrina hugged her mother tight and then drew back to look at her face. "You look wonderful." And she did—her face almost glowed with happiness. "I like the new haircut."

Mama fluffed the shorter, bouncy cut.

"Thank you. I got it done on the cruise. I wasn't sure, but Mason says he likes it."

Behind her, Mason appeared at the door and stepped outside, smiling. "Hello, Sabrina."

"Mason, it's nice to see you." She hesitated, not sure how to greet him, but they managed an awkward hug. "I appreciate you letting me stay at your house."

"Don't be silly. You're family." He put an arm around Mama's shoulders and she beamed up at him. "In fact, your mother and I are hoping when you get this job, you'll stay with us for a while, until you get settled."

He sounded sincere, as if he really wanted a stranger living in his home. "That's very generous of you. But one step at a time. First I have to do the interview tomorrow."

"You'll be great," Mama declared. "Where's the little doggie I've heard so much about? Did you not bring him?"

"No, I left him in a boarding kennel." Clara or Autumn would probably have dog-sat for her, but she couldn't very well tell her co-workers where she was going on her days off.

"You could have brought him," Mama said. "Mason's two cats rule the roost around here, but they're good with dogs. Too bad. I was looking forward to spending time with my granddog."

Mason chuckled. "Once Sabrina gets that job and moves here, you'll be able to spoil your granddog all you want." He picked up Sabrina's suitcase. "Now let's get out of this heat."

"Yes, come inside." Mama reached for her hand. "I made all your favorites for dinner, and you can tell us about your adventures in Alaska."

Mason shut the door behind them. "That picture you sent last week was incredible. What's the name of that mountain?"

"Denali."

"That's right. Formerly Mount McKinley. The highest peak in North America. I looked it up. We're thinking of taking the Alaska cruise and tour package next year. You'll have to tell us all about Denali Park and what to see there."

Sabrina could feel the smile on her face getting tight, but she nodded. She could flip through the photos of the park on her phone and feign enthusiasm, but she couldn't tell them the truth. It had been glorious that day in the park, but when she thought of Denali, only one impression stayed with her: the image of Leith's face when she broke his heart.

LEITH LET TAL out of the car before retrieving a grease-stained paper sack containing his dinner from the passenger seat. She followed him inside to the kitchen, which no longer seemed warm and inviting, but was simply empty. He sat down at the table and unwrapped the burger, which had gone cold. He considered microwaving it, but what difference did it make? He took a bite.

Tal flopped on the floor nearby with her chin resting on her paws and gave a deep sigh. She missed that goofy little terrier almost as much as he missed Sabrina.

He should be used to it. He'd been here before. But somehow this time was different. With Nicole, he'd felt angry and betrayed. He'd done everything she'd asked of him, and in return, she'd used and discarded him. But, if he was perfectly honest, he'd gone along with everything to get a break from her constant complaints and demands. He'd been infatuated with Nicole, but he'd only married her because she insisted, and he didn't want to lose her. Did he ever really love her? He wasn't sure he even knew what love was, before Sabrina.

And look where love had gotten him. Sitting alone in a kitchen with a depressed dog, eating a cold burger and trying to ignore the giant hole in his heart. Yesterday, when he'd driven Emma home from soccer practice, he'd had to confess to Volta that he and Sabrina were over, that he'd given her an ultimatum and she'd chosen a job over him. And to demonstrate what pathetic shape he must be in, instead of the hassle he expected, Volta had given him a hug.

Tal raised her head and let out a single *woof*. A car door slammed. Leith went to the front window, to see an airport limousine pulled up to the curb in front of his house. The driver opened the back door and a familiar blonde woman climbed out. Oh, man, this day just got better and better.

His former wife picked her way up the flagstone path toward the porch, careful not to get her high heels caught between the stones. Leith waited, expecting the simmering resentment he always felt in his stomach when he was reminded of her betrayal, but instead of anger, all he felt was weariness. He was tired of this fight.

Nicole looked the same, just as beautiful as she'd been when he married her, and yet it was like seeing a stranger walking up to his house. She was just an unpleasant memory from the past, and no longer had any bearing on his life. He walked through the living room to open the door just as she rang the bell.

She looked up, startled. "Leith."

"Hello, Nicole."

She raised her chin. "I assume you know why I'm here."

"I'd imagine you want those annulment papers."

"So you did get them? Because I have another set in the car if you need them."

"I have them." He stepped back from the doorway. "You may as well come in."

She stepped inside. Tal moved out from behind the door. "Oh, is this the puppy I got for you? Talkeetna?" She bent down to stroke the dog's head. Tal gave a polite wave of her tail and stepped away. Nicole straightened. "Leith, I need you to sign these papers. This is important to me."

"I suppose if you came all the way to Alaska to get them, they must be."

She crossed her arms. "Look. I understand why you're mad at me. I treated you badly, and I'm sorry. But why not sign the annulment papers? Yes, we repeated vows, but I don't think I even understood the concept of 'till death do us part.' We were just a couple of kids, playing house. Honestly, can you say it was a real marriage?"

He considered her words. "Maybe not. A marriage should be a partnership, where both people care about each other's happiness."

She narrowed her eyes. "You're saying I didn't care about yours?"

He turned his hands palms-up. "Did you?"

"I—" She wiggled her shoulders as if to shoo off an annoying insect. "I was immature. I guess I was too busy trying to figure what I needed to pay much attention to your needs." She tried a little smile. "Although I did buy you a dog for your birthday."

"Yes." Leith rubbed Tal's ears. "That was probably the most thoughtful thing you ever did for me—getting me a companion right before you moved out of state to play with your lover while I footed the bill."

"I was working on my degree," she huffed.

He raised an eyebrow.

"Okay, and I was having an affair. Yes, I was a bad wife. But that's my point. It wasn't a real marriage. The annulment papers just confirm that."

"And now? This guy you're marrying. Are you committed to him, or to what he can do for you?"

She took half a step backward. "You really don't think much of me, do you, Leith?"

"Can you blame me?"

"Maybe not." Her face softened. "I love him. I really, truly love him. I've made a lot of mistakes in my life, but I'm devoted to him. And he's devoted to me. For life."

"And what if I won't sign the papers?"

"Then we'll marry anyway, but it won't be in a church, with his family, the way he wants it. And I want him to have the wedding he deserves."

He searched her face. During their marriage he'd learned that when she lied, she tended to smile with her lips while her eyes remained hard and focused. Today, though, he saw no sign of deception. For once in her life, she seemed completely sincere.

"Come with me." He turned and led her through the door to the kitchen, where the envelope containing the annulment papers rested in the drawer of the built-in desk.

She looked around the space. "This is nice. I like the copper accents. It really brings a sense of warmth to this room."

A sense of warmth. That was exactly what Sabrina had brought into the kitchen. Into his life. And without her, everything seemed cold and pointless. He opened the envelope and pulled out the papers. "This says my signature has to be notarized."

"I have a notary in the car."

"Of course you do." She was nothing if not prepared. He grabbed a pen and followed her outside. Two men waited beside the limo. The taller of the two came to meet them halfway to the car and took Nicole's arm, his eyebrows raised in question.

She smiled at him. "It's fine. Leith has decided to sign. Leith, this is my fiancé, Dr. Robin Wilmoth. Rob, Leith Jordan."

They exchanged nods. After showing his driver's license, Leith signed the papers on the hood of the limo, and the notary stamped them. Nicole gave an audible sigh of relief. "There. Was that so hard?"

Surprisingly, it wasn't. Leith should have done it a long time ago instead of letting it drag out.

Nicole's fiancé put his left arm around her waist and offered a hand to Leith. "Thank you."

"You're welcome." Leith shook hands with the doctor. "Best wishes for a happy marriage."

"We appreciate that." For the first time, the man cracked a brief smile. Then he turned to Nicole. "We'd better go, darling. We have reservations."

She nodded. "Goodbye, Leith." At least she didn't say "good riddance."

Leith watched the limo pull away. Maybe she really had grown up. The guy seemed decent enough. Maybe they would be happy together. Maybe not. Either way, his marriage with Nicole wasn't just in the past; it had now been erased. Nicole was completely out of his life.

THE NEXT AFTERNOON, Sabrina pulled up in front of her mother's house. She used the key her mom had given her to let herself inside and strolled through the house to the great room. It was a beautiful place, even nicer than the one she remembered from her childhood. But, unlike that perfectly decorated home, this one had books and magazines scattered on the coffee table, two sleeping tabby cats shedding on the couch cushions and crayon drawings by Mason's grandchildren on the refrigerator. It was a home. A happy home.

The back door opened and Mama came in, carrying two bulging shopping bags. "Oh, good. You're here. Could you help me with the groceries?"

"Sure." Sabrina brought in two more bags. "Is this everything?"

"Yes. Let me get the cold food put away and I'll make us some iced tea." Mama smiled at her. "And you can tell me the good news."

"What makes you think it's good news?"

"Because they'd be stupid not to hire you. And McCormick and Sons didn't get where they are by being stupid."

Sabrina set her phone on the kitchen table and helped Mama put away the groceries. Ten minutes later, they were sipping peach-flavored tea and nibbling on cinnamon cookies from the bakery. Sabrina's phone chimed.

"Who's that?" Mama asked.

Sabrina checked to find a photo of Misty holding up both hands with her fingers crossed. The text read Well?

Sabrina smiled and texted back No news yet. She showed her mother the photo. "It's Misty."

"So you're getting to know your sister." Mama nodded her approval.

"A little bit. She's…interesting. And funny. Speaking of my sister, you could have warned me she was going to call."

"She wanted to surprise you. I told her I wasn't sure that was a good idea, but she made me promise. The girl can be very persuasive."

"That's for sure."

"I hope it wasn't too much of a shock for you."

"It was a shock, but I've discovered I rather

like the idea of a sister. I've scheduled an extralong layover in Seattle on the way back and she's coming to the airport to meet me in person. But what about you? It had to be hard for you when she called."

"Why?"

"*Why?* Because her mother was the reason your husband left. He abandoned us in favor of them."

"None of that is the girl's fault."

"No. But still. Dealing with her had to bring up old wounds."

"You know, I've been thinking about that." Mama took a sip of tea. "It almost destroyed me when your father left us. Almost. But, mostly thanks to you, it didn't. We survived. And I'm much happier now, with Mason, than I ever would have been if your father had stayed. Maybe it all worked out for the best."

"Truly?"

"Truly. That business was his whole identity, and when he lost it…" Mama shook her head. "Don't get me wrong—I don't excuse your father's behavior. I understand why he felt like he needed to get away and start over, but we were his family. Even if he didn't want to be married to me any longer, you deserved his love and his loyalty. The checks he sent didn't make up for leaving you behind."

"No. From a few things Misty has said, I gather her mother was very jealous, and he didn't want to upset her."

"I have to feel sorry for the woman."

"Sorry for the woman who stole your husband?"

"Think about what it must have been like for her. She'd seen him abandon one wife and child. She must have spent her whole marriage wondering if he was going to do it again." She bit into a cookie.

"I've never thought about that."

Mama smiled. "Enough about old history. Tell me about the interview. Are they offering you a bonus if you can start right away?"

Sabrina laughed. "They haven't offered me anything yet, except to pay my travel expenses. It was a good day. I talked with several different people and they gave me a tour. They gave me the impression I'm in the running, but they have more people to interview. They said to expect to hear from them in about a week."

"Then it's just a formality. They're going to hire you and you'll finally be coming home." Mama beamed.

Coming home. Sabrina tried to smile back, but it felt forced. Somehow, the metro area where she'd spent her whole life didn't feel like home anymore. There was no goofy little dog angling for a run, no view of towering green mountains outside the kitchen window, no ugly but serviceable rain jacket on the hook beside the door.

No Leith.

"What's wrong?" Mama had stopped with a cookie halfway to her mouth.

Sabrina shook her head. "Nothing's wrong. Everything I've wanted since I graduated is possible now. If I can get this job with McCormick and Sons, I'm set for life."

"So, you're worried you won't get the job?"

"If not, I'll continue my job at Orson Outfitters. They're a great company, too. I've learned so much since I started there. I think I have a good shot to make it to the management group in Seattle." Sabrina ran a finger down the condensation on the side of her glass. "They're good people to work with. In fact, I feel a little disloyal sneaking off to interview for this job without telling them."

Mama patted her arm. "I'm sure if they're as good as you say, they'd tell you to go for the job that suits you best."

And the thing was, Mama was probably right. Walter believed that the best workers were the people with a passion for their job, and he would advise her to work where her passion led her. Which made Sabrina feel even worse about deceiving him.

"Besides," Mama continued, "you're almost done with this training period in Anchorage. You'll be moving away from that store one way or the other anyway. And just in time. Last week, I saw that show where they're driving trucks on the ice." She shuddered. "You don't want to be in that place in the winter."

Sabrina smiled. "That's on the North Slope, all the way to the other end of the state. Leith says Anchorage is warmer than Minneapolis in January and gets less snow than Flagstaff."

"Well, that's not saying much. Who's Leith?"

Sabrina almost said "a friend." He'd been her best friend, and more. Much more. But now what were they? Former friends? Misaligned soul mates? "He's someone I know in Anchorage."

"Ah, tell me about this Leith. What does he do for a living?"

"He's a survival instructor."

"Survival instructor?" Mama fanned herself with her hand. "Oh, my."

Mama was probably imagining a picture from some Hot Alaskan Men calendar. And with those incredible blue eyes and fit body, Leith could be a cover model for one. But that wasn't what made him so attractive. The images that stuck in Sabrina's mind were of Leith patiently coaching Emma on fishing, of his fingers flying over the guitar strings as he led the group in campfire songs, of conversation and laughter over so many meals. That was why she loved him.

She loved him! *Cielos!*

Mama was eyeing her now, no doubt planning her strategy to extract information. Sabrina pushed back her chair. "Excuse me just a minute."

Mama said something, but Sabrina couldn't hear it over the pounding in her ears. She escaped into the powder room under the stairs and splashed cool water on her flushed face. The image in the mirror stared back at her with frightened eyes. How could she have let this happen?

CHAPTER FIFTEEN

"Hey, Sabrina." Sabrina had barely stepped inside the store when Clara beckoned her over from her spot at register one. "Over here."

Sabrina had only been back in Anchorage for two days since her trip to Arizona. She wove her way past stacks of camping guides and bug spray to reach Clara. "Hi. What's up?"

"Your career," Clara whispered. "Kate from management is here again, and I overheard her and Walter talking about you. He says sales are way up in women's clothing since you took over the department, and Kate was agreeing with everything he said. I think she's here to tell you that you made the cut."

A stab of guilt ran through Sabrina's chest. Here was Walter, advocating for her to make the team, and she was sneaking away interviewing for another job. "They're not scheduled to make that announcement for a while yet."

"Maybe she's just here to interview you

before they make the final selections, then, but I can tell she's impressed." Clara grinned at her like a proud parent. "You're going to get the Seattle job, and you'll be great at it."

Sabrina felt tears well up at Clara's faith in her. She blinked them away. "It means a lot that you think so."

Clara patted her on the shoulder. "Hey, don't get all emotional on me. Remember, you're moving to management at headquarters. You have to be all icy and professional."

Sabrina laughed. "I'll keep that in mind. Thanks, Clara." She made her way back to her department, sweeping her gaze over the colorful fleece vests and T-shirts, so different from the silk dresses and designer bags displayed in the front window of McCormick and Sons. Regardless of which job she landed, she was going to miss her coworkers here at the store.

A scary thought suddenly crossed her mind. Could word somehow have gotten out that she was interviewing for another job, and Kate was here to tell her she was being dropped from the program? Sabrina licked her dry lips. What if she didn't get the McCormick job, and it got her kicked out of the management program, too?

No, they wouldn't waste an executive's time traveling all the way to Alaska to tell her she was out. And Walter wouldn't have been discussing her sales record in front of Clara if she was in trouble. It was just her guilty conscience talking.

She'd barely had time to dump her bag in her locker and return to her department when Walter appeared. "Good morning, Sabrina." He seemed to be all smiles this morning, further reassuring her they didn't know about Scottsdale. "I'm glad you're in early today. Kate's here from Seattle, and she has something to talk with you about. She's waiting in my office."

"Oh, okay. Thanks." Sabrina took long, deep breaths in a futile attempt to slow her heart rate as she strode past the break room toward Walter's office.

Kate sat at Walter's desk leafing through some papers. Sabrina recognized them as copies of the design sketches she'd shown Kate at their last meeting. Kate looked up and smiled. "Good morning. Have a seat. We have a lot to talk about."

Sabrina greeted Kate and perched on the edge of the same chair where she'd sat her first day here, when Walter had given her his welcome speech.

Kate gathered up the papers and tapped them into a neat stack. "Sabrina, are you familiar with Caribou Pass and Hidden Glacier?"

"The outdoor clothing brands, you mean?"

"Yes. What's your opinion of their products?"

"Well, from what I've seen of their catalogs, they seem to have a broad selection. The online reviews are favorable."

"Yes, but what do you think of their clothes? Do you own any of them?" Kate grinned. "This is not a test of loyalty. I'll admit I have a Caribou Pass down coat I adore."

Sabrina laughed. "No. I don't own any, but that's because I can't afford it."

"Ah, that's what I thought you'd say. But you'd like to be able to afford more stylish outdoor gear than what Orson Outfitters offers. Am I right?"

"Honestly, yes. I hate to say it, but most of Orson's women's wear just seems like a man's product in a different size. I'd like outdoor gear that was more stylish and designed for a woman."

Kate nodded. "Lots of women would. That's why I've convinced the board to introduce a new line of women's wear. Orson will keep the existing line of basics—the board insisted on that—but we'll add some more fashion-oriented clothes as well. We'll have to work out the details, but I estimate we can sell them for about twenty-five percent more, with a slightly higher profit margin. I showed the board a photo of the vest you remade, and how it was still functional but more attractive. That's what sold them on the idea."

They liked her vest! "That's great. I'll look forward to seeing what you come up with."

"Actually, I'm hoping you'll do more than that. I'm here to offer you a job as designer for the new line."

"Me?" Sabrina had always loved working with fabrics and creating fashion, but after learning more about the industry, she'd decided security was more important than creativity. Could she have both?

"You'd work with our production department. At the beginning, we plan to offer just a few select items. These sketches you came up with are a great start."

Could she really do this? "You realize I'm not a designer. That is, I've taken design classes in college, but I haven't worked in the field at all."

"Yes, we understand that, but we think it's important to have someone who comprehends the function of the clothes and not just the aesthetic. Your designs have both."

Sabrina swallowed. It was time to come

clean. "Okay, confession time. I don't have that much experience with outdoor clothing, either. Before I came to Alaska, I'd never even been camping."

Kate laughed. "Yes, I suspected that might be the case."

"You knew all along?"

"I noticed whenever the group discussed their outdoor adventures, you were conspicuously quiet. But you had other skills and experience that I thought could benefit the company. Camping isn't that hard, and judging from what I saw of you at Walter's, you're a quick study."

"I burned the cobbler."

"Because you were busy saving a baby from choking. Hey, you can be forgiven for getting a little distracted." Kate leaned forward in her chair. "Sabrina, you turned that vest from ho-hum into something eye-catching without sacrificing function. In your jacket design you arranged different pockets to make it easy for a woman to find her cell phone or sunglasses or warm her hands. Your designs are well-thought-out and practical. And if you need expert advice on what features to include for various types of clothing, you have an entire store here full of outdoor enthusiasts as consultants."

"You mean, I could do that job from here?"

"Here, Seattle, anywhere with internet, really. You'd need to travel, of course, to find the right fabrics and meet with the production team, but you could base wherever you wanted. That's one of the perks of this position. There are negatives as well."

"Like what?"

"First of all, accepting this position would take you out of the running for the management team, and I won't lie—you're on track to make it." Kate handed her a paper with a salary figure. "Initially, your salary as designer would be a little higher than what you would have earned on the next step in the management training path, but you'd lose out on the potential for promotion and corresponding salary growth opportunities."

"So, less money in the long term."

"Most likely. Secondly, this is an experiment. We would only be signing you to a one-year contract. It took some arm-twisting to convince the board to expand the women's clothing line, and if the new designs don't sell, they won't hesitate to jettison the whole project."

"And if that happened, could I transfer to the management team?"

"I'm afraid not. They will have filled all the

positions and moved to the next rung by that time. You could, of course, apply again from scratch, but we run on a four-year cycle, so you'd have to wait for the next opportunity."

"So, if I take this job as designer instead of the management position, it would mean potentially less money and I could be out of a job in one year. Is that right?"

Kate gave a rueful smile. "That's about the size of it."

So, no security. But a chance at designing? "May I have some time to think about it?"

"Absolutely. But I'd appreciate it if you'd let me know within a week or so, both because we need to make the final decisions for the management team, and because we need to get rolling if we want to get the clothes in stores by next season."

"I can do that." One week to decide the future course of her life. How hard could it be?

LEITH PULLED INTO the Orson Outfitters' parking lot, but instead of taking the first available space, he cruised up and down the rows, looking for a familiar blue car. It had been ten days since he'd last seen Sabrina. Her interview in Scottsdale would have been almost a week ago. If they offered her the job, it was possible she'd already quit Orson's and moved away.

He turned a corner and there it was, parked on the far side of a minivan at the back of the lot. He pulled into a spot two spaces down and stared, unseeing, through the windshield. What was he doing here? Yes, he'd broken his favorite six-weight fly rod and needed a replacement, but that didn't explain why he was stalking Sabrina's car.

He ran his fingers through his hair. He could come tomorrow instead, when she might be off. But that was stupid; he was here now. He could just go into the fishing department, get the rod and leave. Sabrina would probably be in the back, doing paperwork, anyway. And if she was working the floor and he happened to see her, so what? It didn't change anything.

A glance at the clock on the dash told him if he didn't get a move on, the store would close while he was making up his mind. He climbed out of his car and went inside, heading directly to the fishing department. He found the rod he wanted easily enough. The lights dimmed, and a pleasant voice urged customers to bring their purchases to the register.

Instead, he found himself slipping toward the back of the store. He stopped behind a display of canoe paddles and peered toward Sabrina's department. There she was, bent down over a stroller, talking gibberish to a baby. After a moment, she smiled up at the proud mom. Two little kids chased each other in circles around the department.

The mom said something, and Sabrina went to one of the racks, checked a couple of tags and held up a blue fishing shirt for the woman's approval. One of the kids, dodging away from his sister, ran into a table and knocked a stack of neatly folded shirts to the floor.

The mom grabbed the kids and seemed to be apologizing profusely, but Sabrina just smiled and waved away her offers to help pick up. After a few more words, the woman took the blue shirt and herded her kids forward toward the registers. Sabrina bent to pick up the shirts, but she stopped to wave goodbye to one of the kids before she began refolding them.

Her kindness touched him. Most people would have been annoyed at the very least, but she was as patient with these children as she'd always been with Emma. Sabrina was special. A rock formed in the pit of his stomach when he thought about how he'd pushed her away.

Leith stepped from behind the paddles and walked toward her. She looked up, and the professionally friendly smile slipped off her face. For a long moment, they stared at one another. Then she broke her gaze and finished folding the polo shirt, setting it on the table.

He came closer. "Hello, Sabrina."

"Leith."

He held up the fishing rod. "I, uh, broke my old rod and thought I'd come into the store for a new one."

"I see that." She picked up the next shirt. "All fishing rods are on sale this week, twenty percent off."

"Guess I got lucky."

"I guess so." She set the next shirt on the pile and looked at him. "Is there anything else I can help you with?"

So, this was what he'd been reduced to, just another customer. He supposed he didn't deserve anything more than that. But it hurt to see her looking at him with no warmth, no trace of a smile.

"I was wondering—" he paused to rub the back of his neck "—how your interview in Scottsdale went."

"Were you?" Sabrina picked up another shirt.

"Yes, I was. Would you like to tell me?"

She kept folding. "Actually, it went quite well. They called me today, as a matter of fact, and offered me the job."

"Oh." That rock in his stomach grew into a boulder. "Well, that's good, then. Have you given your notice?"

"I haven't accepted the job in Scottsdale yet."

Hope flickered, but he tamped it down. "Why not?"

"Does it matter?" The shirt she was folding came out crooked. Impatiently, she shook it out and started again. "I went to the interview in Scottsdale. Wasn't that the line you drew in the sand?"

She was right. As much as he wanted to blame her for leaving, he was the one who had laid out the ultimatum. She'd made her decision, and now she was making it clear her life choices were no longer any of his business. "Well, whether you end up in Seattle or Scottsdale, I wish you the best. You deserve all the happiness in the world."

Without waiting for a response, he turned and carried the fishing pole to the checkout. But before he left the store, he craned his neck for one last glimpse of Sabrina.

THE NEXT MORNING, Sabrina locked the door to her apartment and followed Boomer up the stairs. He tugged on his leash, eager to get to the park. Today was a late half day at work, so Sabrina had the morning off, and letting Boomer mark every bush in the neighborhood park followed by a nice long run seemed like a good way to spend it. She had a decision to make and running always helped her think.

She zipped her jacket. No rain this morning, but clouds and a slight breeze chilled her Arizona-bred body. On a day like this, Leith would be wearing hiking shorts and a T-shirt. He never seemed to get cold. On her last morning off before their trip to Denali, they'd hiked in Kincaid Park and spotted a bull moose with an enormous set of antlers lying in a patch of sun. The moose had watched them as though trying to understand why these two-legged creatures insisted on wandering in the woods when there was a nice sunny meadow for relaxing. An Alaska moment. She was going to miss those when she left. If she left.

She reached the park, and Boomer did his thing while she warmed up and stretched. Once he was satisfied that every dog passing this way would know "Boomer was here," Sabrina broke into a run. Boomer dashed along beside her, his little legs a blur.

Tomorrow, she had to give Kate her answer, and she wasn't sure what she would say. Too many variables made what should have been an easy decision impossible. Take the secure job she knew she was good at—working for McCormick and Sons? Stay on the management track at Orson, where she might work her way up the ladder to a high-paying upper-management job? Or try her hand at design, knowing if her designs didn't sell the first year, she was toast?

The obvious answer was McCormick. They had an excellent reputation as an employer, and the people she'd met there seemed nice enough. She'd get to travel to places like Paris, London and Barcelona to find the most fabulous fashions. And most important, she'd know her job was likely safe, which had always been her priority.

So why couldn't she just make the call? She'd signed on to the management-trainee program with Orson, but they had plenty of qualified applicants. It was the design job that tempted her. Or was it? Was it really the chance to design that was enticing her to accept Kate's offer? Or was it that the design job would allow her to stay in Anchorage, with Leith?

Leith. She missed him. Missed his laughter, and his kindness. Missed spending time with him outdoors. Missed the way he could make her feel adventurous and safe at the same time. But just because she missed him was no reason to turn down a secure job. If there was one thing her father's leaving had taught her, it was that you couldn't rely on anyone else. Leith shouldn't factor into this decision.

She and Boomer had made three laps around the park when she stopped to stretch and catch her breath. Boomer gave a sudden bark of greeting and wagged his tail. Sabrina looked up to see Volta approaching. What in the world was she doing here? She lived on the other side of town.

"Hi. Out for a run?" Volta gave a nervous laugh. "I mean, obviously you are."

"Uh-huh. How about you? Did you just happen to decide to walk in a neighborhood park several miles from your house?"

Volta grinned. "No. I called Orson's, and they said you weren't scheduled for work until this afternoon, so I came looking. I knocked on the door of your apartment, and when I didn't hear the dog bark I figured I might find you here."

"That was a lot of detective work. You could have just called."

Volta shrugged. "Yeah, but I was afraid you might not answer."

"Why wouldn't I?"

Volta grimaced. "Leith told me about what happened, how he expected you to choose between the job interview and him. I thought you might not want to deal with anyone associated with that lunkhead."

Sabrina laughed. "I won't hold your brother against you."

"Good, because I want to take you out for an early lunch."

"That's nice of you, but I don't know if I have time for a restaurant meal." Sabrina checked her watch. "I need to finish my run and take a shower before work."

"How about if you finish your run while I pick up some bop and we can eat over there at the picnic table by the lake?"

"Bop?"

"Korean rice bowls. There's a place on Muldoon. They come with vegetables, meat and this amazing sauce. If I call it in, I can be back in fifteen minutes."

"Sounds good to me."

"Great. What kind of meat do you like?"

"Surprise me."

Volta nodded her approval. "See you in a bit."

Sabrina and Boomer had just finished their run and were cooling down when Volta showed up again with a carrier sack and two bottles of water. Sabrina accompanied her across the park to the picnic table, tied Boomer to the table leg and sat down on the bench. Boomer lay with his chin on his paws, looking up at her with sad eyes, as though brokenhearted over her callous treatment of not allowing him in her lap while she ate.

Volta handed her a paper bowl full of food. Sabrina popped off the lid and dug a plastic spork into her bowl, coming up with a spoonful of rice, a mushroom and a tiny meatball. She popped it into her mouth. "Mmm, this *is* good."

"I thought you'd like it." Volta took a bite of her own lunch.

"I do." Sabrina swallowed another bite. "So, now that you've gotten me in a good mood, what did you want to talk about?"

"How did you know I wanted to talk?"

"You're here. And you went to a lot of trouble to find me. Where is Emma, by the way?"

"She went RVing with a friend's family. They're spending the night in Seward and going to the SeaLife Center."

"Sounds fun."

"It's really good. Emma loves the seals. You should go if you get the chance."

"I'll keep it in mind."

"Do." Volta took a drink. "Leith said you interviewed for a job in Scottsdale."

"Yes, with McCormick and Sons."

"McCormick's?" Volta broke into a grin, her spoon halfway to her mouth. "I love that store. When we lived there, Mom and I went to their big semiannual clearance sale. I found this amazing prom dress that had been marked down from three hundred dollars to sixty. Spaghetti straps, beaded bodice, mermaid skirt. It was gorgeous. I had to scramble for a date to the prom the next year, but I had the perfect dress."

"I can picture it on you. Beautiful. My mother used to take me to the sale when I was little, too, and she'd buy me chocolate-covered raisins from the candy department."

"Ooh, chocolate-covered raisins. Yum. Have you heard back from McCormick's yet?"

"Leith didn't tell you?"

"No, I haven't seen Leith in the last couple of days."

"McCormick offered me the job."

"Oh." Volta's face fell, but then she forced a smile. "Congratulations. When do you move to Scottsdale?"

"I haven't accepted yet."

"No? Why not?"

"As it turns out, I've had another job offer."

"What kind of offer?"

Sabrina took another bite before continuing. "It's kind of complicated. Are you sure you want to get into this?"

"Sure, unless you don't want to tell me. Though sometimes it's easier to make a decision if you talk it over with a friend."

She smiled. "I do need to decide."

"Then let's examine all the options. First, tell me about McCormick and Sons. You obviously impressed them in the interview. Did you get a sense of what they would be like to work for?"

Sabrina nodded. "I've always heard it's a great place to work, and everyone I talked to confirmed that. They treat their employees well. It would involve travel, similar to what I was doing before with Cutterbee's."

"You'd travel to fashion shows in Europe and things like that?"

"Yeah. I did that with my other job, but this would include more high-fashion shows."

"It sounds like a good fit," Volta admitted.

"It is a good fit. Plus, my mother lives in Scottsdale. She's already making plans for Sunday dinners and spa weekends."

"I'll bet."

"But then there's the management job with Orson's. If I did well in the company, I could eventually make it to upper management. I don't know how much they make, but it's a lot more than a buyer."

Volta smiled. "Money is always nice."

"And I'd live in Seattle. I have a sister in Seattle."

"You do? For some reason, I thought you were an only child."

"I was, for all intents and purposes. Long story short, my father, who left my mother and me when I was twelve, had another daughter, who I didn't know about. He died earlier this year, and she tracked me down."

"That must be weird. What's she like?"

Sabrina grinned. "Weird isn't far off. Fun, though. She's a college freshman. We met at the airport for a couple of hours on my way back from Phoenix. I'd like to spend more time with her and get to know her better."

"Okay, so job number one—fashion shows, nice company to work for, close to your mom. Job number two—big bucks, get to know your sister. Is that about the size of it?"

"No, there's another choice. Kate Simonton, one of the VPs, offered me a different job designing a new line of women's outdoor clothing for Orson's."

"A whole new line of clothes?"

"Yeah. Outdoor clothing similar to what

we offer now, but with more style. Along the lines of what Caribou Pass and Hidden Glacier are putting out, but more affordable."

"Wow. You'd be really good at that. How's the pay?"

"Comparable to McCormick's."

"Housing is expensive in Seattle," Volta warned.

"The design job isn't necessarily based in Seattle. I could live wherever I want."

"So if you wanted, you could live in Scottsdale, near your mother?"

"I could."

"Or you could stay here, in Anchorage?"

"Yes."

Volta's eyes, the same brilliant blue as her brother's, lit up. "That would be awesome." She held up her hands. "For me. But you need to do what's best for you. You'd rather be a buyer or a manager than a designer?"

"I don't know. I'd love to try my hand at design. But they're only offering a one-year contract. If the line doesn't sell well, they'd discontinue it and I'd be out of a job. Again."

"And if it did sell well?"

"Then I suppose they'd renew my contract and I'd keep on designing. If it were very popular they'd probably grow the line and hire more people."

Volta absently stirred the ingredients in her bowl. "Suppose for a moment everything was equal. Pay, job security, perks, location. Nobody pressuring you to live in one location or another. Which job would you choose?"

"That's silly. You can't make decisions like this in a vacuum."

"But if you could, which job would you take?"

Sabrina paused to take a bite and think it over while she chewed. "I'd love to try my hand at design. But that's irrelevant because everything is not equal. Openings at McCormick and Sons don't happen often. If the designer job doesn't work out, I might never get another chance with them. Even the management training program at Orson's is only every four years. If I started over, I'd be four years behind."

"So, basically, you're choosing between a management job that might make you a lot of money, a secure job doing something you like and a risky job doing something you love."

"Maybe. But, you know, design might not be all that exciting as a permanent job. It's fun to come up with ideas and designs when I'm in the mood, but under pressure it might not be so fun. What with production schedules, suppliers and cost control, it could be a nightmare."

"It sounds to me like you're trying to talk yourself out of what you really want to do."

Was she? Sabrina shook her head and reached for the water bottle. "You've given me something to think about, but let's leave it for now."

"But—"

"Tell me what Emma's been up to lately."

Volta paused as though she was thinking about pushing her point, but she didn't. "Emma." She shook her head. "Emma has decided she's going to be a veterinarian when she grows up, so she performed a stuffing-ectomy on her tiger. Then she decided to try it on one of my mom's down throw pillows. Feathers everywhere. It didn't go over well."

"I'll bet not." Sabrina laughed. "What did your mother do?"

"She sentenced Emma to thirty minutes of solitary confinement for practicing medicine without a license."

"That must have been a long thirty minutes for Emma."

"For both of them. Mom hates it when she has to discipline Emma. She'd rather be the cool grandma and get my dad or Leith to be the heavy."

"Leith as the enforcer?" Sabrina raised her eyebrows.

"Yeah, I know. But Emma listens to him."

"You're lucky to have your family so close."

"I am." Volta turned to watch a duck zoom and skid across the lake before settling into the water. Then she turned back. "After high school I had big plans. I was going to be a physical therapist, and I convinced my parents that the best program for me was to study kinesiology in Hawaii."

"Nice."

"It was. I loved Hawaii, and there was this guy..."

"Ah, the guy."

"Yeah. But—" She let out a long breath. "It didn't work out. It was starting to feel serious, and then—boom—he broke up with me. I finished out the semester and came home. And before long, I met Emma's dad, and instead of finishing up my degree in Hawaii, I married him. Two years later, he died in an accident, and I was alone and pregnant, and only had a part-time job. I moved in with my parents and felt like a failure."

"But look at you. You're a flight paramedic, and a great mom."

"I owe that to my family. After Emma was born, I found a cheap apartment and got a job in a hospital as an aide. It didn't take long before I realized I wanted to become an EMT. And I wanted to do it on my own."

Sabrina nodded. She would have felt the same.

"I got accepted into a program, got loans and childcare lined up and started studying. It wasn't easy, but I was doing okay until Emma began getting recurring ear infections. She couldn't go to day care, and I'd miss class. My grades were falling. One evening, Leith dropped in. Emma was screaming because her ears were hurting, and I started crying, too, because I needed to study for a big test and I couldn't get Emma settled down enough to go to sleep."

"It must have been so hard."

"It was," Volta admitted, "until Leith insisted on taking Emma for the night. He called my mom, and she came to see me the next day. She told me she was proud of me, but that it wasn't a weakness to accept help from the people in your life who love you. She rearranged her work schedule so that she could care for Emma while I was in class and Leith took her lots of evenings. It made all the difference then and later when I was working on my flight certification. It still does. I couldn't do my job if Leith and my parents didn't help out with Emma."

"I don't know who's helping whom. Spending time with Emma is a blast."

Volta grinned. "I'm glad you think so. I'm pretty crazy about her."

"She's a great kid."

"I know." Volta stood and started gathering up the bowls and napkins. "This was fun, but I have an overflowing hamper of laundry to take care of and you have to get ready for work. Let's do it again soon."

Sabrina stood, too. "I don't know if I'll be in town much longer. It depends on what job I take."

"Then I'll look you up when I'm in Seattle or Phoenix. They're major medical centers, so I fly patients there from time to time."

"That would be great."

Volta squatted down and scratched the dog under his chin. "Bye, Boomer. You take good care of Sabrina." She straightened. "One more thing. My brother may be a lunkhead, but he has his reasons."

"You mean because of his ex?"

Volta nodded. "He should never have married that...woman. But he did, and she jerked him around for five years before she cut him loose. Things like that leave scars. When I talked with him last week he was kind of a mess. But he took Emma anyway. Leith has never let me down."

"What do you mean 'kind of a mess'?"

"Upset. Sad. You know, that feeling when you've done something monumentally stupid and you don't know how to fix it?" Volta shook her head. "He's such a guy. But one thing about Leith—once he commits, you can depend on him to stand behind you. No matter what." She smiled. "Just something to keep in mind while you're deciding about your job." She gave Sabrina a quick hug, turned and walked away.

Sabrina watched her go. So she'd really gone to all this trouble just to leave Sabrina with that little endorsement. Volta's tendency to butt into Leith's life drove him crazy, but it was only because she loved him. Leith and his sister always had each other's backs.

It must be nice.

CHAPTER SIXTEEN

SABRINA ARRIVED AT the store in time to give Autumn her lunch break. Two women and a little girl browsed through the clothes on the sales rack. Sabrina waved to let them know she was there if they needed help and left them alone to shop. A few minutes later, the girl wandered over to Sabrina and held out her stuffed animal.

"This is my lamb."

"It's a very nice lamb. May I pet it?"

The little girl nodded, and Sabrina stroked the toy made of an ultrasoft microfleece. The fleece had been textured to resemble a sheep's wool. Sabrina could envision using the fabric on a jacket. She'd use a suede-like brushed fabric for the body and the microfleece to line the collar, cuffs and along the zipper. It would be soft and warm where the jacket touched skin. Her fingers itched to sketch it out.

"Anna, come back over here. You need to stay close to me." The girl smiled at Sabrina and skipped back to her mother, carrying the toy.

It was a typical workday, and yet it seemed somehow surreal, knowing that tomorrow, everything would be different. Tomorrow, Sabrina would have to give Kate and the people at McCormick and Sons an answer. And then she'd tell Walter and her coworkers. And they'd never look at her the same way again.

Autumn returned from her lunch break, leaving Sabrina free to get her paperwork caught up. Just in case Walter decided to decline her two-week notice and sent her packing, she didn't want any loose ends for whoever took over until Marianne returned. At the end of the day, she was washing out her coffee cup in the break room when Tim wandered in. "Hi, Sabrina. Too bad about Marianne."

"What about her?" She hadn't heard any more since the department manager left to help her sister.

"She's not coming back. Her sister had the baby, but he's premature and will need a lot of extra care, and there's a sibling, too. It's more than Marianne's sister can handle alone. Marianne decided to move there permanently so she can help out."

"That's really good of her."

"Yeah. I never thought you'd be able to pry her out of Alaska, but things change. You never know what's going to happen. You just have to adapt."

"That's for sure." Sabrina certainly wouldn't have expected to find herself here. Her excellent job-performance ratings and steady salary increases had led her to believe her job with Cutterbee's was safe, up until the bankruptcy.

But like Tim said, you never knew. Maybe security was an illusion. McCormick and Sons seemed rock-solid, but the same forces that had bankrupted Cutterbee's could impact them as well. Maybe the only real security was knowing you could adapt.

Once the store was closed and she'd made sure everything was in good shape for the next day, Sabrina went out to her car, but she didn't immediately start the engine. Leith had once talked about how he would wake up eager to get to his job almost every day.

She closed her eyes and pictured a workday in Seattle, a bustling, thriving, attractive city. She would commute in with all the other worker bees, and spend her day organizing facts, figures and people. Maybe on the weekend, she'd get to spend some time with Misty.

Or there was McCormick's. A typical day might involve anything from chasing down a supplier to attending a Paris fashion show. She'd done it before, and she knew she could do it again. Mom would be there, hopefully willing to babysit Boomer while Sabrina was out of town.

Finally, there was the design job. Creating a line of functional fashion for Orson Outfitters. Finding the perfect fabrics and making them into something both beautiful and useful, like the jacket she'd been envisioning earlier, with the microfleece trim. And she smiled. That was a job she would look forward to each morning.

She could do it in Scottsdale with Mama, or Seattle with Misty, but she wouldn't. There was only one place she wanted to be, one face she longed to see at the end of the day. Was it too late?

She started the car. This was what she wanted. She just had to screw up enough courage to make it happen. And she never felt more courageous than when she was with Leith. If he would listen.

She stopped by her apartment just long enough to collect Boomer and drove by Learn & Live, but there were no cars in the lot. At Leith's house, the driveway was empty, and when she knocked on the door, there was no answer. Maybe he was at his parents' or Volta's. She pulled out her phone, but before she could press a button, a chime signaled an incoming text. From Leith. Where are you? Need to talk. And then another text. Please.

Hope surged. In your driveway. Where are you?

At your apartment. Stay there. I'm coming.

What was he doing at her apartment? While she waited to find out, she let Boomer nose around the lawn. Some kids rode by on their bikes and waved. Sabrina waved back. She was on the far side of the yard, letting Boomer sniff along the lilac bush beside the fence, when Leith pulled in beside her car. He must have hit every green light on the way there.

He climbed out of the car and paused. She looked back at him, trying to read his expression. Tal, breaking with her usual flawless manners, jumped over into the driver's seat and bounded out of the car and across the lawn, her tail wagging madly. Boomer strained to the end of his leash, pulling toward her. Once she'd reached him, Tal dropped her chest to the ground and Boomer stood on his hind legs to lick at her ears.

Leith made his way to them. "They look happy."

"Yeah, Boomer really missed her." Sabrina gathered her courage. "And I—" she began.

"I have something—" Leith said at the same time.

"You first." They spoke in unison. And laughed.

Leith reached for her hand. "This might take a while. Let's go inside."

He unlocked the front door, and they ended up in the kitchen. This time of day, sunlight poured through the window over the sink, washing the new paint in a warm glow. Now that they were here, Leith seemed in no hurry to continue the conversation. He just looked at her, as if he wasn't quite sure she was real.

Sabrina smiled at him. "You go first."

"All right." He took a deep breath. "First of all, I need to apologize. It wasn't fair to ask you to give up a chance at your dream job to stay here with me and I'm sorry."

"Leith—"

"Wait— let me finish." He reached inside the pocket of his jeans and pulled out what looked like a printout of an email. "I've been in touch with an adventure-guide service based in Scottsdale. They've offered me a job."

"What? Why?"

"I suppose because they think I'm qualified."

"No—why would you apply for a job in Scottsdale?"

"Because ever since that last day when I told you we couldn't be together, I've been miserable. I miss you. I need you in my life." He took a step closer. "I know I acted like a jerk, but if you'll forgive me, I promise to be more flexible. Starting with moving to Scottsdale."

She stared at him. "You hate Scottsdale."

"I hated Scottsdale, but that was when I was a sulky teenager. You've taught me it's all about attitude. This time, I'm not being dragged somewhere against my will. I'm choosing Scottsdale because I want to be there. With you." He reached for her hand. "I love you, Sabrina."

He loved her. It was more than she'd dared hope. He was willing to give up his job, his family and this place he loved so much. For her.

"I love you, too."

"You do?" His smile could melt glaciers.

"I do. I love you." It felt so good to say it aloud.

"Then you forgive me?"

"Absolutely, I do." She reached up to press her hand against his cheek.

He pulled her close, those blue eyes smiling at her for a long moment before his mouth met hers and she let her eyelids drift closed, losing herself in the warmth of his arms, the touch of his lips. Afterward, he held her, his hand stroking her hair. It was several minutes later before he spoke again.

"I guess we need to make plans. When do you report to your new job? Have you given notice?"

She'd almost forgotten what she'd come to talk about in the first place. "Volta didn't tell you?"

"Tell me what?"

"That I'm considering turning down the Scottsdale job."

"No, I haven't talked with Volta for a few days. I thought McCormick and Sons was your dream job."

"It was, but I'm not sure it still is."

He drew back so he could see her face. "Sabrina, don't give it up for me. I can do this guide job in Scottsdale."

"It's not that. Kate Simonton, one of the VPs at Orson Outfitters, has offered me another job."

"You got the management job in Seattle?"

"No... Well, yes, kind of, but there's also something else. They're experimenting with a new line of women's outdoor clothes, and she wants me to design it."

"That's great!"

"I think it could be. But she's just offering a one-year contract. If the line doesn't sell well, that's the end of it. And I'm out of a job."

"It will sell." He spoke without hesitation. "I know nothing about fashion, but I've seen your sketches. Even I can tell they're good. You're great with colors and shapes. And if they're distributing the clothes through the Orson Outfitters' stores and catalog, you'll get great exposure. It's the perfect job for you."

"There's another perk. This designer job would involve a fair amount of travel, but I could be based anywhere I want." She squeezed his hand. "I was leaning toward here."

"Here? In Anchorage?"

"Yes. Here. Doing work I could really enjoy. Being with the man I love."

He smiled, his eyes tender. "Are you sure? I could find something in Seattle if that's better for you. It's cold and dark in Anchorage in the winter. You may hate it."

"Like you hated Scottsdale?"

"As you pointed out, I didn't give Scottsdale a chance."

"Winter could be fun. I have a cashmere sweater I've only worn once. I'd like a chance to try out wool skirts and boots. And I've always wanted to try ice-skating. Do you skate?"

"I was on the state championship hockey team my junior year of high school."

"Of course you were. Leith, I admit, this scares me. I'd love to try my hand at design, but what if I give up my one chance at the security of McCormick's to take this job and I lose it in a year?"

"It's a legitimate concern. But you've been there before and now you have, what, three job offers?" He stroked her hair. "Is that really what you're afraid of?"

"What do you mean?"

"Maybe what really scares you is the possibility that you'll be hurt if you commit to the job here and our relationship doesn't last. I could be wrong—maybe I'm projecting my own fears onto you. I gave you that ultimatum because I wanted to save myself some pain. It didn't work, by the way. But I'm wondering if you might be doing the same."

"You think I'm afraid of loving you?"

"I think you're afraid the love won't last. That you can't count on me to stand by you when things go wrong."

Sabrina thought about what he'd said. "It's not easy to give up a chance at a secure job. After seeing my mom fall apart when my dad left, I made up my mind not to depend on anyone except myself."

"I can understand that. It's hard, giving away your heart, especially after it's been broken. I have a confession to make." He lifted her hand and pressed a kiss to it. "I almost bought you a ring earlier today. Because I wanted to show you that I'm committed to you, to us. But then I realized, based on experience, neither of us can put much faith in a ring. We both know rings and vows are only as good as the people who give them. Sabrina, all I can say is that I love you. That's not going to change. What it comes down to is this—do you trust me?"

She looked into his blue eyes, just as she had that day when she'd panicked on the ledge. Just like then, she saw only goodness and love shining out at her. She saw a man who would do whatever it took to keep her safe and happy. "I do."

"Then trust that you can take a chance on a job you love, and if it doesn't work out, I'll be there. If the design job ends, we'll work together to find a position where you can use your talents, here or somewhere else. I'll be there beside you. Always."

"Always." She smiled. "That's a really nice word."

"It is, isn't it?"

"I love you, Leith." She slipped her arms around his neck and stood on tiptoe to kiss him. "And I always will."

CHAPTER SEVENTEEN

Ten months later

"MILEPOST TWENTY-EIGHT-POINT-SEVEN. Turn here." Sabrina pointed at the sign and Leith turned in. As he drove, Sabrina ducked to peer through the windshield. "There it is, girls. Worthington Glacier."

Misty leaned forward from the back seat. "How can you tell it's a glacier? It just looks like snow from here."

"When we get closer, you'll be able to tell," Leith assured her. He pulled into the parking lot. "You girls up for a short hike?"

"Yeah!" Misty, Emma and the dogs spilled out of the back seat of the Land Cruiser. "Let's go!"

"You need shoes," Sabrina pointed out to Misty. "Flip-flops don't work for glaciers."

Misty laughed and nudged Emma. "Three days with my big sister and she's already bossing me around."

"I'll get your shoes for you." Emma climbed

back into the car and scrambled over the seat to dig Misty's Cheetahs out from under a sleeping bag.

"Thanks, squirt." Misty held out her hand for a high five, and Emma slapped it. Misty kicked off her flip-flops and stepped into her sneakers. "There. I'm wearing shoes. Should I wear a sweater, too, and maybe pin mittens to my jacket?"

Sabrina smirked. "As a matter of fact, yes, you should both wear sweaters because ice is cold. But you can probably skip the mittens." Misty had been teasing her about acting like a big sister ever since Sabrina picked her up at the airport and asked if she ate dinner on the plane.

Sabrina and Leith had been planning this visit for two months, since Misty called to announce she'd bought an airline ticket to Anchorage. Yesterday, after picking up Emma, they'd driven from Anchorage through the tunnel to Whittier, and loaded onto the Alaska Ferry. After a six-hour cruise past glaciers, seals and puffins, they'd disembarked in Valdez and camped out just outside of the town. They'd dined on hot dogs, roasted marshmallows for s'mores and made hot chocolate on Sabrina's new camp stove. Leith had wowed

Misty with his guitar skills. And Boomer and Emma found a chipmunk.

Now they were driving back to Anchorage via the Glenn Highway and stopping to see the sights along the way. Once Misty and Emma had pulled on sweatshirts, they started along the trail toward the glacier with Boomer. Sabrina had managed to teach the terrier a few commands, but unlike Tal, he was prone to sudden fits of deafness when he spotted something interesting, so he had to stay on a leash. Leith and Sabrina followed with Tal heeling at Leith's side. Leith reached for Sabrina's hand. "Having fun?"

"It's been great. Misty and Emma are, too."

"If the level of giggles is anything to go by, they're having a blast."

"Yeah, Misty's getting a kick out of Emma. You know, this sibling thing is a lot of fun."

"Volta might disagree."

"Volta likes to tease, but she adores you. So does your niece. Oh, I just realized—someday if Misty has a baby, I'll get a niece or nephew, too."

"And vice versa."

"Aunt Misty." Sabrina grinned.

As they got closer, they could start to see cracks exposing the deep blue ice through the outer white ice and snow on the surface.

Emma and Misty stopped to look around while Leith and Sabrina caught up with them.

"Wow. The ice is so blue!" Misty said. "Let's take some pictures."

"Uncle Leith, can I borrow your phone for a selfie?" Emma asked.

"Here you go. There's an ice cave over that way." Leith handed her the phone and Misty and Emma ran ahead, with Boomer at their heels, barking as he ran. Tal gave a whimper.

Leith chuckled. "Fine, go with them." Tal broke into a gallop to catch up with Boomer and the girls.

Sabrina stepped closer to a blue fracture in the ice and pulled out her phone to take a photo. "Imagine a down jacket this color. The shell would be something smooth and icy-looking, maybe nylon with a satin finish. Instead of diamonds or boxes, we could use curved lines of quilting, like the way a glacier looks from above."

Leith slipped an arm around her waist. "It would look great on you."

She smiled at him. "You always say that."

"It's always true. You could call it the glacier jacket. You'd sell a million of them."

"You think?"

"People love your designs. I see the Talkeetna vest all over town. In fact, isn't that lady over there wearing one?"

Sabrina looked to where he was pointing. Sure enough, a tourist posing for a photo was dressed in Anne Li jeans, Caribou Pass hiking boots and the dusty plum version of the vest Sabrina had designed. Sabrina's heart did a happy dance. This never got old.

Judging from sales figures, the vests were almost as popular in the rest of the country as they were in Anchorage. The whole line was selling well, too. Sabrina's contract would be up in two months, but she no longer feared it wouldn't be renewed. In fact, Kate had hinted at the possibility of a bonus.

"I think every woman at the Orson's team-builder last month was wearing your vest," Leith said.

Sabrina smiled. "Walter ordered them for all the women employees."

"Your group looked pretty impressive in the shelter-building competition. You've come a long way since last year's team-builder."

She gave him a playful nudge in the ribs. "Are you referring to the infamous exploding-bean incident?"

"Not me." He gave her waist a squeeze. "I've come a long way in the last year, too, since you came into my life."

"Oh, yeah?"

"Yeah. Come with me. There's something I want to show you." Leith led her in the direction the girls had gone. The sun was shining, but a gentle breeze swept across the ice and chilled the air around them. Sabrina was glad to have Leith's warm arm around her.

They climbed over some loose rocks until they came to the ice cave. Fractured walls of azure ice, two stories tall, had melted into strange curves and shapes. A steady stream of melting water flowed away from the glacier.

Sabrina tilted back her head to take it all in. "I love this. It's like being inside of a diamond."

"Speaking of diamonds." Leith pulled something from his pocket and knelt on one knee.

Sabrina gasped and brought her hand to her mouth. "What's this?"

Leith opened the box. "Sabrina, I knew I'd always love you. What I didn't realize is that every day we spent together that love would grow and grow. I want to make it official. Will you marry me?"

The ring was beautiful, a sparkling diamond solitaire in a classic setting. "Leith, it's gorgeous. I don't know what to say."

He grinned. "'Yes' would be good before my knee freezes to the ice."

"Yes!" She grabbed his hands and pulled him up. "Yes, yes, yes!" She threw her arms around his neck and kissed him thoroughly. Giggles alerted her to the presence of Misty and Emma, who were busy snapping photos.

Sabrina looked over at them without taking her arms from Leith's neck. "Were you two in on this?"

Misty just smiled, but Emma spilled the beans. "Uncle Leith showed us the ring this morning, but I promised not to say anything, so you'd be surprised."

"Good job, Emma. It was a wonderful surprise."

"Why don't you try it on?" Leith slid the ring onto her finger. "Ah. Perfect fit."

Sabrina held out her hand, admiring the sparkle on her finger. It contrasted nicely with the pearlized pink of her nails.

"Can I be in your wedding?" Emma asked.

"Absolutely. Both of you. Come here. We need a group hug."

They hurried over. After the hugs, Misty grabbed her hand and examined the ring. "It looks good on you. Your guy has excellent taste."

Emma's eyes sparkled with excitement. "Mommy says when you're married, you'll be my aunt."

"That's right. Won't that be fun?"

"Your uncle will be my brother-in-law," Misty told Emma.

"And we'll be family forever and always, right, Uncle Leith?" Emma asked.

"Yes, we will." Those blue eyes, the same vivid color as the ice of the glacier, met Sabrina's and held. "Forever and always."

* * * * *

For more great romances in the
Northern Lights miniseries from
acclaimed author Beth Carpenter,
please visit www.Harlequin.com
today for these titles:

The Alaskan Catch
A Gift for Santa
Alaskan Hideaway

Get 4 FREE REWARDS!

We'll send you 2 FREE Books plus 2 FREE Mystery Gifts.

Love Inspired® books feature contemporary inspirational romances with Christian characters facing the challenges of life and love.

FREE
Value Over
$20

YES! Please send me 2 FREE Love Inspired® Romance novels and my 2 FREE mystery gifts (gifts are worth about $10 retail). After receiving them, if I don't wish to receive any more books, I can return the shipping statement marked "cancel." If I don't cancel, I will receive 6 brand-new novels every month and be billed just $5.24 for the regular-print edition or $5.74 each for the larger-print edition in the U.S., or $5.74 each for the regular-print edition or $6.24 each for the larger-print edition in Canada. That's a savings of at least 13% off the cover price. It's quite a bargain! Shipping and handling is just 50¢ per book in the U.S. and 75¢ per book in Canada.* I understand that accepting the 2 free books and gifts places me under no obligation to buy anything. I can always return a shipment and cancel at any time. The free books and gifts are mine to keep no matter what I decide.

Choose one: ☐ **Love Inspired® Romance**
Regular-Print
(105/305 IDN GMY4)

☐ **Love Inspired® Romance**
Larger-Print
(122/322 IDN GMY4)

Name (please print)

Address   Apt. #

City   State/Province   Zip/Postal Code

Mail to the **Reader Service:**
IN U.S.A.: P.O. Box 1341, Buffalo, NY 14240-8531
IN CANADA: P.O. Box 603, Fort Erie, Ontario L2A 5X3

Want to try 2 free books from another series? Call 1-800-873-8635 or visit www.ReaderService.com.

LI19R

Get 4 FREE REWARDS!

We'll send you 2 FREE Books plus 2 FREE Mystery Gifts.

Love Inspired® Suspense books feature Christian characters facing challenges to their faith... and lives.

FREE Value Over $20

2018 CHRISTMAS ROMANCE COLLECTION!

You'll get TWO FREE GIFTS & TWO FREE BOOKS in your first shipment, plus a trade paperback by *New York Times* **bestselling author RaeAnne Thayne!**

This collection is packed with holiday romances by internationally famous *USA TODAY* and *New York Times* bestselling authors!

Get 4 FREE REWARDS!

We'll send you 2 FREE Books plus 2 FREE Mystery Gifts.

FREE
Value Over
$20

Both the **Romance** and **Suspense** collections feature compelling novels written by many of today's best-selling authors.

Get 4 FREE REWARDS!

We'll send you 2 FREE Books
<u>plus</u> 2 FREE Mystery Gifts.

Harlequin® Special Edition books feature heroines finding the balance between their work life and personal life on the way to finding true love.

FREE Value Over $20

Get 4 FREE REWARDS!

We'll send you 2 FREE Books
<u>plus</u> 2 FREE Mystery Gifts.

Harlequin® Romance Larger-Print books feature uplifting escapes that will warm your heart with the ultimate feel-good tales.

FREE
Value Over
$20